William Walker

Memoirs of the Distinguished Men of Science of Great Britain

Living in the years 1807-8 - an appendix

William Walker

Memoirs of the Distinguished Men of Science of Great Britain
Living in the years 1807-8 - an appendix

ISBN/EAN: 9783337094546

Printed in Europe, USA, Canada, Australia, Japan

Cover: Foto ©Andreas Hilbeck / pixelio.de

More available books at **www.hansebooks.com**

MEMOIRS

OF THE

DISTINGUISHED MEN OF SCIENCE

OF GREAT BRITAIN

LIVING IN THE YEARS 1807-8.

AND APPENDIX.

WITH AN INTRODUCTION BY

ROBERT HUNT, F.R.S., &c.

COMPILED AND ARRANGED BY

WILLIAM WALKER, JUNIOR.

Second Edition.

" The evil, that men do, lives after them ;
The good is oft interred with their bones."
SHAKSPEARE.

LONDON:
E. & F. N. SPON, 16, BUCKLERSBURY.
—
1864.

CONTENTS.

PREFACE TO SECOND EDITION.

THE following brief memoirs were originally compiled for the purpose of accompanying the Engraving of " The Distinguished Men of Science of Great Britain living in 1807–8, assembled at the Royal Institution." As, however, "The Memoirs" were found to have a considerable sale, independent of the Engraving, it has been found necessary to produce a second edition. All the lives have been carefully revised, and considerable additions made, while, in order to render the present book a more complete compendium of the great men of that period, an Appendix has been added, containing the Memoirs of Black, Cort, Ivory, and Priestly, who unfortunately were, from different reasons, unable to be included in the group in the Engraving.

With the exception of the notices of Trevithick, Tennant, Maudslay, Francis Ronalds, and one or two more, these memoirs necessarily contain little information which has not been previously published in some shape or other. The authorities from which the present particulars have been taken are given at the end of each memoir; and the writer claims no further merit than that of having compiled and arranged the works of others, whose language, in most cases, it would indeed be presumption in him to alter, further than was necessary to present to the public in a clear, brief, and (it is hoped) readable form, the doings of men who must ever be held in the grateful remembrance of their country.

INTRODUCTION.

THE influences of human thought on the physical forces which regulate the great phenomena of the universe,— and the operation of the powers of mind, on the material constituents of the planet, which is man's abiding place, form subjects for studies which have a most exalting tendency. Thought has made the subtile element of the thunderstorm man's most obedient messenger. Thought has solicited the sunbeam to betray its secrets; and an invisible agent, controlled by light, delineates external nature at man's request. Thought has subdued the wild impulses of fire, and heat is made the willing power to propel our trains of carriages with a bird-like speed, and to urge—in proud independence of winds or tides—our noble ships from shore to shore. Thought has penetrated the arcana of nature, and, by learning her laws, has imitated her works. Thus, Chemistry takes a crude mass, —rejected as unworthy and offensive,—it recombines its constituent parts, and gives us, the grateful odours of the sweetest flowers, and tinctures which rival nature in the intensity and the beauty of its dyes.

No truth was ever developed to man, in answer to his laborious toils, which did not sooner or later benefit the race. Every such development has been the result of the continuous efforts of an individual mind; therefore it is that we desire to possess some memorial of the men to whom we are indebted.

We have advanced to our present position in the scale of nations by the efforts of a few chosen minds. Every branch of human industry has been benefited by the discoveries of science. The discoverers are therefore deserving of that hero-worship which, sooner or later, they receive from all.

The following pages are intended to convey to the general reader a brief but correct account of the illustrious dead, whose names *are* for ever associated with one of the most brilliant eras in British science. It will be remembered that, in the earliest years of the present century, the world witnessed the control and application of steam by Watt, Symington and Trevithick; the great discoveries in physics and chemistry by Dalton, Cavendish, Wollaston and Davy,—in astronomy by Herschel, Maskelyne and Baily; the inventions of the spinning-mule and power-loom by Crompton and Cartwright; the introduction of machinery into the manufacture of paper, by Bryan Donkin and others; the improvements in the printing-press, and invention of stereotype printing, by Charles Earl Stanhope; the discovery of vaccination by Jenner; the introduction of gas into general use by Murdock; and the construction (in a great measure) of the present system of canal communication by Jessop, Chapman, Telford and Rennie. During the same period of time were likewise living Count Rumford; Robert Brown, the botanist; William Smith, "The Father of English Geology;" Thomas Young, the natural philosopher; Brunel; Bentham; Maudslay; and Francis Ronalds, who, by securing perfect insulation, was the first to demonstrate the practicability of passing an electric message through a lengthened space; together with many others, the fruits of whose labours we are now reaping.

The following pages briefly record the births, deaths, and more striking incidents in the lives of those benefactors to mankind.

" Lives of great men all remind us we may make our lives sublime."—The truth of this is strongly enforced in the brief memoirs which are included in this volume. They teach us that mental power, used judiciously and applied with industry, is capable of producing vast changes in the crude productions of Nature. Beyond this, they instruct us that men, who fulfil the commands of the Creator and employ their minds, in unwearying efforts to subdue the Earth, are rarely unrewarded. They aid in the march of civilization, and they ameliorate the conditions of humanity. They win a place amongst the great names which we reverence, and each one

" becomes like a star
" From the abodes where the Eternals are."

ROBERT HUNT.

WILLIAM ALLEN, F.R.S.

Born August 29, 1770.   Died December 30, 1843.

William Allen, the eminent chemist, was born in London. His father was a silk manufacturer in Spitalfields, and a member of the Society of Friends.   Having at an early period shown a predilection for chemical and other pursuits connected with medicine, William was placed in the establishment of Mr. Joseph Gurney Bevan in Plough Court, Lombard Street, where he acquired a practical knowledge of chemistry. He eventually succeeded to the business, which he carried on in connection with Mr. Luke Howard, and obtained great reputation as a pharmaceutical chemist. About the year 1804, Mr. Allen was appointed lecturer on chemistry and experimental philosophy at Guy's Hospital, at which institution he continued to be engaged more or less until the year 1827.   He was also connected with the Royal Institution of Great Britain, and was concerned in some of the most exact experiments of the day, together with Davy, Babington, Marcet, Luke Howard, and Dalton.   In conjunction with his friend Mr. Pepys, Allen entered upon his well known chemical investigations, which established the proportion of Carbon in Carbonic Acid, and proved the identity of the diamond with charcoal ; these discoveries are recorded in the 'Philosophical Transactions' of the Royal Society, of which he became a member in 1807.   The 'Transactions' for 1829 also contain a paper by him, based on elaborate experiments and calculations, concerning the changes produced by respiration on atmospheric air and other gases.   Mr. Allen was mainly instrumental in establishing the Pharmaceutical Society, of which he was president at the time of his death.   Besides his public labours as a practical chemist, he pursued with much delight, in his hours of relaxation, the study of astronomy, and was one of the original members of the Royal Astronomical Society. In connection with this science, he published, in 1815, a small work entitled 'A Companion to the Transit Instrument.'

Many years before his death Mr. Allen withdrew from business, and purchased an estate near Lindfield, Sussex. Here while still engaged in public schemes of usefulness and benevolence, he also carried out various philanthropic plans for the improvement of his immediate dependants, and poorer neighbours. He erected commodious cottages on his property, with an ample allotment of land to each cottage, and established Schools at Lindfield for boys, girls, and infants, with workshops, outhouses, and play-grounds. About

B

three acres of land were cultivated on the most approved system by the boarders, who also took a part in household work. The subjects taught were land-surveying, mapping, the elements of Botany, the use of the barometer, rain-gauge, &c., and there was a good library with various scientific and useful apparatus.

Mr. Allen died at Lindfield, the scene of his zealous benevolence, in the seventy-fourth year of his age.—*English Cyclopædia*, London, 1856.—*Monthly notices of the Royal Ast. Soc.* vol. 6, Feb., 1844.

FRANCIS BAILY, F.R.S. &c.

Born April 28, 1774. Died August 30, 1844.

This eminent English astronomer was born at Newbury in Berkshire, and received his education at the school of the Rev. Mr. Best of that town, where he early showed a propensity to physical inquiry, obtaining among his schoolmates the nickname of 'the Philosopher of Newbury.' Francis Baily quitted this school, when fourteen years old, for a house of business in the city of London, and remained there until his twenty-second year, when, desirous of the enlargement of views which travel affords, he embarked for America in 1795. Mr. Baily remained there nearly three years, travelling over the whole of the United States and through much of the western country, experiencing at various times great hardships and privations.

Shortly after his return to England he commenced business in London as a stockbroker, and was taken into partnership by a Mr. Whitmore, in the year 1799. While engaged in this business he published several works on Life Annuities, one of which, entitled 'The Doctrine of Life Annuities and Insurances analytically investigated and explained,' was published in 1810, with an appendix in 1813, continuing to this day to be a standard work on the subject, and it may serve to give some idea of the estimation in which it was held, to mention, that when out of print, copies used to sell for four to five times their original value.

Although Mr. Baily was thus actively devoting himself to matters of a direct commercial interest, he was still able to find time for works of a more general nature: in 1810 he wrote his first astronomical paper on the celebrated Solar Eclipse, said to have been predicted by Thales, published in the 'Philosophical Transactions for 1811, and in 1813 published a work entitled 'An Epitome of Universal History.' Astronomy, however, was his chief pursuit; and shortly after the celebrated fraud of De Beranger on the Stock Exchange in 1814, (in the detection and exposure of which Baily had a considerable share), this science absorbed more and more of his attention. His accounts of the Eclipse of 1820; of the Annular Eclipse of 1836, which he observed at Jedburgh; and the Total Eclipse of July 8, 1842, with its marvellous revelation of the rose-coloured protuberances of the solar atmosphere, since known as ' Baily's Beads,' are among the most interesting and classical of his writings.

In January, 1823, the Royal Astronomical Society was founded, chiefly through the suggestions of Francis Baily and Dr. Pearson, and for the first three years of its existence Mr. Baily filled the office of Secretary, sparing no exertions on its behalf, watching over its early progress with paternal care, and as the Society grew and prospered, contributing to its transactions many copious and valuable papers.

In 1825 Baily retired from the Stock Exchange, having acquired a considerable fortune, and shortly afterwards took a house in Tavistock Place, giving his whole attention to the furtherance of astronomical science. Here, he executed that grand series of labours which has perpetuated his name, and the building in which the Cavendish experiment of weighing the earth was repeated, its bulk and figure determined, and the standard of British measure perpetuated, must continue to be a source of interest to scientific men for many generations to come. The chief works to which Mr. Baily devoted himself during this later portion of his life are:—

1. The Remodelling of the Nautical Almanac.
2. The Determination of the length of the Seconds Pendulum.
3. The Fixation of the Standard of Length.
4. The Determination of the Density of the Earth.
5. The Revision of the Catalogues of the Stars.
6. The Reduction of Lacaille's and Lalande's Catalogues; and
7. The Formation of a New Standard Catalogue.

The benefits which not only astronomy but all England have derived from these laborious investigations, can hardly be too much appreciated. But a short time elapsed, after Baily had completed his observations on the pendulum, and determined the standard of length,—being thereby enabled to compare his new scale with the imperial standard yard,—when the conflagration of the Houses of Parliament in 1834 took place, and both the latter standard, and the original one by Bird (that of 1758) were destroyed. When it is considered that Baily's repetition of the Cavendish Experiment involved untiring watching for more than 1200 hours, and this, too, by one who in early life seemed only able to find food for his vigorous mind amidst the hardships and fatigues of travel, it affords a remarkable instance how a man, active and full of ardour in early youth, can yet be enabled, by the strength of his character, to concentrate the full force of his powers upon a series of researches apparently the most wearying and full of disappointment, an example

well fitted for the earnest consideration of all who imagine that the
energies of their minds can alone be satisfied by stirring scenes or
a life full of activity and adventure. Mr. Baily's last public appearance was at Oxford, to which place he went with some difficulty, to
receive the honorary degree of Doctor of Civil Law. He was distinguished by great industry, which was made more effective by his
methodical habits; and also by a suavity of manner which greatly
enlarged the circle of his friends. In fact, Mr. Baily effected in the
last 20 years of his life, a greater number of complete and refined
researches than most other philosophers have accomplished during
a whole lifetime.—*Memoir of Francis Baily, by Sir John Herschel,
Bart.* London, 1856.

SIR JOSEPH BANKS, BART., C.B., P.R.S.

MEMBER OF THE INSTITUTE OF FRANCE, ETC.

Born February 12, 1743. Died June 19, 1820.

Sir Joseph Banks, President of the Royal Society for upwards of
forty years, was born in Argyle Street, London, He was the eldest
son of Mr. W. Banks, a gentleman of considerable landed property,
whose family was originally of Swedish extraction, although it had
been settled in England for several generations. The early life of
Joseph Banks was passed principally at Revesby Hall, his father's
seat in Lincolnshire, and his education was for several years entrusted to a private tutor; in his ninth year he was sent to Harrow
and four years after to Eton, from whence he proceeded to Christ's
College, Oxford.

During his residence at college, he made considerable progress in
classical knowledge, but evinced at the same time a decided predilection for the study of natural history. Botany in particular was
his favourite occupation, and one to which his leisure hours were
devoted with enthusiastic ardour and perseverance. An anecdote is
told of Mr. Banks being on one occasion so intent on exploring
ditches and secluded spots, in search of rare plants, as to have
excited the suspicions of some countrymen, who, conceiving that
he could have no innocent design in acting thus, seized the young
naturalist, when he had fallen asleep exhausted with fatigue, and
brought him as a suspected thief before a neighbouring magistrate.
After a strict investigation he was soon liberated, but the incident
occasioned much amusement in the neighbourhood.

In the year 1761 Mr. Banks lost his father, and in 1764, on coming of age, was put in possession of his valuable estates in Lincolnshire. Mrs. Banks, soon after the death of her husband, removed with her family from Lincolnshire to Chelsea, as a spot likely to afford her son Joseph peculiar advantages in the study of botany, from the numerous gardens in the vicinity devoted to the culture of rare and curious plants of every description. And now it was that the great merit of Mr. Banks shone forth. With all the incitements which his age, his figure, and his station naturally presented to leading a life of idleness, and with a fortune which placed the more vulgar gratifications of sense or of ordinary ambition amply within his reach, he steadily devoted himself to scientific pursuits, and only lived for the studies of a naturalist. He remained out of Parliament, went little into any society but that of learned men, while his relaxation was confined to exercise and to angling, of which he was so fond, that he would devote days and even nights to it. Whilst living at Chelsea, Mr. Banks formed the acquaintance of Lord Sandwich, afterwards first Lord of the Admiralty, who as it happened had the same taste, and to the friendship of whom he was in after life indebted for essential aid in the furtherance of his numerous projects for the advancement of scientific knowledge. Soon after attaining his 21st year, Mr. Banks undertook a voyage to Newfoundland and the Labrador coast, for the purpose of exploring the botany of those unfrequented regions. On his return, he brought home valuable collections not only of plants, but also of insects and other natural productions of that district. In 1768, he obtained leave from Government, through the interest of Lord Sandwich, to embark in the ship commanded by the great navigator Cook, who had been commissioned to observe the transit of Venus in the Pacific ocean, by the observation of which phenomenon the sun's parallax might be measured, and to fulfil also the usual object of a voyage of discovery.*

In order to turn to the best account all opportunities that might occur during the voyage, Mr. Banks made most careful preparations. He provided himself with the best instruments for making all kinds of scientific observations, and for preserving specimens of natural history, and persuaded Dr. Solander, a distinguished pupil of Linnæus, to become his associate in the enterprise. He also took with him two draughtsmen, to delineate all objects of interest that did not admit of being transported or preserved, and four servants. This voyage occupied three years; during that period all engaged in it incurred many and severe hardships; several, including three of the attendants of Dr. Solander and Mr. Banks, losing their lives. The results were highly important, the observations necessary for making the solar parallax were made with perfect success. The

* The portable observatories used in this expedition were constructed by Smeaton the engineer.— *Wild's History of the Roy. Soc.* vol. 2, p. 37.

manners of the natives in the Society Islands had been examined,
and the singular state of their society ascertained. Their products,
vegetable, mineral, and animal, as well as those of New Holland,
New Zealand, and New Guinea, had been fully explored, and a considerable share of the fame, which accrued to Captain Cook and his
associates in the enterprise, was due to Mr. Banks, who brought
home a splendid collection of specimens from those countries.

No sooner had Mr. Banks returned from this expedition than he
commenced, with unabated vigour after a few months repose, preparations for another. Having been prevented from joining Captain
Cook's second expedition, chiefly through the influence of Sir Hugh
Pallisser with the admiralty, he undertook the equipment of a ship
at his own expense; and, taking with him Dr. Solander, Dr. Lind,
Dr. Von Troil, a Swedish naturalist, and others, he sailed for Iceland
in 1772. After exploring during two months that interesting region
of volcanoes he returned to England, enriched with many valuable
specimens, and still more valuable information respecting the productions of the country. A fine collection of books and manuscripts
were purchased and presented by Mr. Banks to the British Museum,
and Dr. Von Troil, in whose hands Mr. Banks, with his wonted
aversion to literary fame, left the subject, published a full and interesting account of the voyage.

A great part of the knowledge resulting from the various travels
of Mr. Banks were communicated by him, at different times, in
papers to the Royal Society, of which he had been elected a fellow
as early as the year 1766. On the resignation of Sir John Pringle,
in 1778, Mr. Banks was elected President of this Society, an honour
he continued to hold until his death. During the whole of his life
Sir Joseph enjoyed the favour of the king, forming a kind of connecting link between his scientific compeers, and the courtly circles
of the aristocracy. In 1781 he was made a baronet; in 1795 was
invested with the order of the bath; and, in 1797, became a member
of the privy council. He did not, however, engage much in politics,
but used the influence he had acquired chiefly in the promotion of
scientific objects, and the encouragement of those who pursued
them.

Sir Joseph Banks's published works bear little proportion either
to his scientific labours or his exertions on behalf of learned men,
nor are his real claims to the gratitude of posterity much known.
He it was who may truly be said to have planted and founded the
colony of Botany Bay. He was the real founder of the African
Association, and by his scientific exertions the productions of other
climates were diffused over each portion of the globe. Thus he
brought over into Europe the seeds of the South Sea lands, having
previously distributed to the latter those of Europe. To him are
we indebted for many of the beautiful plants which adorn our
gardens and shrubberies. The sugar-cane of Otaheite was trans-

planted by him into the colonies, the bread fruit tree of the Pacific introduced into the tropical soil of America, and the flax of New Zealand brought into Europe. While among animals, the black swan and the kangaroo were brought from Australia and introduced into this country by this eminent man.

Sir Joseph Banks was married but had no family. He continued to fill the honourable office of President of the Royal Society for the unprecedented period of nearly forty-two years, enjoying, during that time, the correspondence and confidence of most of the distinguished men of learning both of this and other nations. His name was enrolled amongst the associates of almost every academy and learned society in Europe. His house and table were ever open for the reception and entertainment of all those who were eminent for their scientific attainments, with that spirit of liberality so conducive to the union of interests and co-operation of efforts, requisite for the cultivation of knowledge. During the latter part of his life Sir Joseph Banks was a great sufferer from the gout, and during the last fourteen years was almost deprived of the use of his feet and legs. At last, he gradually sank under the exhausting effects of this ailment, and died at his villa at Spring Grove, Hounslow, in the seventy-eighth year of his age. He was succeeded in the chair of the Royal Society by Dr. Wollaston for the remainder of the year, until the election of Sir Humphry Davy on the anniversary of the Society in November.—*Memoir of Sir J. Banks, by Dr. P. M. Roget, Encyclopædia Britannica,* Eighth Edition.—*Welds' History of the Royal Society, with Memoirs of the Presidents.* London, 1848.—*Brougham's Lives of Philosophers.* London and Glasgow, 1855.

BRIGADIER-GENERAL SIR SAMUEL BENTHAM.

Born January 11, 1757. Died May 31, 1831.

Sir Samuel Bentham was the youngest son of Jeremiah Bentham, and brother of Jeremy, the celebrated jurist. He was placed when very young at a private school, from whence, at the age of six, he was sent to Westminster. His father occupied a house in Queen's Square Place, in the stable-yard of which were spacious workshops, let to a carpenter; here Samuel used to spend all his leisure time, and soon acquired considerable skill in handling tools, for when only thirteen years old he had managed to construct with his own hands a carriage, for a young friend and playmate, Miss Cornelia Knight At the age of fourteen he exhibited so strong a taste for naval matters, that his father yielded to his wishes, and bound him apprentice to the master shipwright of Woolwich Dockyard. At that time the superior officers of a royal dockyard were exempted from keeping their apprentices at hard labour, so that time might be allowed for general instruction. Samuel, however, soon perceived that practical manipulation was no less essential than theoretical knowledge, and used therefore to work at the dock side till breakfast-time, and devote the rest of the day to scientific acquirements. In time, Samuel and his master were removed from Woolwich to Chatham Dockyard, by which he was enabled to obtain a practical knowledge of the behaviour of vessels at sea; for he was often permitted to sail in the British Channel, and sometimes extended his voyages further. About this period his brother, Jeremy Bentham, had returned from college, and used to instil into him many of the first ideas of political economy : on these occasions Samuel would take advantage of the Saturday afternoons to *walk* from Chatham to his brother's chambers in Lincoln's Inn.

At the end of his seven years' apprenticeship, Samuel spent another year in the other royal dockyards, and at the Naval College at Portsmouth. He then went to sea as Captain Macbridge's guest, whose ship was one of Lord Keppel's fleet, and on this occasion he suggested sundry improvements in the apparatus of a ship, which were executed in Portsmouth Dockyard. In consequence of the abilities manifested by Bentham, many advantageous appointments were offered him; these were, however, refused, and in 1780 he embarked for the Continent, in order to obtain greater experience in the different practices in the art of naval construction. After having visited Holland he proceeded to Russia, and was well received at St. Petersburgh by the English Ambassador, Sir James Harris, who introduced him to the best society, and through whose means he became acquainted, among others, with Prince Potemkin, and the celebrated traveller, Pallas. Whilst on a visit to the large manufactory of Count Demidoff, Bentham constructed a sort of amphibious vehicle, in the form of a boat, and capable of serving as an ordinary wheel-carriage, and also, when necessity required, of being navigated across, or along a stream of water. This invention he subsequently patented, and likewise extended its utility by constructing the carriages so as to serve as army baggage-waggons, a supply of which Prince Potemkin ordered to be furnished to a regiment at Jassy. They were also introduced into England about the year 1793, when the Duke of York requested that one should be built for the English service, which was successfully tried on the River Thames. In gratitude to Count Demidoff for the facilities which he had afforded him in constructing this carriage, Bentham invented for the use of the Count's factory, a wood-planing machine, which could also be used for making mouldings by changing the cutting tool.

Bentham's stay in Russia was prolonged for a greater period than he originally intended, from his having become attached to a Russian lady of considerable rank and beauty; but although this attachment was mutual, nothing came of it, owing to the opposition of the lady's relatives, on the score of Bentham being a foreigner. During this period Bentham had the direction of the Fontanka Canal, in connection with which he invented a peculiar form of pile-driving machine, in which the weight was attached to a sort of endless ladder, moved by a man stepping on it, on the principle that a man's weight exceeds considerably his muscular strength.

After the completion of the canal, Prince Potemkin induced Bentham to accept military service, and appointed him to the command of a battalion stationed at Critcheff, in White Russia, with the rank of lieutenant-colonel. As the prince's manufactories were in the neighbourhood of Critcheff, Bentham offered to superintend them. This offer was gladly received; and as the management of the works had been previously grossly misconducted, the lieutenant-colonel soon perceived the necessity of his own constant inspection of what was going on, and for this purpose contrived a panoptican building or inspection-house, the centre of which commanded a view of all its parts. His brother Jeremy was on a visit whilst he was devising this panoptican, and the contrivance has frequently on this account been attributed to Jeremy, although in his works Jeremy repeatedly says it was his brother's. Up to this time the panoptican principle has only been adopted in gaols; but Jeremy Bentham has shown that it is equally desirable for a great variety of buildings.

Bentham's next invention was a sort of jointed vessel, for the conveyance of the Empress Catherine down the Dnieper and its affluents, which were shallow, tortuous, and their navigation much impeded by sandbanks and sunken trees. This vessel was in six links, drawing only six inches of water when loaded, and with 124 men at the oars on board. Many more were constructed on the same principle, for carrying the produce of the prince's establishments and manufactories to the Black Sea.

On the breaking out of war with Turkey, Bentham was sent to the south with his battalion, of which, according to orders, he had made sailors and shipwrights; and shortly afterwards, by the joint order of Souvaroff and Admiral Mardvinoff, he was commanded to fit out vessels at Cherson to oppose the enemy. It happened that he had the sole command of the arsenal at Cherson, in which he found an immense stock of ordnance of all descriptions, but no better navigable vessels than the pleasure-galleys which had brought the empress and her suite down the Dneiper. But nothing daunted, Bentham set to work. He reflected that it is not size of vessel which ensures victory, but that it is gained by the fleet that can throw the heaviest weight of missile in the shortest time, joined to the facility of manœuvring vessels. Strengthening his vessels as well as he could, he fitted them with as heavy artillery as they could possibly bear, and when all was finished, took the command of the flotilla himself, and had the satisfaction of engaging the Turks on three separate days, in all of which actions he was equally victorious, notwithstanding the enemy's flotilla were doubly as numerous and powerful. For these three victories Bentham received from the empress a like number of honourable rewards—rank in the army, a gold-hilted sword, and the Cross of the Order of St. George.

Sir Samuel Bentham now returned to the army, and by his own choice was appointed to the protection of the eastern frontier of Siberia, his command extending from the northern part of the Ural Mountains to the confines of Russia in the Chinese dominions. After holding this appointment for a couple of years, during which period he established schools for his troops, and introduced other improvements into their condition, Bentham obtained leave of absence to visit England.

Here commences another epoch in Sir Samuel's life. Arrived in England, he found his brother Jeremy absorbed in investigations relative to jurisprudence. Jeremy, however, had not forgotten his brother's Panopticon, but had proposed its adoption for the County Gaol of Middlesex. This led to some explanations with the ministers, who ultimately entrusted Jeremy Bentham with a thousand convicts, of whose labour he was to make the best use he could. In the meanwhile Samuel went to visit the principal manufactories in England; he found that steam-engines were used for giving motion to machinery for spinning cotton, but in no case were they applied to machinery for the working of wood, metal, &c.; nor, in fact, were there any mechanical apparatuses for saving labour, with the exception of turning-lathes, and some boring tools worked by horses, for making ships' blocks. Bentham therefore patented, in 1791, his machinery for planing and making mouldings, specifying the improvements which he had made on the machine constructed ten years before for Count Demidoff. His brother's arrangements for the industrial employment of convicts having been concluded, Sir Samuel considered that the most profitable means of employing them would be the working of machines for saving manual labour, which at the same time ensured accuracy of work; he therefore exerted his mechanical genius to perfect several engines he had previously contrived in Russia, and patented his inventions in the specification (No. 1951). This specification includes machines for sawing, boring, and many other operations necessary for the working of wood or metal.

Nor did the general confine himself to mere verbal descriptions of his machines; many of them were constructed and erected under his own eye, in Queen's Square Place, amongst which may be mentioned an apparatus for making wheels, and another for making all the parts of a window-sash frame; both of these leaving nothing for the skilled workman to do, save putting the pieces together. There were also planes of various descriptions, saws for cutting extremely fine veneers, machines for boring, dovetailing, cutting stone, &c., &c. Machines for metal-work were not, however, attempted, on account of the difficulty of obtaining the necessary power for working them, the Queen's Square Place apparatus being all worked by men. The fame of this machinery attracted many visitors, amongst others Mr. Secretary Dundas (afterwards Lord Melville), who stated in the House of Commons that it opened a new era in the manufacturing prosperity of the country.

But the circumstance which completely changed Bentham's future destiny, was the frequent visits of Earl Spencer and the Lords of the Admiralty, who soon perceived the advantages which would accrue to the state by engaging the general in the British service. Various proposals were made by the Admiralty to engage him permanently in the public service; but Bentham refused all in which he had not the individual responsibility. Ultimately a new office was created for him, under the name of Inspector-General of Naval Works; not, however, without the fierce opposition of the Naval Board, who, although unable to change the title of the office, managed to reduce the salary from the sum of 2000*l.* per annum, as originally proposed, to 750*l.* nominal, with an addition finally agreed upon of 500*l.* a year—in all, 1250*l.* per annum. Notwithstanding this opposition, Bentham, convinced of the services he could render, gave up the honours and riches which awaited him in Russia—amongst others, an estate promised him on his return—and determined to devote his energies to his native country, regardless of all pecuniary advantages. During the interval which elapsed before the actual institution of his new office, Bentham was authorized by the Lords of the Admiralty, early in 1795, to build seven experimental vessels; into these he introduced many improvements, amongst which may be mentioned diagonal braces, metallic tanks for water, metallic canisters for powder, means for filling the magazine with water in case of fire, safety lamps, &c.

Appointed Inspector-General of Naval Works in 1796, the whole of Sir Samuel's energies were henceforward directed towards the improvement of naval arsenals, and the introduction of his machinery for shaping wood, with steam-power to give it motion. This introduction of steam-power into the naval dockyards of Great Britain experienced at first the most violent opposition; and it was not until 1797 that any progress was made towards the furtherance of his object. During the same year Sir M. Isambard (then Mr.) Brunel presented himself to the general, for the purpose of bringing before his notice certain machinery for making blocks. Bentham was at that time fully engaged by Lord St. Vincent in organizing a better mode of managing timber in the royal dock-

yards, and it occurred to him that Brunel would be likely to influence the public in favour of machinery for working wood, and
therefore proposed that he should be engaged for that purpose,
recommending at the same time the adoption of his apparatus for
shaping blocks, to which Brunel's machines were solely confined*—
a measure which has had the effect of giving almost the entire
merit of the Portsmouth machinery to Brunel. This statement is
made without any intention of detracting from Sir Isambard's well-
earned reputation, but simply in justice to Bentham, who, singularly free from an inventor's jealousy, himself officially stated:—
"In regard to the machinery, I was afterwards satisfied that Mr.
Brunel had skill enough to have contrived machinery to have
answered the same purposes, had he not found mine ready to his
hand."

To describe all Bentham's subsequent improvements, not only in
machinery, but also in the economy of the management of the
dockyards, would take too much space. By his energetic efforts
and inventive genius, the wood mills, metal mills, and millwrights'
shop were established at Portsmouth. In 1800, he proposed to the
Admiralty a steam dredging-machine, of which he gave drawings,
similar to the ones now in such general use; and the efficacy of
this invention has since realized the most sanguine hopes of its
designer. Notwithstanding the great value of Bentham's services, he seems to have experienced little gratitude on the part of
the government. During the year 1805, he was requested by the
Admiralty to proceed to Russia, and commence building in that
country ships of war for the British navy. On his consenting, and
arriving at St. Petersburgh, he found, much to his surprise, that
nothing had been done to facilitate his mission; and although personally received with great kindness by the emperor, he was unable
to obtain the required permission to build vessels of war for Great
Britain.

Returning to England in 1807, he learnt that his office had been
abolished, and that henceforth he would be amalgamated with the
Naval Board. Nothing but the necessity of supporting his family,
made Bentham accept this new post, which gave him the title of
Civil Engineer and Architect of the Navy—an employment for
which he had manifested peculiar talents, although not educated
for it, but excluding him at the same time from all interference in
ship-building, for which he had served a regular apprenticeship, and
had subsequently manifested extraordinary talents. When this
office also was abolished, about the year 1812, Sir Samuel, by the desire of Lord Melville, applied for some compensation for loss of office,

---

* Mr. Samuel Bentham had amongst his other contrivances for shaping wood,
described one in his patent of 1793, for shaping the shells of blocks, but with a
singular degree of candour and generosity, he at once acknowledged the superiority of Brunel's machinery.—*Smiles's Industrial Biography*. London, 1863.

and likewise for a remuneration for his services. On account of the loss of office, Bentham's salary was continued; but during the discussion which arose regarding the statement of services which Sir Samuel had drawn up at the request of the Admiralty, although, on coming to the metal mills, Lord Melville said, "There Sir Samuel stands upon a rock," it proved a slippery one; for under the pretext that it would be necessary to apply to parliament for so large a sum as a year's savings effected by the introduction of the metal mills, no remuneration was ever accorded to Bentham for any one of his services.

After the restoration of peace in 1814, Sir Samuel retired to France, for the economical education of his children. In 1827 he returned to England, where he remained until his death in 1831, at the age of seventy-four.—*Papers and Practical Illustrations of Public Works of Recent Construction, &c.* London, 1856.

MATTHEW BOULTON, F.R.S. L. and E. &c.

Born at Birmingham, Sept. 3, 1728. Died Aug. 17, 1809.

This skilful, energetic, and farseeing man, who, by his extended views and liberal spirit of enterprise, contributed so greatly towards the successful introduction of Watt's condensing steam-engine, commenced life at Birmingham as a maker of buttons and shoe-buckles. Matthew Boulton received an ordinary education at a school at Deritend. He was, however, gifted with rare endowments, and of these he made the best use; with a thorough knowledge of business, great prudence, and admirable tact, he combined boldness of spirit, quickness of thought, and promptitude of action. At the death of his father, Boulton became possessed of considerable property, and desirous of extending his commercial operations, purchased, about the year 1762, a lease of Soho, near Handsworth, where he founded that establishment which has become renowned as the nursery of English mechanics. The hill from which this place derived its name was, at that time, a bleak and barren heath, at the bottom of which rippled a small stream. Boulton's instinctive mind saw the uses to which these waters might be turned. By collecting them into a pool, and pouring their united weight upon a water wheel, he became possessed of a motive-power sufficient to set in motion various machines, by whose agency were fabricated articles in gold, silver, and tortoise-shell, and plated and inlaid works of the greatest elegance and perfection. On the side of the hill, Boulton built extensive workshops, and dwellings capable of holding many hundreds of workmen, and erected a mansion for himself surrounded by beautiful grounds, where he lived as a prince among his people, extending hospitality to all around. In 1767, Boulton, finding that the motive-power which he possessed was inadequate to the various purposes of his machinery, erected a steam-engine upon the original construction of Savery. This, however, in turn was found to be insufficient for the objects required, and Boulton then had the discernment to perceive that they might be very completely attained by the adoption of the various improvements lately made in the steam-engine by James Watt. In 1773 he entered into partnership with this great scientific inventor, and induced him to settle at Soho and superintend personally the erection of his new steam-engines. This bold but clear-sighted act of Boulton was destined to crown with honour a reputation, already rising, and built upon the firm foundation of uprightness and integrity. "Had Watt searched all Europe," says Playfair, "he could not have found another man so calculated to introduce the machine to the public in a manner worthy of its reputation." Its sale as an article of commerce was entirely conducted by him, and the skilful and liberal way in which he performed this difficult task brought in time its own reward; yet as great a sum as 47,000l. had to be expended upon the steam-engine before any profit resulted to its owners. In process of time, however, wealth flowed into the hands of Boulton and Watt; and in the year 1800 Mr. Watt was enabled to retire from the firm possessed of a large competency, and leaving the exclusive privilege of the sale of the engine to Boulton. Boswell, who visited Soho in 1776, shortly after the manufacture of steam-engines had been commenced there, was greatly struck by the vastness and contrivance of the machinery. "I shall never forget," he says, "Mr. Boulton's expression to me when surveying the works: 'I sell here, sir, what all the world desires to have—*Power*.' He had," continues Boswell, "about 700 people at work; I contemplated him as an iron chieftain, and he seemed to be the father of his tribe."*

In 1785 Mr. Boulton was elected a Fellow of the Royal Society, and two or three years after this, turned his attention to the subject of coining, to the improvement of which art he devoted the last twenty years of his life. He erected extensive machinery for this purpose, and by uniting some processes originating in France with new kinds of presses, he was enabled to obtain great rapidity of action combined with the utmost perfection in the articles produced; so much so, that having been employed by the British Government to recoin the whole of the British specie, he rendered counterfeits nearly impossible by the economy and excellence of his work. In addition to this, Mr. Boulton planned and directed the arrangement of the machinery in the British Mint, and executed that for the

* *Quarterly Review*, October, 1858.

coining department. He also constructed the machinery for the great national mints of St. Petersburgh and Copenhagen; his son, to whom the establishment at Soho devolved upon his death, doing the same for the extensive and splendid establishments of the East India Company at Bombay and Calcutta.

Boulton died August 17, 1809, in his eighty-first year, and his remains were borne to the grave by the oldest workmen connected with the works at Soho; five hundred persons belonging to that establishment joined in the procession, which numbered among its ranks several thousand individuals, to whom medals were given recording the age of the deceased and the date of his death.— *Stuart's Anecdotes of the Steam Engine.* London, 1829.—*Muirhead's Translation of Arago's Life of J. Watt.* London, 1839.

JOSEPH BRAMAH.

Born April 13, 1749. Died December 9, 1814.

This eminent practical engineer and machinist was born at Stainborough, in Yorkshire. His father rented a farm on the estate of Lord Strafford, and Joseph, being the eldest of five children was intended for the same employment; but fortunately for his subsequent career, an accidental lameness, which occurred when he was sixteen years old, prevented his following agricultural pursuits. When quite a boy, Bramah exhibited unusual mechanical talent; he succeeded in constructing two violoncellos, which were found to be very tolerable instruments, and also managed to cut a violin out of a single block of wood, by means of tools which were forged for him by a neighbouring smith, whom in after life he engaged in London as one of his principal workmen. After having served an apprenticeship to a carpenter and joiner, Bramah obtained employment in the workshop of a cabinetmaker in London, and soon afterwards established himself as a principal in the business. The history of his life after this is perhaps best given by a record of his numerous inventions, all of which are, more or less, of a highly useful character. For the manufacture of those, Bramah first took up his residence in Denmark Street, Soho, but subsequently removed to Piccadilly, and established the various branches of his manufactory in some extensive premises at Pimlico. In 1783 he took out a patent for an improved watercock, and in the year following, completed the invention of his famous lock, which for many years stood unrivalled in ingenuity of construction, workmanship, and powers of resistance against all attempts to pick.* Bramah's indefatigable spirit of invention was stimulated to fresh efforts by the success of his lock, and he now entered upon a more important and original line of action than he had yet ventured upon. In his patent of 1785 he indicated many inventions, although none of them came into practical use—such as a Hydrostatical Machine and Boiler, and the application of the power produced by them to the drawing of carriages and the propelling of ships, by a paddle-wheel fixed in the stern of the vessel. For different modifications of pumps and fire-engines, Mr. Bramah took out three successive patents, the two last being dated in 1790 and 1798. But in the year 1795 he produced and patented the most important of all his inventions, namely, 'The Hydraulic Press,' a machine which gives to a child the strength of a giant, enabling him to bend a bar of iron as if it were wax. The chief difficulty which Bramah experienced in constructing this press was that of devising an efficient packing for the ram or solid piston, which, while capable of keeping out the water under the tremendous internal pressure exercised by the pump, should, on the withdrawal of that pressure, allow the ram to sink into its original place. This was at length accomplished by the invention of the self-tightening leather-collar, which was firmly secured in a recess at the top of a cylinder, with the concave side downwards. Consequently, when the water was pumped into the cylinder, it immediately forced its way between the bent edges of the collar; and the greater the pressure of water, the tighter became the hold which the collar took of the solid piston. It appears from the testimony of Mr. James Nasmyth, that Bramah was indebted for this simple but beautiful contrivance, to Henry Maudslay, who was at that time a workman in his shop, and who had already greatly assisted him in the construction of his lock.

Bramah continued his useful labours as an inventor for many years, and his studies of the principles of Hydraulics, in the course of his invention of the press, enabled him to introduce many valuable improvements in pumping machinery. By varying the form of the piston and cylinder, he was enabled to obtain a rotary motion, which he adopted in the well-known fire-engine. In 1797 he took out a patent for the beer-machine, now in such general use in public houses, and in the description of this he includes a mode of converting every cask in a cellar into a force pump, so as to raise the liquor to any part of the house; a filtering machine; a method of making pipes; a vent peg, and a new form of stop-cock. Bramah also turned his attention to the improvement of the steam-engine, but in this, Watt's patent had left little room for other inventors: and hence Bramah seems to have entertained a grudge against Watt, which was shown strongly in the evidence given by him in the case

* For Maudslay's connection with this lock, see Maudslay.

of Boulton and Watt *versus* Hornblower and Maberly, tried in December 1796. On the expiry, however, of Boulton and Watt's patent, Bramah introduced several valuable improvements in the details of the condensing engine, the most important of which was his " four-way cock," which was so contrived as to revolve continuously instead of alternately, thus insuring greater precision with less wear of parts. In this patent, which he secured in 1801, he also proposed sundry improvements in the boilers, as well as modifications in various parts of the engine. In the year 1802, Bramah obtained a patent for a very elaborate and accurate machine for producing smooth and parallel surfaces on wood and other materials. This was erected on a large scale at Woolwich Arsenal, and proved perfectly successful. The specification of the patent includes the description of a mode of turning spherical surfaces either convex or concave, by a tool moveable on an axis perpendicular to that of the lathe, and of cutting out concentric shells, by fixing in a similar manner a curved tool, nearly of the same form as that employed by common turners for making bowls. Bramah also invented machinery for making paper in large sheets, and for printing by means of a roller, composed of a number of circular plates, each turning on the same axis, and bearing twenty-six letters capable of being shifted at pleasure, so as to express any single line by a proper combination of the plates. This was put in practice to number bank-notes, and enabled twenty clerks to perform the labour which previously had required one hundred and twenty. In 1812 he projected a scheme for main-pipes, which was, however, in many respects, more ingenious than practicable. In describing this, he mentions having employed a hydrostatic pressure equal to that of a column of water twenty thousand feet high (about three and a half tons per square inch). Mr. Bramah made several improvements in the bearings of wheels, and suggested the use of pneumatic springs formed by pistons sliding in cylinders, in place of the usual metal springs for carriages. He likewise improved the machines for sawing stones and timber, and suggested some alterations in the construction of bridges and canal locks. He died in his sixty-sixth year, his last illness having been occasioned by a severe cold caught during the month of November, while making some experiments with his hydraulic press on the tearing up of trees in Holt Forest. He was a cheerful, benevolent, and affectionate man, neat and methodical in his habits, and knew well how to temper liberality with economy; greatly to his honour he often kept his workmen employed solely for their sake, when the stagnation of trade prevented him from disposing of the products of their labour. As a manufacturer he was distinguished for his promptitude and probity, and was celebrated for the exquisite finish which he gave to his productions. At his death he left his family in affluent circumstances, and his manufacturing establishments have since his death been continued by his sons. Unfortunately, Mr.

Bramah had an invincible dislike to sitting for his portrait, and there
consequently exists no likeness of this distinguished man; for,
although a cast of his face was taken after death by Sir Francis
Chantry, this, together with many others was destroyed by Lady
Chantry after the death of her husband.—*Memoir by Dr. Brown.—
Stuart's Anecdotes of the Steam Engine.* London, 1829.—*Smiles's
Industrial Biography.* London, 1863.

ROBERT BROWN, D.C.L., F.R.S., P.L.S, &c.

MEMBER OF THE INSTITUTE OF FRANCE.

Born December 21, 1773.   Died June 10, 1859.

Robert Brown, whom Humboldt has designated as the " Prince of
Botanists," was the second and only surviving son of the Rev.
James Brown, Episcopalian Minister, of Montrose.   Several generations of his maternal ancestors were, like his father, ministers of
the Scottish Episcopalian Church, and from them he appears to
have inherited a strong attachment to logical and metaphysical
studies, the effects of which are so strikingly manifested in the
philosophical character of his botanical investigations.   At an early
age he was sent to the grammar-school of his native town, and
in 1787 entered at Marischal College, Aberdeen, where he immediately obtained a Ramsay Bursary in philosophy.   About two years
afterwards, on his father quitting Montrose to reside in Edinburgh,
he was removed to the University of that city, in which he continued
his studies for several years; but without taking a degree, although
destined for the medical profession.

In the year 1791, at the age of seventeen, Brown laid before the
Natural History Society, of which he was a member, his earliest
paper, which contained, together with critical notes and observations, an enumeration of such plants as had been discovered in
North Britain subsequent to the publication of Lightfoot's " Flora
Scotica."   Although this paper was not intended for publication, it
brought the young botanist into communication with Dr. Withering,
and laid the foundation of a warm and intimate friendship between
them.   In the year 1795, soon after the embodiment of the Fifeshire
Regiment of Fencible Infantry, Brown obtained in it the double
commission of ensign and assistant surgeon, proceeding with the
regiment to the north of Ireland, in various parts of which he was
stationed until the summer of 1798, when he was detached to
England on recruiting service.

Fortunately for himself and for science, this service enabled him to pass some time in London, where his already established botanical reputation secured him a cordial reception from Sir Joseph Banks, of whose library and collections he availed himself to the utmost. In 1799 he returned to his regimental duties in Ireland, from which he was finally recalled, in December of the following year, by a letter from Sir Joseph Banks, proposing for his acceptance the post of naturalist in the expedition for surveying the coasts of New Holland, then fitting out under the command of Captain Flinders.

In the summer of 1801 he embarked at Portsmouth and set out on this expedition. His absence from England lasted more than four years, during which period the southern, eastern, and northern coasts of New Holland, and the southern part of Van Diemen's Land were thoroughly explored; and he arrived in Liverpool, in the month of October, 1805, enriched with a collection of dried plants amounting to nearly 4000 species, a large proportion of which were not only new to science, but likewise exhibited extraordinary combinations of character and form. Immediately on his arrival in England, Brown was appointed librarian of the Linnean Society, of which he had been elected an associate in 1798. The materials which he had been indefatigable in collecting during this voyage, and the vast store of facts and observations in relation to their structure and affinities which he had accumulated, opened out to him new views upon a multitude of botanical subjects, which he was enabled by his position in the Linnean Society to enlarge, and to perfect, and ultimately to lay before the world in a series of masterly publications, which at once stamped upon him the character of the greatest and most philosophical botanist that England had ever produced.

In 1810 appeared the first volume of his 'Prodromus Floræ novæ Hollandiæ et Insulæ Van Diemen.' This important work, together with his memoirs on Proteaciæ and Asclepiadeæ, which immediately followed, and his 'General Remarks, Geographical and Systematical, on the Botany of Terra Australis,' appended to the 'Narrative of Captain Flinder's Voyage,' published in 1814, by displaying in the most instructive form the superior advantages of the Natural System, gave new life to that system, which had hitherto found little favour in France, and speedily led to its universal adoption. A series of memoirs followed the above works, chiefly in the Transactions of the Linnean Society, or in the appendices to various books of travel and survey, which gave fuller and more complete development to his views upon almost every department of botanical science, and induced the illustrious Humboldt not only to confer upon Brown the title mentioned at the beginning of this memoir, but also to designate him as the "Glory and Ornament of Great Britain."*

* In the dedication of the 'Synopsis Plantarum Orbis Novi,' Roberto Brownio, Britanniarum Gloriæ atque Ornamento, totam Botanices Scientiam ingenio mirifico complectenti.

At the close of the year 1810, on the death of his learned and intimate friend Dryander, Mr. Brown succeeded to the office of Librarian to Sir Joseph Banks, who (on his death in 1820) bequeathed to him for life the use and enjoyment of his library and collections. These were subsequently, with Mr. Brown's consent, and in conformity with the provisions of Sir Joseph's will, transferred, in 1827, to the British Museum; and from this latter date, until his death, he continued to fill the office of Keeper of the Botanical Collections in the National establishment. In 1849 Mr. Brown was elected President of the Linnean Society, of which, soon after the death of Sir Joseph Banks, he had resigned the Librarianship, and had become a fellow.

In 1811 he had been made a fellow of the Royal Society; and in 1839 received its highest honour in the Copley medal, awarded to him " for his discoveries during a series of years on the subject of vegetable impregnation." In the meantime, honours and titles flowed in upon him from all quarters. In 1832 the University of Oxford conferred on him, in conjunction with Dalton, Faraday, and Brewster, the honorary degree of D.C.L.; and, in the succeeding year, he was elected one of the eight foreign associates of the Academy of Sciences of the Institute of France, his name being selected from a list, including those of nine other savans of world-wide reputation, nearly every one of whom has since been elected to the same distinguished honour. During the administration of Sir Robert Peel, he received, in recognition of his great eminence in botanical science, a pension on the Civil List of 200*l.* per annum, and shortly afterwards the King of Prussia decorated him with the cross of the highest Prussian Civil Order—' Pour le Merite.'

Of Mr. Brown's later publications the most important are, his ' Botanical Appendix to Captain Burt's Expedition into Central Australia,' published in 1849; and his Memoir ' On Triplosporite, an undescribed Fossil Fruit,' published in the Linnean Transactions for 1851. The pervading and distinguishing character of all these writings, is to be found in the combination of the minutest accuracy of detail with the most comprehensive generalization; and no theory is propounded which does not rest for its foundation on the most circumspect investigation of all attainable facts. Among the most important anatomical and physiological subjects of which they treat, particular mention is due to the discovery of the nucleus of the vegetable cell, the development of the stamina, together with the mode of fecundation in Asclepiadeœ and Orchideœ; the development of the pollen and of the ovulum in Phœnogamous plants, and the bearing of these facts upon the general subject of impregnation; also the origin and development of the spores of mosses; and the discovery of the peculiar motions which take place in the "active molecules" of matter when seen suspended in a fluid under the microscope. Of structural investigations, the most important are those which establish the relation of the flower to the axis from which it is derived, and of the parts of a flower to each other, as regards both position and number; the analogy between stamina and pistilla: the neuration of the corolla of compositœ, their œstivation and inflorescence; and the structure of the stems of cycadeœ, both recent and fossil.

Mr. Brown was also strongly attached to the study of fossil botany, and, with a view to its prosecution, he formed an extensive and valuable collection of fossil woods, which he has bequeathed, under certain conditions, to the British Museum.

After the death of Sir Joseph Banks, who bequeathed to him his house in Soho Square, Mr. Brown continued to occupy that portion of it which opened upon Dean Street; and it was in the library of that illustrious man, the scene of his labours for sixty years, surrounded by his books and by his collections, that Robert Brown breathed his last, on the 10th of June, 1859, in the eighty-fifth year of his age.—*Memoir by John J. Bennett, F.R.S.*, read at the Anniversary Meeting of the Linnean Society, May, 1859.

SIR M. ISAMBARD BRUNEL, V.P.R.S., &c.

Born April 25, 1769.   Died December 12, 1849.

This celebrated engineer was born at Haqueville, in Normandy, where his family had for several centuries held an honourable position, numbering among its members the eminent French painter Nicholas Poussin. Brunel was educated at the seminary at Rouen, with the intention of his entering holy orders, but he displayed so decided a taste for mathematics and mechanics,* that by the advice of the superior of the establishment he was removed to follow a more congenial career.

His father then destined him for the naval service, which he entered on the appointment of the Mareschal de Castries, the Minister of Marine, and made several voyages to the West Indies. While in this position, although only fifteen years old, his mechanical talents showed themselves on many occasions, and he surprised his captain by the production of a sextant of his own manufacture, with which he took his observations.

In 1792 Brunel returned to France, where he found the revolution at its height, and, like all who entertained Royalist principles, was

---

* At eleven years of age, Brunel's love of tools was so great that he once pawned his hat to buy them; and at the age of twelve he is said to have constructed different articles with as much precision as a regular workman.

compelled to seek safety by flight, which with difficulty he effected,* taking refuge in the United States of America. Here, driven by necessity to the exercise of his talents, he followed the bent of his inclination, and became a civil engineer and architect. His first engagement in this capacity was on the survey of a tract of land near Lake Erie; he then became engaged in cutting canals, and was employed to erect an arsenal and cannon foundry at New York, where he erected several new and ingenious machines. He was also engaged to design and superintend the building of the Bowery Theatre, New York, since destroyed by fire, the roof of which was peculiar and original in its construction. Brunel now rose high in the estimation of the citizens of New York; they appointed him their chief engineer, and in that capacity he organized an establishment for casting and boring ordnance, which at that time was considered unsurpassed for its novelty of design and general practicability. Previously to this the idea of substituting machinery for manual labour in making ships' blocks had long occupied Brunel's mind, and in 1799, having matured his plans, he determined upon coming to England, finding that the United States were unable to afford full occupation for his inventive genius.

In the month of May of the same year Brunel took out his first patent in England, which was for a duplicate writing and drawing machine. His next invention was a machine for twisting cotton-thread and forming it into balls; it measured the length of thread which it wound, and proportioned the size of the ball to its weight and firmness. This machine was not, however, patented, and it became rapidly and generally adopted without bringing any advantage to the inventor.

Brunel's next contrivance was a machine for trimmings and borders for muslins, lawns, and cambrics, somewhat of the nature of a sewing machine. Shortly after this he patented his famous block-machinery, which he submitted for the inspection of the Admiralty in 1801.

Earl St. Vincent was at that time at the head of the Admiralty, and after many delays and difficulties, which were ultimately overcome chiefly through the influence of Earl Spencer and Sir Samuel Bentham, Brunel's system was adopted; and he was enabled to erect the beautiful and effective machinery, which has continued until the present time, without any alteration or improvement, to

---

* Brunel had scarcely left the shores of France when he found that he had lost his passport. This difficulty he, however, got over by borrowing a passport from a fellow-traveller, which he copied so exactly in every particular, down to the very seal, that it was deemed proof against all scrutiny. He had hardly completed his task when the American vessel was stopped by a French frigate, and all the passengers were ordered to show their passports. Brunel, with perfect self-possession, was the first to show his, and not the slightest doubt was aroused as to its authenticity.

produce nearly all the blocks used in the Royal Navy.* The construction of this block machinery, completed in 1808, was entrusted to the late Mr. Henry Maudslay, from whom Brunel had already derived considerable assistance in the execution of his models and working out of his designs. It was erected in Portsmouth Dockyard, and the economy produced by the first year's use of these machines was estimated at about 24,000l., two-thirds of which sum was awarded to the ingenious inventor, who was soon after engaged by the government to erect extensive saw mills, and carry out other improvements at Chatham and Woolwich. Brunel was essentially an inventor; besides the above-mentioned machines, he took out patents for "the manufacture of tin-foil," for "copying presses," for "stereotype printing plates," a contrivance for making the small boxes used by druggists, and a nail-making machine.

He likewise introduced the system of cutting veneers by circular saws of a large diameter, to which is mainly due the present extensive application of veneers of wood to ornamental furniture.

A short time before the termination of the war with France he devised a plan for making shoes by machinery, and under the countenance of the Duke of York the shoes so manufactured were introduced for the use of the army, on account of their strength, cheapness, and durability; but at the peace in 1815, the machines were laid aside, manual labour having become cheaper, and the demand for military equipments having in a measure ceased. Steam navigation also attracted Brunel's attention, and he became deeply interested in establishing the Ramsgate steam vessels, which were among the first that plied effectively on the River Thames. About this period, after much labour and perseverance, he induced the Admiralty to permit the application of steam for towing vessels to sea, the experiments being made chiefly at his own expense, a small sum in aid having been promised, but eventually withdrawn before the completion of the trials, the Admiralty considering the attempt too chimerical to be seriously entertained.

In the year 1824 Brunel, undeterred by the two previous failures of Dodd and Trevethick, commenced his great work—the Thames Tunnel. It is said that the original idea occurred to him as applied to the Neva at St. Petersburgh, in order to avoid the inconvenience arising from the floating ice; a plan which he offered to the Emperor Alexander, on the occasion of his visit to this country in 1814. During the above-mentioned year a company was formed for the execution of this work, under the auspices of the Duke of Wellington, who had always entertained a favourable view as to its practicability; and after numerous accidents, and frequent suspensions of the works, this great and novel undertaking was successfully

* The total number of machines employed in the various operations of making a ship's block by this method was forty-four, and 16,000 blocks of various sizes could be turned out in the course of a year.

accomplished, and opened to the public in the year 1843. In the prosecution of this undertaking Sir Isambard derived great assistance from his son, the late Mr. I. K. Brunel.

The shield, as it was termed, under shelter of which the excavation beneath the bed of the river was carried forward, required very peculiar contrivances to adapt it to its purpose. It was made in sections or compartments contained in a strong square frame, each section or compartment being moved forward by screws, as the men working in them proceeded with the excavation; the entire shield was thus enabled to be moved forward, and the brickwork, consisting of two tunnels, was built up to the extent that it had been advanced.

After the completion of the Tunnel, Brunel's health became seriously impaired from the labours he had undergone in its execution, and he was unable to mix in active life; he expired on the 12th of December, 1849, in his eighty-first year, after a long illness.

He received the honour of Knighthood in 1841, and the order of the Legion of honour in 1829; he was also a corresponding member of the French Institute, a Fellow of the Royal Society, and a member of the Institution of Civil Engineers, which he joined in the year 1823.—*Annual Report of the Institution of Civil Engineers.* December 17, 1850.—*Beamish's Life of Brunel.* London, 1862.

EDMUND CARTWRIGHT, D.D., F.R.S., &c.

Born April 24, 1743.   Died October 30, 1823.

Dr. Cartwright, whose invention of the power-loom may be considered as one of the valuable elements of our national manufacturing superiority, was born at Marnham in Nottinghamshire, and was the youngest of three brothers, all of whom were remarkable men.* He was educated under Dr. Clarke, at the Grammar School of Wakefield, and had he been permitted to follow the bent of his own inclination in the choice of a profession, would have preferred the navy; but two of his brothers being already designed for that service, it was thought advisable that Edmund should enter the Church. Dr. Cartwright began his academical studies at University College, Oxford, where he was entered at fourteen years of age, and during the vacations was placed under the private tuition of Dr. Langhorne, the editor of 'Plutarch's Lives.'

* Dr. Cartwright was the younger brother of Major John Cartwright, the well-known English Reformer of the reign of George III., to whose memory a bronze statue is erected in Burton Crescent, London.

In process of time he became distinguished for his literary abilities, and was elected a Fellow of Magdalen College. He likewise evinced a considerable taste for poetry, and published in 1770 a legendary tale, entitled 'Armine and Elvira,' which went through seven editions in little more than a year, and was greatly admired for its pathos and elegant simplicity. Some years subsequent to this, Cartwright wrote 'The Prince of Peace,' published in 1779, and was also for several years a principal contributor to the 'Monthly Review.'

In the year 1772 he married the daughter of Richard Whittaker, Esq., of Doncaster, and after his marriage resided first at Marnham, and afterwards at Brampton in Derbyshire, to the perpetual curacy of which he was presented by the Dean of Lincoln, Dr. Cust. It was while attending to his clerical duties at this latter place, that Cartwright discovered the application of yeast as a remedy for typhus fever. In 1779 he was presented to the living of Goadby Marwood in Leicestershire, and continued to reside there until the summer of 1796, when he removed with his family* to London, as being a situation more favourable for the cultivation of the scientific pursuits in which he had by that time become engrossed.

Dr. Cartwright had attained the mature age of forty, before his attention was drawn towards the subject of weaving, by the following accidental occurrence:—In the summer of 1784, he happened to be on a visit at Matlock, in Derbyshire, and in the company of some gentlemen from Manchester. The conversation turned upon Arkwright's spinning machinery; and fears were expressed by one of the company, that, in consequence of the recent improvements, so much cotton would soon be spun, that hands would not be found to weave it. To this the doctor replied, that the only remedy for such an evil would be to apply the power of machinery to weaving as well as spinning. The discussion which ensued upon the practicability of doing this, made such an impression on Cartwright's mind, that on returning home he determined to try and see what he could do.

His first attempts, as might be supposed, were very clumsy, but he at length succeeded in constructing a machine (for which he took out a patent in 1785), which, although rude and cumbersome in its action, was yet capable of weaving a piece of cloth. Up to this time he had never turned his mind to anything mechanical, either in theory or practice, and his invention was consequently susceptible of great improvement. To accomplish this, he now examined with care the contrivances already in use among the weavers, and availing himself of their general principles, produced in the year 1787 a far more complete and valuable machine, since known as the power-loom.

* Dr. Cartwright was married twice. His first wife died in 1785, and in 1790 he married the youngest daughter of the Rev. Dr. Kearney.

Shortly after he had brought his loom to perfection, a manufacturer who had called upon him to see it at work, after expressing his admiration at the ingenuity displayed in it, remarked, that wonderful as was Dr. Cartwright's skill, there was one thing that would effectually baffle him, and that was, the weaving of patterns in checks, or, in other words, the combining in the same web a pattern or fancy figure with the crossing colours which constitute the check. The doctor made no reply to this at the time; but some weeks afterwards, on receiving a second visit from the same person, he showed him a piece of muslin, of the description mentioned, beautifully executed by machinery, which so astonished the man, that he roundly declared his conviction that some more than human agency must have been called in on the occasion.*

Dr. Cartwright being precluded by his clerical character from entering himself into the manufacture of his machines, a weaving factory was erected at Doncaster, by some friends, with his licence, but it was unsuccessful; and another establishment, built at Manchester, containing 500 looms, was destroyed by an exasperated mob in 1790. Cartwright, however, still continued his inventions, and shortly afterwards contrived a wool-combing machine, which met with even fiercer opposition from the working-classes, who went the length of petitioning parliament to suppress all such obnoxious machines. Their great utility, however, caused them by degrees to be generally adopted; and at the time of Cartwright's death, steam-looms had increased so rapidly, that they were performing the work of 200,000 men.

Notwithstanding the great advantages which the cotton and wool manufacturers reaped from these inventions, their author had as yet obtained no emolument from them, but, on the contrary, had incurred a heavy loss. In consideration of this, and on the petition of several influential cotton-spinners, Parliament in 1810 made the doctor a grant of 10,000l.—a sum which, although munificent as a present, hardly covered what he had expended in his experiments. Having received the sum awarded by Parliament, and being now sixty-six years of age, Dr. Cartwright was desirous of passing the remainder of his life in retirement and tranquillity, and for this purpose purchased a small farm at Hollenden, in Kent. At this place he spent the remainder of his life, occupied in various scientific and mechanical experiments.

Dr. Cartwright was the author of many other inventions in the arts and agriculture, for some of which he received premiums from the Board of Agriculture and Society of Arts. He also contrived an ingenious modification of the steam-engine, in which he made use of *surface condensation*, and metallic spring packing for the piston.

Till within a few days of his death, Dr. Cartwright retained full

* *Pursuit of Knowledge*, vol. 2.

possession of his mental faculties, and attained, at the time of his decease in 1823, the age of eighty-one. His remains were interred in the church at Battle, in Sussex. *Memoir of Dr. Edmund Cart-wright.* London, 1843.—*Stuart's Anecdotes of the Steam-Engine.* London, 1829.

=====

THE HON. HENRY CAVENDISH, F.R.S.

Born October 10, 1731.   Died February 24, 1810.

Henry Cavendish, the third in order of time among the four great English pneumatic chemists of the eighteenth century,[*] was the younger son of Lord Charles Cavendish, whose father was the second Duke of Devonshire. His family trace back their descent in unbroken and unquestionable links to Sir John Cavendish, Lord Chief Justice during the reign of Edward III. The great majority of the distinguished chemists of Great Britain have sprung from the middle and lower ranks of the people, but in this respect Henry Cavendish presents a remarkable exception. He was moreover immensely wealthy, so much so, that it has been epigrammatically remarked of him, "That he was the richest of all wise men, and probably, too, the wisest of all rich men;" yet no one could well be more indifferent than he, to the external advantages which are conferred by birth and fortune. Few particulars are known of his early life. He was born at Nice, whither his mother, who died when he was two years old, had gone for the sake of her health.

In 1742 Cavendish became a pupil at Dr. Newcome's school at Hackney, continuing his studies there until he had reached his seventeenth year, when he went to Cambridge, where he matriculated in the first rank on the 18th of December, 1749. He remained at this university until 1753, but did not graduate.

After leaving Cambridge, the personal history of Cavendish becomes a blank for the next ten years. He joined the Royal Society in 1760, but did not contribute anything to its 'Transactions' until the year 1766, when he published his paper 'On Factitious Airs,' which contains the first distinct exposition of the properties of hydrogen, and the first full account of those of carbonic acid; and a paper published by him in the following year may be considered as a still further extension of his research into the properties of this acid.

For some considerable time after this, Cavendish appears to have

[*] The other three being Hales, Black, and Priestly.

laid aside Chemistry for other departments of physics. In 1771 he published an elaborate paper on the theory of the principal phenomena of electricity; and in 1776 appeared the curious and interesting account of his attempts to imitate the effects of the torpedo, by an apparatus constructed in imitation of the living fish, and placed in connection with a frictional electrical machine and a Leyden battery. In this imitation he succeeded so well, that all doubts were removed as to the identity of the torpedinal benumbing power with common electricity. In 1776 Cavendish was selected by the Royal Society, in whose 'Transactions' all his previous papers had been published, to describe the various meteorological instruments which were made use of in their apartments; and the succeeding year to this marks the period when he commenced his most important chemical researches, entitled 'Experiments on Air,' which were carried on with frequent and sometimes long interruptions until 1788, no part of them, however, having been published before the year 1783. They led to the discovery of the constant quantitative composition of the atmosphere, the compound nature of water, and the composition of nitric acid. To solve the important problems, whether the atmosphere is constant in its composition, and if so, what is its composition? Cavendish experimented in 1781 for some sixty successive days, making many hundred analyses of air. The honour of the discovery of the compound nature of water, by which perhaps his name has become most famous, is also claimed by James Watt. Cavendish, however, seems at all events entitled to the honour of having first supplied the data on which that discovery was founded, whilst Watt appears to have supplied the conclusion.

Between the years 1783 and 1788, Cavendish published his papers on 'Heat,' and his 'Experiments on Air;' the former are three in number, and relate chiefly to the phenomena of congelation, and embody some of the results of experiments made as early as the year 1764. The first of these papers refer to quicksilver, demonstrating the true freezing-point of this metal to be 39° or 40° below zero, while the second and third refer to the freezing of the mineral acids and of alcohol.

His experiments on air, which led to the important results already referred to, supplied materials for four papers, besides leading to the observation of many phenomena which were never made public. With the last of these papers published in 1788, Cavendish closed his chemical researches, his remaining publications referring to meteorology and astronomy.

In 1798 appeared the celebrated enquiry into the density of the earth, communicated by Cavendish, in a paper to the Royal Society, in which he determined, by means of an apparatus contrived by the Rev. John Mitchell, the density of our globe to be 5·4,—or, in other words, nearly five-and-a-half times heavier than the same bulk of water would be. The experiments made with this apparatus consisted in observing, with many precautions, the movements of a long lever delicately suspended by the centre, so as to hang horizontally, and furnished at either extremity with small leaden balls. When two much larger and heavier balls of the same metal were brought near the smaller ones, the latter were attracted towards them with a certain force, the measurement of which supplied one essential datum for the determination of the mean density of the earth. No greater compliment to the accuracy of the 'Cavendish Experiment' (as the researches taken as a whole are generally called) can be afforded, than the slight difference which appeared when the experiment was repeated at a later period by Francis Baily, who, with extraordinary precautions to ensure a correct result, and with all the improvements which forty fertile years had added to mechanical contrivances, determined the density to be 5·6, or a little more than five-and-a-half times that of water.

The last paper which Cavendish published, on an improvement in the manner of dividing astronomical instruments, appeared in 1809,—a year before his death. His published papers give, however, but an imperfect notion of the great extent of ground over which he travelled in the course of his investigations, and of the success with which he explored it. He was an excellent mathematician, electrician, astronomer, meteorologist, and geologist, and a chemist equally learned and original. He lived retired from the world among his books and instruments; he never meddled with the affairs of active life, but passed his whole time in storing his mind with the knowledge imparted by former inquirers, and in extending its bounds. His dress was of the oldest fashion; his walk was quick and uneasy; he never appeared in London unless lying back in the corner of his carriage; and he probably uttered fewer words in the course of his life than any man who ever lived to fourscore years. His private character has been thus described by Dr. George Wilson, from whose comprehensive life of Cavendish the present memoir has been chiefly taken :—

"Morally it was a blank, and can only be described by a series of negations. He did not love, he did not hate, he did not hope, he did not fear, he did not worship as others do. He separated himself from his fellow men, and apparently from God. There was nothing earnest, enthusiastic, heroic or chivalrous in his nature; and as little was there anything mean, grovelling or ignoble. He was almost passionless. An intellectual head thinking, a pair of wonderfully acute eyes observing, and a pair of very skilful hands experimenting or recording, are all that I recognize in his memorials. His brain seems to have been but a calculating engine; his eyes inlets of vision, not fountains of tears; his hands instruments of manipulation, which never trembled with emotion, or were clasped together in adoration, thanksgiving or despair; his heart only an anatomical organ necessary for the circulation of the blood. A sense of isolation from his brethren made him shrink from their society and avoid their presence; but he did so as one conscious of an infirmity, not boasting of an excellence. He was like a deaf mute, sitting apart from a circle whose looks and gestures show that they are uttering and listening to music and eloquence, in producing or welcoming which he can be no sharer. Wisely therefore he dwelt apart. He was one of the unthanked benefactors of his race, who was patiently teaching and serving mankind, whilst they were shrinking from his coldness or mocking his peculiarities. He could not sing for them a sweet song, or create a 'thing of beauty,' which would be 'a joy for ever,' or touch their hearts, or fire their spirits, or deepen their reverence or their fervour. He was not a poet, a priest, or a prophet, but only a cold clear intelligence, raying down pure white light, which brightened everything on which it fell, but warmed nothing—a star of at least the second, if not of the first magnitude in the intellectual firmament."

As Cavendish had lived, so he died—alone. He died after a short illness, probably the first as well as the last under which he ever suffered. His habit of curious observation continued to the end; he was desirous of marking the progress of disease and the gradual extinction of the vital powers. With this view, that he might not be disturbed, he desired to be left alone. His servant returning sooner than he had wished was ordered again to leave the chamber of death, and when he came back a second time he found his master had expired. Although in many respects of a highly liberal character, so great was the frugality of his ordinary mode of living in comparison to his income, that at his death Cavendish left the enormous sum of 1,200,000*l.* to be divided among his relations.— *Life of the Hon. Henry Cavendish, by George Wilson, M.D., F.R.S.E.* London, 1851.—*Brougham's Lives of Philosophers.* London and Glasgow, 1855.

WILLIAM CHAPMAN, M.R.I.A.

Born 1749.   Died May 29, 1832.

William Chapman, Civil Engineer, was born at Whitby, in Yorkshire, of a respectable and wealthy family, who had resided in that town for several generations. He inherited the freedom of Newcastle-upon-Tyne from his father, who, in common with all the chief people of Whitby, was engaged in shipping, and was besides particularly distinguished for his attainments in mathematics and other scientific pursuits. William Chapman derived great advantage from his father's knowledge of these subjects, contracting a strong taste for similar occupations. After receiving a liberal education at different public schools, he was put in command, at the early age of eighteen, of a merchant vessel, in which he enjoyed the opportunity of visiting numerous harbours, both in Great Britain and other countries. He continued thus occupied for a period of three years, losing no opportunity of making himself acquainted with the circumstances of the various harbours he was in the habit of visiting, and he thus acquired that valuable practical knowledge on the subject of these works for which he became afterwards so highly distinguished.

After leaving the merchant service, Mr. Chapman was fortunate enough to become acquainted with James Watt, with his partner Matthew Boulton, and also with Mr. Wooller, Engineer to the Board of Ordnance. By these eminent men he was strongly advised to become an engineer, and follow as a profession that which he had already closely studied as an amusement. Chapman accordingly accompanied Mr. Boulton into Ireland, about the close of the year 1783, but although well introduced, was unable to obtain any employment of consequence in that country, until he had written a prize essay on the effects of the river Dodder on the Harbour of Dublin. Shortly after this, he was appointed resident engineer to the County of Kildare Canal, the works of which were carried on under the surveillance of the Duke of Leinster, the county members, and other leading men. In the execution of this undertaking, Mr. Chapman was requested not to alter the direction of the roads intersected by it, although one of them deviated from the right angle across the canal upwards of 50 deg. To meet this difficulty, and knowing that a bridge of the ordinary construction, with any obliquity, could not possibly stand, Chapman invented, and put into practice, the method of building oblique or skew bridges, which has since been so generally adopted throughout the country, in railway, canal, and other bridges. Before this period, (1787), whenever a road crossed the course of a canal or river, requiring the construction of a bridge, it had been usual to deviate the course, either of the road or the object it crossed, so that the crossing should be at right angles; a practice which occasioned a great waste of land and considerable expense as well as awkward and dangerous bends in the roads thus treated. In some few cases where the bridge was required to be of only a small opening, no alteration in the direction was made, but a bridge built of an oblique form, that is with abutments forming oblique angles with the road passing over it, the courses of the arch being built in lines parallel with the abutments, and the ends of the voussoirs bevelled off to coincide with the direction of the road. Bridges built in this manner consequently became highly dangerous when the span was great, or the obliquity considerable. The value of Chapman's invention consists in this, that he gave the means of building bridges on the skew principle, in any required situation, without altering the direction of the roads or wasting material, and at an expense little above that of ordinary rectangular bridges. This he accomplished by the principle of building the courses of voussoirs at right angles to the face of the arch, meeting the abutments at oblique angles, being the very reverse of the system previously practised.

During the progress of the Kildare Canal, Mr. Chapman, at the request of the Duke of Leinster, became overseer, conjointly with him and the Hon. Mr. Ponsonby Moore, for the building a bridge of five arches over the Liffey, to replace the former one which had been carried away by a flood. The bridge itself was a plain structure, but the means employed in forming and securing the foundations attracted general attention, and brought Mr. Chapman into still greater notice. From this time the number and importance of his professional engagements continued to increase, and he was engaged to survey and report upon several projects for the improvement of the navigations of various rivers, of which plans the most important was the navigation of the river Barrow, from Athy downwards. During this period he was appointed consulting engineer to the Grand Canal of Ireland, of which undertaking Mr. Jessop was directing engineer; and under the joint superintendence and surveys of these two gentlemen, the extension of the Grand Canal from Robarts Town to Tullamore was laid out, as well as the Dock between Dublin and Ringsend, and the canal of communication by the line of the circular road. The projected canal from near Tullamore passed through extensive bogs, some of which were thirty feet in depth, and in consequence of its difficulties was laid out by Mr. Chapman himself. The directors of the Grand canal had expended upwards of 100,000l. in a very short space of ground between Robarts Town and Bathangar, from not being acquainted with the extent of the subsidence of bogs under superincumbent weight, or when laid dry by drainage. Mr. Chapman, therefore, availed himself of their dearly bought experience, and adopted the following ingenious method of comparing different kinds of bogs and their relative subsidence. He provided himself with a cylindric implement of steel plate, sharp at the lower edges, and containing exactly one hundredth part of a cubic foot, and having divided the strata of the bogs into as many leading classes and subdivisions as were necessary, he filled the cylinders with a specimen of each, by twisting them round so as to cut the fibres of the bog. The samples thus taken were carefully cut off at the level of the cylindric guage, and their weight having been ascertained, they were left to dry during the space of several months; and when in a firm state and consequently greatly contracted, were again weighed, the result being that the originally wettest bog was found to have lost 10–11ths of its weight, and the firmest 2–3rds, the rest in due progression between. It therefore became a simple process to ascertain pretty nearly the extent of subsidence in any bog to be passed through, and of course to lay out the line of the canal with such levels, that after subsidence, its surface should be at the required depth below the surface of the bog.

Amongst Mr. Chapman's other extensive employments in Ireland, he caused, at the instance of the Irish Government, a survey to be made of the harbour of Dublin to beyond the Bar at Howth; and on this occasion projected a pier from the Clontarf shore to a due distance from the lighthouse, and then to the westward to a proper distance from the north wall, so as to confine all the tidal water covering that vast space, and to cause it to pass down the channel of Pool Beg, in place of being permitted to flow inwards and outwards over the North Bull.

In the year 1794 Mr. Chapman returned from Ireland, and fixed his general residence at Newcastle-upon-Tyne. About this time the great project of a canal communication between the German Ocean and the Irish Sea, was engaging general attention in the North of England, and Mr. Chapman was fixed upon to survey the line of country for this proposed canal between Newcastle and the Solway Firth. His reports on this subject, which were made during the years 1795 and 1796, are still extant; and although the work to which they relate was never executed, the documents connected with it are of a very interesting nature. In 1808 this project, which had lain dormant for many years, was again revived, and Mr. Telford was employed to survey and report upon the best line of canal between Carlisle and a suitable port on the Solway Firth. Although Mr. Telford's plan was highly approved of, the time had not yet arrived for the carrying out of even this small portion of the original great scheme; and it was not until the year 1818, when Mr. Chapman drew up a plan and report upon this line from Carlisle to Bowness, that a Bill was brought into Parliament, for which an act was obtained early in 1819. The canal which has been in successful operation for many years, is eleven-and-a-half miles in length, and cost about 120,000*l.* It commences on the south-eastern side of Carlisle, and falls into the sea, through a height of seventy feet, by means of nine locks.

About the year 1796 Mr. Chapman became a member of the Society of Civil Engineers, which at that time numbered amongst its members Watt, Jessop, and Rennie, and amongst its honorary associates Sir Joseph Banks, and other leading men of the day. In conjunction with Mr. Rennie, Chapman was then occupied in designing the London Docks, and subsequently the southern dock and basin at Hull. He was also engaged as engineer for the construction of Leith, Scarborough, and Seaham Harbours, the last named work being undertaken for the Marquis of Londonderry.

In addition to his regular professional occupations, Mr. Chapman devoted a portion of his time to the publication of works bearing on engineering. Amongst the most important of these were the following : ' A Treatise on the various inventions for effecting ascents in rivers ;' 'Hints on the necessity of Legislative interference for registering the extent of workings in the Coal Seams, and preventing such accidents as arise from want of that knowledge ;' ' An Essay on Cordage ;' and 'A Treatise on the preservation of Timber from premature decay.' Mr. Chapman also took out a patent for an improvement upon Captain Huddart's system of manufacturing ropes. This method was successfully carried into effect in all the rope grounds on the river Tyne, and in some of those on the Wear and Tweed. His next invention was for an expeditious and easily practicable method of lowering coal waggons, with their contents, immediately over the hatchways of ships, so as to prevent the great breakage of coals which attended the usual method of shooting them through long spouts; this system, after the expiration of the patent became universal upon the Tyne.

. Mr. Chapman possessed a robust constitution, and practised through life the most temperate habits ; he was thus enabled to retain the full enjoyment of his faculties, and to continue employed upon various public works, in drainages, canals, and harbours, up till within a very short period of his decease, which occurred in 1832, in the eighty-third year of his age.—*Life of Chapman.* London, John Weale.

SIR WILLIAM CONGREVE, BART., F.R.S.

Born in Middlesex, May 20, 1772. Died May 3, 1828.

Sir William Congreve was the son of the first baronet, an Artillery officer of the same name. He entered early into the branch of military service his father had pursued, and, in 1816, attained in it the rank of Lieutenant-Colonel. He was also at this time equerry to the Prince Regent, which office he retained on the occasion of his quitting the military service in 1820. Congreve very early distinguished himself by his inventions in the construction of missiles. He invented the rocket which bears his name in the year 1808, and succeeded in establishing this destructive engine of warfare as a permanent instrument in military and naval tactics, both at home and abroad. It was used by Lord Cochrane in his attack on the French squadron in the Basque roads, in the expedition against Walcheren, at Waterloo, and with most serviceable effect in the attack on Algiers. It was also used at the battle of Leipzig in 1813, and for its service on this occasion the Order of St. Anne was conferred on Sir William by the Emperor of Russia. Since that time the rocket has been much improved and modified, and has become an essential part of every armament, not in England alone, but universally.

Sir William Congreve was elected a Fellow of the Royal Society in the year 1811. In 1812 he became a Member of Parliament for Gatton, and in 1820 and 1826 for Plymouth. He succeeded his father as baronet in 1814. Besides the above important invention, Sir William wrote and published in 1812 an 'Elementary Treatise on the Mounting of Naval Ordnance,' and in 1815 'A Description of the Hydro-Pneumatic Lock.' During the course of the same year he obtained a patent for a new mode of manufacturing gunpowder. This invention consisted, first, of a machine for producing as perfect a mixture as possible of the ingredients ; and, secondly, of an improved mode of passing the mill-cake under the press, and a new granulating machine. In 1819 a patent was granted to him for an improved mode of inlaying or combining different metals, and another for certain improvements in the manufacture of bank-note paper for the prevention of forgery.

The last public service performed by Sir William was the drawing up and publishing, in 1823, a very interesting report on the gaslight establishments of the metropolis. In 1826, he became mixed up in the speculative mania which prevailed at that period, and was ultimately compelled to seek refuge on the continent at Toulouse, where he shortly afterwards died at the age of fifty-six.—*Annual Register*, 1828.

SAMUEL CROMPTON.

Born December 3, 1753. Died June 26, 1827.

Few men, perhaps, have ever conferred so great a benefit on their country and reaped so little profit for themselves as Samuel Crompton, inventor of the Spinning Mule. He was born at Firwood, in the township of Tonge near Bolton, where his parents occupied a farm, and spent their leisure hours according to the custom of the period—in the operations of carding, spinning, and weaving. Soon after the birth of Samuel, the Cromptons removed to a cottage near Lower Wood in the same township, and afterwards, when their child was five years old, to a portion of the neighbouring ancient mansion called Hall-in-the-Wood. Almost immediately after this last removal Samuel's father died, at the early age of thirty seven, and he was left to be brought up under the care of his mother, a prudent and virtuous woman, who took care that her son should have the benefit of all available means of education. Samuel first attended the school of Mr. Lever in Church Street, Bolton, but was very early removed to the school of William Barlow, a master well known at that time for his success as a teacher of writing, arithmetic, and the higher branches of mathematics.

From the exigencies of her situation, Mrs. Crompton was compelled to take advantage of her son's assistance, as soon as she possibly could, and there is little doubt that Samuel's legs must have been accustomed to the loom almost as soon as they were long enough to touch the treddles. Little, however, is known of his early life until the year 1769. He was then sixteen years old, and continued to reside with his mother, occupied during the day at the loom and spending his evenings at a school in Bolton, where he advanced his knowledge of algebra, mathematics, and trigonometry. For some years previous to this period there had been a greatly increased demand for all kinds of cotton goods, particularly for imitations of the fine muslins imported from India; and many attempts were made by the manufacturers in Lancashire and Scotland to produce similar fabrics, but without success, for the handspun yarn of this country could not compete with the delicate filaments produced by Hindoo fingers. Still, the demand for fine cottons of various kinds was so considerable, that the weavers, for the sake of high wages, were stimulated to make great exertions. But they were continually impeded by the scarcity of yarn for weft, which often kept them idle half their time, or compelled them to collect it in small quantities from the cottages round about.

Another important cause of this scarcity had been the invention of the fly-shuttle, by Kay of Bury, in 1738, which by doubling the speed of the weaver's operations, had destroyed the arrangement which, up to that time, existed between the quantity of yarn spun and the weavers' demand for it. This natural balance, the fly-shuttle suddenly disturbed, and, notwithstanding the great efforts of others, it was not again adjusted until after Crompton's invention was in full operation. Such was the weavers' state of starvation for yarn, when, in 1767, Hargreaves invented the jenny, which enabled a number of threads to be spun at the same time.

It was on one of these machines with eight spindles, that Samuel Crompton was in the habit of spinning the yarn which he afterwards wove into quilting, and he continued thus occupied for the five following years. During this period, being debarred from company and accustomed to solitude, he began to show a taste for music; to gratify which he was led to the first trial of his mechanical skill in making a violin, upon which he commenced learning to play. With this musical friend Crompton would beguile many a long winter night, or during the summer evenings wander contemplatively among the green lanes, or by the margin of the pleasant brook that swept round the romantic old residence of Hall-in-the-Wood. He had, however, little leisure in general to spend with his favourite instrument; the necessities of his situation compelled him to perform daily a certain amount of weaving, and he only succeeded in performing this at the expense of much time lost in mending the ever breaking ends of the yarn spun on Hargreave's machine, which was of a very soft nature, and quite unfitted for warps or for the muslins so much in demand.

During this same period Arkwright had risen to eminence, by adopting and carrying into practice the ideas of Highs,* and one Kay a clockmaker, and had constructed his water-frame, which by means of rollers produced thread of a very superior texture and firmness. It remained, however, for Crompton to combine in his machine the improvements of Hargreaves and Arkwright, and hence was derived the name given to it of the Spinning-Mule.

Crompton commenced the construction of this machine, which for many years was known by the name of the ' Hall-i'-th'-Wood Wheels,' in the year 1774. His first spinning-mule was constructed chiefly in wood, by the aid of a scanty supply of tools which had been left by his father, who, enthusiastically fond of music, had shortly before his death commenced making an organ. With the help of these tools, and the assistance which a small wayside smithy afforded him, Samuel Crompton completed that invention which, from the extended benefits it has conferred upon our commerce, entitles him to rank amongst the greatest inventors Britain has ever produced. The important part of his invention was the spindle carriage, and the principle of there being no strain upon the thread until it was completed. This was accomplished by causing the carriage with the spindles to recede by the movement of the hand and knee, just as the rollers delivered out the elongated thread in a soft state, so that it would allow of a considerable stretch, before the thread had to encounter the stress of winding upon the spindle. "This," as the late Mr. Kennedy of Manchester truly said, "was the corner stone of his invention."

When Crompton was on the eve of completing his first mule, about the year 1779, the Blackburn spinners and weavers, who had previously driven Hargreaves from his home, again commenced their riotous proceedings, and began to destroy all the jennys round about, which had more than twenty spindles. Crompton, fearful lest his new machine should meet with a similar fate, took it to pieces and kept it hid in a loft above the ceiling of his room during several weeks. In the course of the same year, however, the Hall-i'-th'-Wood Wheel was completed, and the yarn spun on it proved fit for the manufacture of muslins of an extremely fine and delicate texture.

* Highs or Hays was a reedmaker at Leigh, and in 1767 took up the plan of attempting to spin by rollers running at different speeds, previously invented by Lewis Paul in 1738. Highs employed Kay to carry out his plans, from whom Arkwright obtained the requisite information.

Shortly before this, Crompton had married Mary Pimlott, the daughter of a gentleman residing at New Keys Hall, near Warrington. After his marriage he lived in a cottage attached to the old Hall, though he still continued to occupy part of the mansion, in one of whose large rooms he now operated upon the mule with the utmost secrecy and with perfect success, startling the manufacturing world by the production of yarn which both in fineness and firmness had hitherto been unattainable. This seems to have been the happiest portion of Crompton's life. He was then twenty-seven years of age, and the acknowledged inventor of a machine which, from the first hour of its operation, altered the entire system of cotton manufacture in this country. Its merit was universally acknowledged by all engaged in the trade who had an opportunity to examine the yarn spun on it, or the fabrics made from that yarn; but paradoxical as it may appear, the very *perfection of his principle of spinning*, was in a measure instrumental in depriving him of the harvest for which he had so laboriously worked.

The demand for his yarn became so extensive and urgent, that the old Hall was literally besieged by manufacturers and others from the surrounding districts—many of whom came to purchase yarn, but many more to try and penetrate the mystery of the new wheel, and to discover if possible the principle of its operations. All kinds of stratagems were practised in order to obtain admission to the house; and one inquisitive adventurer is said to have ensconced himself for some days in the cockloft, where he watched Samuel at work through a gimlet-hole pierced through the ceiling.

Crompton, at length wearied out, and seeing the utter impossibility of retaining his secret, or of spinning upon the machine with the undisturbed secrecy he desired, yielded to the urgent solicitations, and liberal but deceitful promises of numerous manufacturers, and surrendered to them not only the secret of the principle upon which he spun the much prized yarn, but likewise the machine itself. This he did on the faith of an agreement drawn up by themselves, in which they promised to subscribe certain sums as a reward for his improvement in spinning. No sooner, however, was the mule given up to the public than the subscriptions entirely ceased, and many of those who had previously put down their names evaded or refused payment; some actually denounced Crompton as an impostor, and when he respectfully put before them their own written agreement, asked him how he dared to come on such an errand!

The gross sum of money realized by this subscription amounted to between 50 and 100*l.* Mr. Crompton himself says:—" I received as much by way of subscription as built me a new machine, with only four spindles more than the one I had given up—the old one having forty-eight, and the new one fifty-two spindles." This shameful treatment rested in Crompton's memory through life, and

to the morbid distrust of his fellow-men, which it engendered, may
be ascribed many of the misfortunes which attended his succeeding
life.

About the year 1785 Mr. Crompton removed from the 'Hall-in-
the-Wood' to a farmhouse at Oldhams, in the township of Sharples,
about two miles from Bolton. Here he farmed several acres of land,
and kept three or four cows; while in the upper story of the house
was erected his spinning mule, upon which he continued to spin
with as much privacy as possible. He was, nevertheless, still
troubled by many curious visitors, who were desirous of seeing the
improvements he was supposed to have made on it. Among others
he received two visits from the first Sir Robert Peel, then an
eminent though untitled manufacturer, who came with the hope of
inducing Crompton to join his establishment, and on his second
visit made him an offer of partnership. It is much to be regretted
that this offer was declined, as Mr. Peel's enterprising business
character was exactly that most suited for supporting Crompton's
great inventive genius. Had these two men continued as partners
at this particular time, the successful development of the cotton
trade would have been hastened by at least twenty years, while a
large and well deserved fortune might have been secured to
Crompton and his children.

Excelling all other spinners in the quality and fineness of his
yarn, Crompton continued to obtain a high price for all he could
produce, but his production was restricted to the work of his own
hands, (an increasing family having deprived him of the aid of his
wife); for whenever he commenced to teach any new hands to
assist him in his work, no matter how strictly they were bound to
serve him by honour, by gratitude, or by law, as soon as they
acquired a little knowledge and experience under his tuition, they
were invariably seduced from his service by his wealthy competitors; so that he was ultimately compelled to renounce the use
of his mules, and betake himself to his original occupation of
weaving, or at least to spin only such yarn as he could employ in
his own looms as a small manufacturer.

In 1800 some gentlemen of Manchester, among whom ought to
be mentioned Mr. George Lee and Mr. Kennedy, sensible that Mr.
Crompton had been illused and neglected, agreed, without his
knowledge, to promote a subscription on such a scale as would
result in a substantial reward for his labours. But this scheme,
although generous and noble in its intention, in a great measure
failed. Before it could be carried out, the country suffered severe
distress from a failure in the crops; in addition to this the horrors
of the French Revolution approached their crisis; war broke out,
and trade was all but extinguished. Ultimately, all that could be
realized amounted to about 450l., and this was handed over to
Crompton to enable him to increase his operations in spinning and
weaving.

In October, 1807, Mr. Crompton, in the hopes of gaining the patronage of Sir Joseph Banks, wrote a letter to him, but unfortunately addressed it to Sir Joseph Banks, President of the Society of Arts, and it is probable that Sir Joseph never read the letter, but transmitted it to the Society to which it was addressed; in any case, no notice was taken of this letter, and Crompton's too morbidly sensitive mind thus received an additional wound.

Two or three years after this, his family circumstances became very precarious, and in the undefined hope of yet obtaining some recompense for his labours which might better his position, Crompton, in the year 1811, commenced a statistical investigation into the results of his invention. For this purpose he visited the various manufacturing districts of Great Britain, and, from the information he obtained, calculated that between four and five millions of mule spindles were then in actual use. But this estimate was afterwards found to be much too low, as it did not include any of the numerous mules used in the manufacture of woollen yarn.

A story is told of Mr. Crompton, that, when at Glasgow engaged in collecting this information, he was invited to a complimentary dinner, but his courage was unable to carry him through so formidable an ordeal; and so when the time came for going, to use his own words, " rather than face up, I first hid myself and then fairly bolted from the city."

Mr. Crompton laid the result of his investigation before some kind friends* at Manchester, who undertook to draw up a memorial to Parliament on his behalf. But in this matter Crompton's continued ill-fortune was singularly displayed. When the time came for the grant to be proposed to Parliament (May 11, 1812), Mr. Percival, the Chancellor of the Exchequer, who had intended proposing 20,000*l.* as the sum to be awarded, was assassinated while entering the lobby of the House of Commons. Crompton's petition was consequently postponed, and ultimately 5000*l.* was all that was awarded to the *Inventor of the Spinning-Mule;* and thus, after having haunted the lobby of the House of Commons for five wearisome months, Samuel Crompton went back to Bolton with this shadow of a national reward.

Late in life Mr. Crompton's family became dispersed, and as old age crept on he became less and less fitted for business, and now for the first time sank into actual poverty.

A noble effort was, however, made by some of the inhabitants of Bolton to rescue him from his distressing position, and by their efforts an annuity of 63*l.* per annum was secured to him for the remainder of his life.

In the year 1827 Samuel Crompton's melancholy life came to an end. He died at his house in King Street, Great Bolton, aged

* Mr. Lee, Mr. Kennedy, and Mr. George Duckworth.

seventy-three, of no particular complaint, but by the gradual decay of nature. His body was placed in a grave near the centre of the parish churchyard, underneath a flagstone with the following inscription:—" Beneath this stone are interred the mortal remains of Samuel Crompton, of Bolton, late of Hall-i'-th'-Wood, in the township of Tonge, inventor of the spinning machine called the *Mule*; who departed this life the 26th day of June, 1827, aged seventy-two years."*—*The Life and Times of Samuel Crompton, &c.*, by *Gilbert J. French, F.S.A.*, &c. Manchester and London, 1860.

JOHN DALTON, D.C.L., L.L.D., F.R.S., L. and E.

MEMBER OF THE INSTITUTE OF FRANCE.

Born September 5, 1766. Died July 27, 1844.

John Dalton was born at Eaglesfield, a small village in Cumberland, near Cockermouth. His father, Joseph Dalton, was a woollenweaver, and at the birth of his second son, John, gained but a scanty subsistence by weaving common country goods. At the death of his elder brother, however, he inherited a small estate of sixty acres, which enabled him to give up weaving. John Dalton had consequently few opportunities of obtaining a good education; he was emphatically self-taught, and from his very childhood began to acquire those habits of stern self-reliance and indomitable perseverance which in after life, rather than any direct inspirations of genius (as Dalton himself used to affirm), enabled him to work out his grand discovery of the 'Atomic Theory.'

Dalton attended the schools in the neighbourhood of Eaglesfield until eleven years old, by which time he had gone through a course of mensuration, surveying, and navigation. At the age of twelve he began to teach in the village school, and for the next two or three years continued to be partially occupied in teaching and in working on his father's farm. When fifteen years old he removed to Kendal, to become an assistant in a boarding school established there; and, after remaining in this capacity for four years, he determined to undertake, with the assistance of his elder brother, the management of the same school. Dalton continued to be connected with this school for the next eight years, during which time he occupied his leisure in studying Greek, Latin, French, and Natural Philosophy, and was also a frequent contributor to the 'Gentleman's

---

* There is an unaccountable mistake of one year in Mr. Crompton's age as engraved on his tombstone.

and Lady's Diaries,' two periodicals then in considerable repute. While residing at Kendal, Dalton became acquainted with Mr. Gough, a man who, though blind from infancy, was yet possessed of high scientific attainments. With this gentleman he contracted an intimate friendship, and in 1793 was invited, chiefly through Mr. Gough's favourable recommendation, to join a college, established in Manchester by a body of Protestant dissenters, as tutor in the department of mathematics and natural philosophy. He resigned this appointment after holding it for a period of six years, but continued to reside in Manchester during the whole of his subsequent life.

In September 1793 Dalton published his first work, entitled 'Meteorological Observations and Essays,' the materials of which were, however, collected, and the work entirely completed during his residence at Kendal. A second edition was printed in 1834, and he continued to pay much attention to this subject until within a short period of his death, by which time he had recorded upwards of 200,000 meteorological observations.

In the year 1794 Dalton became a member of the Literary and Philosophical Society of Manchester, of which, during the course of his life, he filled in succession all the more important offices; including that of the presidentship, which he held from the period of his election in 1817, until his death in 1844. On the 31st of October, 1794, he read his first paper to this Society, entitled, 'Extraordinary Facts relating to the Vision of Colours,' in which he gives an account of a singular defect in his own vision, known by the name of colour-blindness, which rendered him incapable of distinguishing certain colours, such as scarlet and green. He first became aware of this defect in his sight from the following circumstance. When a boy he had gone to see a review of troops, and being surprised to hear those around him expatiating on the gorgeous effect of the military costume, he asked, "In what a soldier's coat differed from the grass upon which he trod," a speech which was received by his companions with derisive laughs and exclamations of wonder.* Until Dalton had announced his own case, and described the cases of more than twenty persons similarly circumstanced, this peculiar form of blindness was supposed to be very rare. In the annals of the above-mentioned Society, Dalton published a long series of important essays, among the most remarkable of which are some papers read in the year 1801, entitled, 'Experimental Essays on the Constitution of Mixed Gases;' 'On the Force of Steam or Vapour and other liquids at different temperatures in a vacuum and in air;' 'On Evaporation,' and 'On the Expansion of Gases by Heat.' In January 1803 he read to the same Society an inquiry 'On the tendency of Elastic fluids to diffusion through each other,' and in October of the same year wrote an Essay containing

* Memoir, by Dr. T. S. Trail, *Encyclopædia Britannica*.

an outline of his speculations on the subject of the composition of bodies, in which he gave to the world for the first time a ' Table of Atomic Weights.' In the following year he communicated his views on the theory of definite proportions to Dr. Thomas Thomson, of Glasgow, who at once published an abstract of them; and in 1808 Dalton himself published the first volume of his new system of Chemical Philosophy, in which he placed the Atomic Theory on a firm and clear basis, and established the law of Multiple Proportions. The value of Dalton's researches on this great subject is immense; by the promulgation of his views Chemistry became for the first time a science, and one great law or theory was seen to govern its actions; before it was a series of separate facts, but by this fundamental law and its branches, and by this only, it is preserved as a science.

Dalton's theory incurred much opposition before it was finally accepted by scientific men, and among the unbelievers in it may be mentioned Sir Humphry Davy. The baronet, however, in the year 1826, clearly acknowledged and accurately defined Dalton's discoveries in his anniversary discourse, when he made known that the first award of the Royal Society's Prize, founded by George IV. in the year before, would be given to Mr. John Dalton, "for the development of the chemical theory of Definite Proportions, usually called the Atomic Theory, and for his various other labours and discoveries in physical and chemical science."

During his later life Dalton continued to gain his living as professional chemist, lecturer, and teacher of Chemistry and Mathematics, and contributed to the advancement of science many valuable papers chiefly relating to Chemistry; he was also accustomed in his analytical researches to use the graduated dropping tube, and may be considered as the originator of analysis by volume. Mr. Dalton was present at the first meeting of the British Association held in York in 1831, and continued to feel a lively interest in its prosperity, and to attend the annual meetings as long as his health permitted him. On the occasion of the second meeting at Oxford in 1832, the honorary degree of D.C.L. was conferred upon him, in conjunction with Faraday, Brown the botanist, and Sir David Brewster. In the summer of the following year, at the meeting of the same society in Cambridge, it was announced by Professor Sedgewick, that the King had conferred on Dalton a pension of 150*l.* per annum, which was increased in 1836 to 300*l.*; and as his brother Jonathan died about the same time and left him heir to the paternal estate, he became comparatively wealthy. He, however, still continued working according to his strength, and so late as 1840 published four Essays, entitled, 'On the Phosphates and Arseniates;' 'Microcosmic Salt;' 'Acids, Bases, and Water;' and 'A New and Easy Method of Analysing Sugar.' In 1837-8 Dalton was attacked by paralysis, which greatly enfeebled him; he, however lived till the year 1844, when a third attack occurred, from which he never recovered, but died shortly afterwards in his seventy-eighth year.

Dr. R. Angus Smith thus describes Dalton's mode of life while living with the family of the Rev. W. Johns, of George Street, Manchester, with whom Dalton continued to reside for twenty-six years: "He rose at about eight o'clock in the morning; if in winter, went with his lantern in his hand to his laboratory, lighted the fire, and came over to breakfast when the family had nearly done. Went to the laboratory and staid till dinner-time, coming in a hurry when it was nearly over, eating moderately, and drinking water only. Went out again and returned about five o'clock to tea, still in a hurry, when the rest were finishing. Again to his laboratory till nine o'clock, when he returned to supper, after which he and Mr. Johns smoked a pipe, and the whole family seems much to have enjoyed this time of conversation and recreation after the busy day.—*Life of J. Dalton, by William Charles Henry, M.D., F.R.S., &c.* London, 1854.—*Life of J. Dalton, by Robert Angus Smith, Ph.D., F.R.S., &c.* London, 1856.

SIR HUMPHRY DAVY, BART., LL.D., P.R.S., &c.,

MEMBER OF THE INSTITUTE OF FRANCE, ETC.

Born December 17, 1778.   Died May 30, 1829.

This eminent philosopher was born at Penzance, in Cornwall. As a child he was remarkably healthy and strong, displaying at the same time great mental capacity. The first school he ever attended was that of Mr. Bushell, at which reading and writing only were taught. In these rudimentary branches of education he soon made such progress, that he was removed, by the master's advice, to the grammar school kept by the Rev. Mr. Coryton. He was then only six years old. Here Davy received the elements of his education until 1793, when he went to the grammar school of Truro, conducted by the Rev. Mr. Cardew, at which place he continued for about a year.

Both Davy and his family received much assistance from the disinterested friendship of Mr. Tonkin, a respectable medical practitioner at Penzance, who had adopted the mother of Davy and her sisters, under circumstances of deep distress, extending his kindness to all her family, particularly to Humphry.

Soon after leaving Dr. Cardew's school, Davy's father died in 1794;

and in the following year Humphry was apprenticed to Mr. Bingham Borlace, a gentleman at that time practising as surgeon-apothecary in Penzance. While yet very young, Davy had exhibited traces of an ardent and inquisitive mind, displaying also a great predilection for poetry; but from this period he directed his attention more particularly to the study of chemistry and natural philosophy His efforts at attaining an experimental knowledge of the above sciences were, however, greatly retarded by the defects of his apparatus, which was necessarily very limited, and consisted chiefly of phials, wine-glasses, tobacco-pipes, and earthen crucibles. But about this time he had the good fortune to make the acquaintance of Mr. Davies Giddy Gilbert and Mr. Gregory Watt,* by whose instrumentality the subject of our memoir was introduced to Dr. Beddoes, who engaged him to superintend a pneumatic medical institution, which that able but eccentric man had just then established at Clifton, for the purpose of trying the effects of gases upon various diseases. This event took place in 1798, Mr. Borlace readily giving up Davy's indenture, which had not as yet expired. During his residence at Clifton, Davy was placed in a sphere where his genius could expand; he was associated with men engaged in similar pursuits, was provided with suitable apparatus, and enabled to speedily enter upon that brilliant career of discovery which has rendered his name illustrious among philosophers.

Soon after he had removed to the neighbourhood of Bristol, Davy's first published paper, on 'Heat, Light, and Respiration,' appeared in 'Beddoes' West Country Contributions.' His earliest scientific discovery was the detection of siliceous earth in the epidermis of canes, reeds, and grasses.

About the same period, he began to investigate the properties of gases, and discovered the respirability of nitrous oxide, giving in a letter to his friend Mr. Davies Gilbert (dated April 16, 1799), the first intimation of the intoxicating qualities of that gas. Shortly afterwards he examined its properties more accurately, administering it to various individuals, and published an account of his discoveries in a volume entitled 'Researches Chemical and Philosophical chiefly concerning Nitrous Oxide and its Respiration.' While the favourable impression from this publication was still fresh on the public mind, the establishment of the Royal Institution, under the auspices of Count Rumford, had taken place, and a lecturer of talent was wanting, to fill the chemical chair. Through the recommendation of Dr. Hope of Edinburgh, with whom he had become acquainted Davy received the appointment, and became lecturer to the institution and director of the laboratory.

It is a singular fact, that although Davy's attention had never been confined to his favourite science, for he had studied general literature as well as poetry, yet he was of so uncouth an exterior

* Youngest son of James Watt.

and manners, notwithstanding an exceedingly handsome and expressive countenance, that Count Rumford, a leading director of the Institution, on seeing him for the first time, expressed no little disappointment, even regretting the part he had taken in promoting the engagement. But these feelings were of short duration. Davy was soon sufficiently humanized, and even refined, to appear before a London and a fashionable audience of both sexes with great advantage, and by his ingenuity, and happy facility of illustration, he rendered his lectures so popular, that at the early age of twenty-two, he found his company courted by the choicest society of the metropolis. An anecdote is told illustrative of his popularity, even among the more humble classes. While passing through the streets one fine night, he observed a man showing the moon through a telescope to the surrounding bystanders; Davy stopped to have a look, and having satisfied his curiosity, tendered a penny to the exhibitor. The man had, however, in the meanwhile, learnt the name of his customer, and exclaimed, with an important air, that he could not think of taking money from a ' brother philosopher.' Davy's style of lecturing was animated, clear and impressive, notwithstanding the naturally inharmonious tones of his voice; whilst the ingenuity of his happily devised experiments, the neatness of their execution, and above all the ingenious enthusiasm which he displayed for his subject, fixed and arrested the attention of his hearers.

At this time, experimental chemistry began to be the fashion of the day. Voltaic electricity had just been found to possess extraordinary powers in effecting the decomposition of chemical compounds; and by the liberality of the Royal Institution, Davy was put in possession of a battery consisting of 400 5-inch plates, and one of 40 plates, 1-foot in diameter, with which batteries his early and most brilliant investigations were conducted.

In 1801 he made his first important discovery, which was communicated to the Royal Society under the title ' An Account of some Galvanic Combinations formed by an Arrangement of Single Metallic Plates and Fluids,' read in June of the same year. In this paper, he showed that the usual galvanic phenomena might be energetically exhibited by a single metallic plate, and two strata of different fluids; or that a battery might be constructed of one metal and two fluids, provided one of the fluids was capable of oxidizing the surface of the metal. In the following year to this, Davy was appointed professor to the Board of Agriculture, and in 1803 was admitted a member of the Royal Society, of which he became first the secretary, and ultimately the president.

To the ' Philosophical Transactions' of this society he continued to contribute papers on different branches of experimental philosophy; and it is on these papers that his claims to celebrity almost entirely rest. From 1802 to 1805, Davy published several minor papers; but in the following year appeared his first Bakerian lecture, read to the Royal Society in November, 1806, in which he detailed the phenomena of electro-chemical decomposition, and laid down its laws; while in his second lecture, read in the November following, he announced the successful application of these principles, and the discovery of the metallic bases of the fixed alkalies, witnessed by the production of two new metals, which he named potassium and sodium.* This splendid discovery was fully confirmed by Guy Lussac and Thenard, who, in the following year, succeeded in decomposing potash by iron filings, in a red-hot gun barrel. From 1808 to 1810, Davy gave three more lectures, in which he announced the results of his further chemical investigations. It may be interesting to remark that the original batteries of the institution were so worn during the course of his experiments, as to be unserviceable; a liberal voluntary subscription, however, amongst the members, in July 1808, put him in possession of the most powerful voltaic battery ever constructed, consisting of 2000 double plates, with a surface equal to 128,000 square inches. The results produced by this tremendous power did not, however, add to science one new fact of any importance. All Davy's great voltaic discoveries were made before it was in use, and it only served to show the phenomena of galvanism with greater brilliancy.

Mr. Davy's reputation was now at its height, and he was invited by the Dublin Society to give a course of lectures on electro-chemical science. For these lectures, which were commenced on the 8th, and concluded on the 29th of November, 1810, he received 500 guineas. In the following year he was invited to give two more courses, on the Elements of Chemical Philosophy, and on Geology, for which he received 750l.,—the Provost and Fellows of Trinity College also conferring on him the degree of LL.D. In 1812, Davy dissolved his connection with the Royal Institution, by giving a farewell lecture on the 9th of April; on the preceding day he had received the honour of knighthood from the hands of the Prince Regent, and on the 11th of the same month was married to Mrs. Apreece, daughter and heiress of Charles Kerr, of Kelso, and the possessor of an ample fortune. During the next two or three years, Sir Humphry communicated several papers to the Royal Society, but they contained little of importance to science.

Whilst experimenting, in the latter part of 1812, upon azote and chlorine, he was severely wounded in the eye by the explosion of these substances; and it is a strong proof of his energy, that when his eye was sufficiently recovered, he renewed his experiments upon the same bodies, and was again wounded in the head and hands, but this time slightly, as he had taken the precaution of defending his face by a plate of glass.

In the autumn of 1813 he obtained the permission of Napoleon to

---

* Davy also reduced by voltaic electricity alumina, but aluminium was first obtained in a perfectly separate state by Wöhler in 1827.

travel in France, whither he proceeded, accompanied by his lady and Mr. Faraday. From France, Davy proceeded to Italy, where he spent the winter, returning to London on the 23rd of April, 1814. During his stay in Italy, he collected specimens of the colours used by the ancients in their pictures. This formed the subject of a memoir to the Royal Society, the most interesting part of the paper being the announcement that the fine blues of the ancients were formed of silex, soda, and copper, and that they may be exactly imitated by strongly heating together, for the space of two hours, three parts of copper filings, fifteen of carbonate of soda, and twenty of powdered flint.

In the year 1816, Davy turned his attention to a method of preventing the dreadful accidents in coal mines, from explosions of the fire-damp. After considerable investigation, he found that this gas would not explode when mixed with less than six times or more than fourteen times its volume of atmospheric air; and in the course of experiments made for the purpose of ascertaining how the inflammation takes place, he was surprised to observe that flames will not pass through tubes of a certain length or smallness of bore. He then found that if the length was diminished, and the bore also reduced, that flames still would not pass; and further, that the length of the tubes might safely be diminished to hardly anything, provided their bore was proportionably lessened. Working from these principles, he proposed several kinds of lamps, but all were finally superseded by the simple one known as the Davy safety-lamp, in which a small oil light is covered by a cylinder of wire gauze, the small apertures* of which flame will not pass through, and the explosion is thus prevented from extending outside the wire gauze. The introduction of this beautiful invention, although freely given to the public, was for a time violently opposed by prejudice and passion. Experience, however, showed the comparative safety which the miners who used it possessed, and the coal-owners of Newcastle and the vicinity presented Davy with a superb service of plate, as some recognition of the important benefit he had conferred on them.

During the later years of Sir Humphry Davy's life, various communications appeared from him to the Royal Society, none, however, presenting any very remarkable features. In November, 1820, a few months after the death of Sir Joseph Banks, he was elected president of the above society. In 1823 he repeated the interesting experiment of Mr. Faraday, as to the condensation of gases by mechanical pressure, and succeeded in converting sulphurous acid and prussic acid gases into liquids, by heating them in strong sealed tubes. During the same year he investigated the causes of the rapid decay of copper sheathing on ships, and attributing this to

---

* The meshes or apertures of the wire gauze ought not to be more than one twenty-second of an inch in diameter.—*Brougham's Lives of Philosophers.*

electro-chemical action, succeeded in preventing it, by attaching plates of iron or zinc to the copper. This, however, on being tried practically, introduced the unlooked for evil, of excessive fouling of the bottoms of ships so protected, which became liable to marine deposits in an equal manner with wooden bottoms. Davy's plan was thus rendered utterly useless, much to his mortification.

During the later portion of his life, Sir Humphry was in very infirm health, and in 1828 he determined to go abroad. Proceeding into Italy, he fixed his residence at Rome, whence he sent his last communication to the Royal Society, viz., ' Remarks on the Electricity of the Torpedo.' The chief peculiarity of this paper was the discovery that the electricity of this curious creature had no effect on the most delicate galvanometer. While staying at Rome, Sir Humphry was seized with a paralytic attack, which greatly alarmed his friends. Shortly afterwards he left Rome for Geneva, on reaching which city an attack of apoplexy seized him during the night, which terminated fatally. The funeral took place on the 1st of June, 1829, with all the honour and respect the inhabitants of Geneva could testify. His remains were deposited in the burying-ground of the city, without the walls, the spot being marked by a simple monument, with a Latin inscription, erected by Lady Davy. —*Life of Sir H. Davy, by his brother, John Davy*, M.D., F.R.S. London, 1839.—*Memoir by Dr. Thomas Trail, Encyclopædia Britannica.*— *Weld's History of the Royal Society, with Memoirs of the Presidents.* London, 1848. — *Brougham's Lives of Philosophers.* London and Glasgow, 1855.

PETER DOLLOND.

Born February 2, 1731. Died July 2, 1820.

Peter Dollond, the subject of the present memoir, was the eldest son of John Dollond, the celebrated inventor of the Achromatic Refracting Telescope, who, during the greater portion of his life, was engaged in the business of a silk-manufacturer, in Stuart Street, Spitalfields. Here Peter Dollond was born and spent the early portion of his life. On reaching manhood he engaged in the same occupation as his father, and for several years they carried on their manufactures together in Spitalfields. Peter Dollond had, however, acquired some knowledge of the theory of Optics, and he determined, if possible, to turn the knowledge he had gained to the improvement of himself and his family. He accordingly commenced business as an optician, under the direction of his father, in

D

the year 1750, occupying a small house in Vine Street, Spitalfields. In 1752 John Dollond, who up till then had pursued his original occupation, grew weary of pursuits so little in accordance with the natural bent of his mind, and entered into partnership with his son, in a house near to Exeter Change, in the Strand. Here father and son began and continued that series of experimental researches which, in June 1758, led to the memorable conclusion on which was founded the construction of the Achromatic Refracting Telescope. In the following year a patent was obtained for the exclusive sale of these telescopes, but so limited were the means of the authors of this invention, that, in order to defray the expenses of the patent, they were compelled to sell a moiety of its value to an optician, with whom they entered into partnership. Notwithstanding the great practical value of this discovery, it produced little benefit for some years to the owners of the patent. In 1761 John Dollond died, leaving to his son Peter the task of carrying on the business in partnership with the optician who had paid for the patent. This connection was, however, of short duration, for the conduct of his partner was so unsatisfactory, that in 1763 Mr. Dollond purchased from him his share in the business for 200*l.*, the full commercial value of this most important discovery being considered at that time to be worth only 400*l.* Peter Dollond was now in possession of the entire patent, and he was soon called upon to contest its validity with the very man who had so lately been concerned in protecting it. These suits were uniformly decided in favour of Dollond, and although vexatious in their character, were of advantage to him, not only in their immediate issue, but also in extending the name, reputation, and sale of the object whose right of owner-ship was contested.

Mr. Dollond now began to be more generally known, and made the acquaintance of many of the philosophical men of the time, becoming intimate with Dr. Maskelyne, the Astronomer Royal at that period, and with Mr. James Short, a man highly distinguished in arts and science. To this latter gentleman he, in 1765, proposed an improvement in the Achromatic Telescope, which Mr. Short laid before the Royal Society, at the same time signifying that it had his entire concurrence and approval. Among other works of Dol-lond are an improvement of Headley's Quadrant, communicated to the Royal Society, in 1772, by the Astronomer Royal; and an apparatus for the improvement of the Equatorial instrument, laid before the Society, through the same medium, in 1779.

Mr. Dollond had now earned for himself a well-deserved reputa-tion. In 1786 the American Philosophical Society, unsolicited, and with the approval of Benjamin Franklin, elected him a member of their society.

About the year 1766 the optical business had been removed from the Strand to St. Paul's Churchyard, where it became so extensive and prosperous, that Mr. Dollond took into partnership his brother John. For nearly forty years the brothers resided here, endeavouring, by their cordial and united efforts, to improve and extend each branch of their profession. In 1804 John, the younger brother, died, and in the following year his place was supplied by a nephew, George Huggins, who, on being admitted into partnership, changed his name to Dollond, and eventually succeeded to the whole concern. In 1817 Peter Dollond took up his residence at Richmond Hill, remaining there till June 1820, when he removed to Kennington Common, where he breathed his last, having arrived at his 90th year.—*Memoir by the Rev. Dr. Kelly.*

BRYAN DONKIN, F.R.S., &c.

Born March 22, 1768.   Died February 27, 1855.

Bryan Donkin was born at Sandoe, in Northumberland. His father, who followed the business of a surveyor and land agent, was acquainted with John Smeaton, the eminent engineer, from having had occasion to consult him frequently on questions relating to the bridges and other works on the Tyne. Donkin early showed a taste for science and mechanics, and when almost a child was to be found continually occupied in making various ingenious mechanical contrivances. He commenced life in the same business as his father, being engaged for a year or two as land agent to the Duke of Dorset. Donkin, however, soon showed the bent of his natural genius by quitting this agency, and going to consult Smeaton as to how he could best become an engineer. By Smeaton's advice, he apprenticed himself to Mr. Hall, of Dartford, in the carrying on of whose works he was soon able to take so active a part, that in 1801-2 he was principally entrusted with the construction of a model of the first machine for making paper, the execution of which had been put into Messrs. Hall's hands by the Messrs. Fourdrinier. The idea of this machine originated with Mr. Roberts, and formed the subject of a patent, which was assigned to Messrs. Bloxam and Fourdrinier. After considerable expense had been incurred, and many trials made with the model, the paper produced was found to be of too inferior a quality for sale. The model remained at Mr. Hall's works for some time, till at length Donkin agreed with the owners to take the matter in hand himself, and for this purpose took premises at Bermondsey (still occupied by his sons). In 1804 he succeeded in producing a machine which, on being erected at Frogmore, Herts, and set to work, was found to be successful, although still far from perfect. A second one, in which still further improvements were introduced, was consequently made the following year and erected at Two-waters; and in 1810 eighteen more of these complex machines were erected at various mills, some of which are even now at work. The practical difficulties having been at length overcome, these machines soon superseded, both at home and abroad, the ordinary method of making paper by hand; and although the original idea was not Mr. Donkin's, still to him the credit is due of having developed, and practically introduced into general use, these most useful and complete mechanical contrivances, by means of which the process of making paper is carried on uninterruptedly from the liquid pulp to the perfect sheet ready for writing or printing.

About the year 1812 Donkin's attention was turned to the subject of the preservation of meat and vegetables in air-tight cases, and he erected a considerable manufactory for this purpose at Bermondsey. Mr. Donkin was also one of the first to introduce improvements into printing machinery. In 1813 he, in conjunction with Mr. Bacon, secured a patent for a Polygonal printing machine, and in the same year invented and brought into use composition rollers, by which some of the greatest difficulties experienced at that time in printing by machinery were overcome. Among other inventions and mechanical contrivances of Donkin's are a very beautiful screw-cutting and dividing machine; an instrument to measure the velocity of the rotation of machinery; and a counting engine: for the two last gold medals were awarded by the Society of Arts. In 1820 Mr. Donkin was much engaged with Sir William Congreve in contriving a method of printing stamps in two colours, with compound plates, for the prevention of forgery; and with the aid of Mr. Wilks, who was at that time his partner, he produced the beautiful machine now used at the Excise and Stamp Offices, and by the East India Company at Calcutta.

Mr. Donkin was an early member of the Society of Arts, and became one of the vice-presidents. From this society he received two medals, one for his invention of an instrument to measure the velocity of the rotation of machinery, and another for his counting-engine.

During the last forty years of his life he was greatly occupied as a civil engineer, and was one of the originators and a vice-president of the Institution of Civil Engineers, which was founded by one of his pupils, Mr. Henry Palmer, and a few other gentlemen, the Royal Charter being obtained by Mr. Telford and himself. He died in his eighty-seventh year, having passed a long life in an almost uninterrupted course of usefulness and good purpose.—From the *Proceedings of the Royal Society*, Nov. 30, 1855.

WILLIAM JAMES FRODSHAM, F.R.S.

Born July 25, 1778.   Died June 29, 1850.

William J. Frodsham was born in London, and brought up under
the care of his grandfather, a great admirer of John Harrison, the
inventor of the timekeeper for ascertaining the longitude at sea.
From thus spending his early life with his grandfather, young
Frodsham acquired a strong desire to engage in the business of
chronometer making, he was consequently apprenticed to a man
eminent in that art.   Shortly after completing his apprenticeship
Mr. Frodsham, in the year 1800, entered into partnership with Mr.
W. Parkinson of Lancaster, and hence arose the celebrated firm of
Parkinson and Frodsham.

During his entire life Mr. Frodsham devoted himself to the advancement of the art he had engaged in, and being ably assisted
by his partner effected various improvements in chronometers,
watches, and other timekeepers, and was also the author of a paper
on pendulum experiments.   Mr. Frodsham lived to an advanced
age, surviving his partner by many years.   During his career he
acquired a large fortune, which he bequeathed to his family, leaving
at the same time a sum of 1000*l.* to the Clockmakers' Company, of
which he had been Master several times during his life.   Mr.
Frodsham died at Chatham Place, Hackney, and was buried in
Highgate Cemetery.

DAVIES GIDDY GILBERT, D.C.L., P.R.S.

Born March 6, 1767.   Died December 24, 1839.

Davies Giddy Gilbert was born at Tredrea, in the parish of St.
Erth, in the west of Cornwall.   His paternal name was Giddy, his
father being the Rev. Edward Giddy of St. Erth.   His mother, an
heiress of very considerable property, was Catherine Davies, allied
to the noble family of Sandys, and a descendant of William Noye,
attorney general in the reign of Charles the First.   Young Giddy,
not being of very robust health, was reared with great care, and
his education chiefly superintended by his father, who was an
accomplished scholar, and a man of acknowledged ability and
attainments.

As Gilbert grew up, it was thought desirable to place him in the
grammar school at Penzance ; and for this purpose his parents

removed for about eighteen months to that town. In 1782 they
went to Bristol, where their son's studies were assisted for some
time by Mr. Benjamin Donne. In 1785 Gilbert matriculated at
Oxford, and became a gentleman-commoner of Pembroke College.
He was already master of a considerable amount of mathematical
and physical knowledge, the greater portion of which he had
acquired by almost unassisted application. While residing at the
University he associated with the senior members of his college,
preferring their company to that of students of his own age; and
considering the natural bent of his tastes, which led him to prefer
the study of the severer sciences to the elegancies of classical
literature, it is not surprising that such should be the case. Dr.
Parr, writing at this time to the late Master of Pembroke, speaks
of Mr. Giddy, then twenty-three years old, as 'the Cornish Philosopher,' and adds that he deserved that name.

During his residence at Oxford, Gilbert was a regular attendant
at the lectures on anatomy and mineralogy, delivered by Dr.
Thompson, at Christ Church. He also attended with assiduity the
lectures on chemistry and botany of Drs. Beddoes and Sibthorp,
with whom he contracted a friendship, which terminated only with
their lives. To the former of these two gentlemen Gilbert subsequently introduced his friend Sir Humphry Davy, at that time in
comparatively humble life, but whose extraordinary combination of
poetical and philosophical genius had attracted Gilbert's attention,
and he thus had the merit and good fortune of contributing to
rescue from obscurity one of the greatest discoverers in modern
chemistry.

Mr. Gilbert continued to reside principally at his college until the
year 1793, when, having previously taken the honorary degree of
M.A., he returned to Cornwall to serve as sheriff, and to divide
his time, between the cultivation of science and literature, and the
duties of a magistrate in a populous and busy town. Previous to
this, in the year 1791, he had been elected a Fellow of the Royal
Society, his certificate describing him as being "devoted to mathematical and philosophical pursuits." It was signed by Thomas
Hornsby, Savilian professor of astronomy, G. Shuckburgh, N. Maskelyne, George Staunton, and other Fellows. In 1804 Mr. Gilbert
became a member of Parliament for Helstone, and at the general
election in 1806, was chosen to represent Bodmin, continuing to sit
for that borough until December, 1832. He was emphatically the
representative of scientific interests in the House of Commons, and
was continually appointed to serve on committees of inquiry touch-
ing scientific and financial questions. He acted as Chairman of the
committee for rebuilding London Bridge, causing it to be widened
ten feet more than originally proposed, and he greatly contributed
by his exertions to carry many very important public projects,
amongst which may be mentioned, the Breakwater at Plymouth,

and the bill for the revision of weights and measures, of which he was appointed a commissioner. He was also a member of the Board of Longitude.

On the 8th of April, 1808, he married Mary Ann Gilbert, only niece of Charles Gilbert of Eastbourne in Sussex, under whose will he came into possession of considerable estates in that county; and, in compliance with its conjunctions, obtained permission to assume the name and arms of Gilbert.

Mr. Gilbert contributed several important papers on mathematical subjects to the 'Philosophical Transactions.' In July, 1819, he succeeded Samuel Lyons in the office of treasurer to the Royal Society, which office he retained until elected President in 1828. He was also the author of numerous papers in the 'Quarterly Journal of Science and Arts,' and presented the world with the fruits of his labours as an antiquary, by publishing, in 1838, 'The Parochial History of Cornwall,' in four volumes 8vo., founded on the manuscript histories of Mr. Hals and Mr. Tonkin. Mr. Gilbert was a diligent collector of ancient traditions, legendary tales, songs, and carols, illustrating the manners of the Cornish peasants, and printed various ballads at his house at Eastbourne. He possessed great memory and powers of quotation and anecdote; his conversation has been described as being a continued stream of learning and philosophy, adapted with excellent taste to the capacity of his auditory, and enlivened with anecdotes to which the most listless could not but listen and learn.

" His manners," says Dr. Buckland, " were most unaffected, childlike, gentle, and natural. As a friend, he was kind, considerate, forbearing, patient, and generous; and when the grave was closed over him, not one man, woman, or child, who was honoured with his acquaintance, but felt that he had a friend less in the world."

Mr. Gilbert retired from the chair of the Royal Society in 1830, and two years later from Parliament; he did not, however, resign himself to repose, but continued in many ways still to advocate the cause of science. In 1839 he became much weaker in health and spirits; and although he made a journey to Durham, and afterwards into Cornwall, where he presided for the last time at the Anniversary of the Royal Geological Society of Cornwall (of which he had been President since its institution in 1814), he was evidently unequal to the exertions he was making. His last visit was to Oxford, which University had some years before conferred on him the title of D.C.L. From that period he never went into public, but, bidding farewell to London, retired to his house at Eastbourne on the 7th of November, 1839, where he died on the 24th of the following December. His body was borne to the grave by his own labourers, and followed by his widow and family, which consisted of one son (the present J. D. Gilbert, F.R.S.) and two daughters.—*Weld's History of the Royal Society, with Memoirs of the Presidents.* London, 1848.

CHARLES HATCHETT, F.R.S.

Born January 2, 1765.   Died March 10, 1847.

Charles Hatchett was born at a house in Long Acre, where his father carried on the business of a coachmaker. He was sent to a school known by the name of Fountayne's, situated in what was formerly called Marylebone Park. On leaving school, Mr. Hatchett continued to live for some time with his father, purposing to follow the same business; he, however, never took kindly to it, but spent the chief part of his time in perusing books of science, or in attending lectures on scientific subjects; and his father, perceiving the bent of his inclination, made him a handsome allowance, to enable him to prosecute his studies.

An amusing story is told by the Rev. Mr. Lockwood, Rector of Kingham, who was an intimate friend of Mr. Hatchett's, that one day he remembered asking Hatchett what first led him to turn his attention to the study of chemistry; he replied, that he believed it was his love for raspberry-jam; for, when quite a boy, he used to accompany his mother to the storeroom, and on one occasion, while as usual entreating for some jam, she locked the door, and putting the key in her pocket, told him he might now get as much as he could. This somewhat nettled the lad, and setting his wits to work, he remembered having read of the power of certain acids to dissolve metals. Young Hatchett accordingly purchased what he thought would suit his purpose, and applying it to the lock of the cupboard, gained an entrance,.and carried off in triumph the pot of jam.

On the 24th of March, 1786, when just one-and-twenty, Mr. Hatchett married the only daughter of Mr. John Collick, of Saint Martin's Lane, and shortly afterwards, in company with his wife, visited Russia and Poland, where they remained for nearly two years. On returning to England, Mr. Hatchett established himself in a house at Hammersmith, which he fitted with an excellent laboratory, so as to be able to pursue his chemical studies. On the 9th of March, 1807, he was elected into the Royal Society, his first paper having appeared in their 'Transactions' in 1796; it was entitled, 'An Analysis of the Carinthian Molybdate of Lead, with Experiments on the Molybdic Acid; to which are added, some Experiments and Observations on the Decomposition of the Sulphate of Ammonia.' This paper was followed by fifteen others, on various subjects, exhibiting the extent and research of his chemical investigations. In one of these, published in 1802, and entitled an 'Analysis of a Mineral Substance from North America, containing a metal unknown,' Mr. Hatchett gives an account of his discovery of the metal Columbium.

During the later portion of his life, Mr. Hatchett was often called upon committees, whenever points of chemistry or other sciences were to be discussed. In 1818, he formed one of the commission, comprising amongst others Dr. Wollaston, Sir Joseph Banks, Sir William Congreve, Davies Gilbert, &c., appointed to authorize an inquiry into the best means of preventing the forgery of bank notes; he was also one of the chemists (consisting of Brande, Hatchett, Wollaston, and Young) who met at Sir Joseph Banks's house, to decide on the respective merits of Sir Humphry Davy and George Stephenson, in the matter of the safety-lamp.

Besides his scientific attainments, Hatchett possessed great conversational powers; he was good-humoured, full of drollery, and never at fault for some jocular or pleasant story, to amuse the company he might be with. At the Royal Society Club, of which he was a member, he was a great favourite, particularly with Sir Joseph Banks, who, after Dr. Johnson, used to call him a clubable man. Sir John Barrow gives the following anecdote:—That "one day, at the club, Hatchett amused us with the story of a dream, which he prefaced by saying that, although it was 'such stuff as dreams are made of,' it still contained a reality in its conclusion, which had very much distressed him. He dreamt that he had lost his way, but came to a dark and dismal-looking building, into which he passed through a forbidding sort of gate, opened by a black-looking porter, who closed it immediately after him. He walked on, and everywhere observed clumps of ill-looking people skirmishing and fighting, while a little beyond were other groups, weeping and in great distress; further on still were flames of fire. Beginning to think he had got into a very bad place, he endeavoured to retrace his steps and get out again; but the black doorkeeper refused to let him pass. A furious fight ensued, and he pummelled the negro-looking rascal, first with one fist and then with another. At length he was brought to his senses by a scream, which, to his dismay, proceeded from his poor wife, and he found that, instead of pummelling the black doorkeeper, he had given Mrs. Hatchett a black eye."

In 1809, Mr. Hatchett was elected one of the chosen few of the Literary Club, originally instituted by Dr. Johnson and Sir Joshua Reynolds; and on the death of Dr. Burney, in 1829, was appointed to the chief official station of treasurer to the club.

In 1810 he took up his residence at Belle Vue House, Chelsea, where he continued for the remainder of his life, which terminated in 1847, Mr. Hatchett having then attained the advanced age of eighty-two.—*Sketches of the Royal Society and Royal Society Club, by Sir John Barrow, Bart., F.R.S.* London, 1849.

WILLIAM HENRY, M.D., F.R.S., &c.

Born December 12, 1774. Died September 2, 1836.

Dr. William Henry, the distinguished chemical philosopher, was
born at Manchester. His father, Mr. Thomas Henry, was a zealous
cultivator of chemical science. The earliest impressions of Henry's
childhood were, therefore, such as to inspire interest and reverence
for the pursuits of science; and he is said, when very young, to
have sought amusement in attempting to imitate, with such means
as were at his disposal, the chemical experiments which his father
had been performing. A severe accident which occurred in early
life, by disqualifying him for the active sports of boyhood, also contributed to determine his taste for books and sedentary occupations.
This injury, occasioned by the fall of a heavy beam upon his right
side, was of a very serious nature, and materially checked his
growth; it left as its consequence acute neuralgic pains, which
recurred from time to time, with more or less severity, during the
remainder of his life.

Dr. Henry's earliest instructor was the Rev. Ralph Harrison, who
possessed considerable repute as a teacher of the ancient languages,
and was considered at that period to be one of the best instructors
of youth in the North of England. Immediately on leaving Mr.
Harrison's academy at Manchester, Henry had the good fortune to
become the private secretary of Dr. Percival, a physician of great
general accomplishments and refined taste, whose example and
judicious counsels were most instrumental in guiding the tastes of
his young companion, and in establishing habits of vigilant and
appropriate expression. In this improving residence Dr. Henry
remained for the space of five years; he was then removed, in the
winter of 1795-6, to the University of Edinburgh, after having
acquired some preliminary medical knowledge at the Infirmary at
Manchester. Prudential considerations compelled him to leave the
University at the end of a year, and commence general medical
practice in company with his father. A few years' experience,
however, showed the inadequacy of his delicate frame to bear up
against the fatigues of this branch of the medical profession, and he
was permitted, in the year 1805, to return to the University, at that
time adorned by the learning of Playfair and Stewart. So powerful
was the stimulus given to his mental powers during his residence
at the University, that he often declared that the rest of his life,
active as it was, appeared a state of inglorious repose when con-
trasted with this season of unremitted effort. The period interven-
ing between Dr. Henry's two academic residences, although passed
in the engrossing occupations of his profession, to which was added
the superintendence of a chemical business previously established

by his father, was yet marked by several important contributions
to science. In 1797 he communicated to the Royal Society an
experimental memoir (the first of a long series with which he
enriched the ' Transactions' of that body), the design of which was
to re-establish the title of carbon to be ranked among elementary
bodies, which had been denied by Austin, Beddoes, and other
eminent chemists. In this paper he subsequently discovered a
fallacy in his own reasoning, which he exposed before it had been
detected by any other chemist. In 1800 he published in the ' Philosophical Transáctions' his experiments on muriatic acid gas, and in
1803 made known to the Royal Society his elaborate experiments
on the quantity of gases absorbed by water at different temperature
and under different pressures, the result of which was the establishment of the law that " water takes up of gas, condensed by one, two
or more additional atmospheres, a quantity which would be equal to
twice, thrice, &c. the volume absorbed under the ordinary pressure
of the atmosphere." In 1808 Henry was elected a Fellow of the
Royal Society, and in the same year described in their ' Transactions'
a form of apparatus adapted to the combustion of larger quantities
of gases than could be fired in eudiometric tubes. This apparatus,
though now superseded, gave more accurate results than had ever
before been attained. In the following year (1809) the Copley gold
medal was awarded to him for his valuable contributions to the
' Transactions' of the Royal Society. For the next fifteen years
Dr. Henry continued his experiments on gases, making known to
the Society the results from time to time. In his last communication, in 1824, he claimed the merit of having conquered the only
difficulty that remained in a series of experiments on the analysis of
the gaseous substances issuing from the destructive distillation of
coal and oil—viz., the ascertaining by chemical means the exact
proportions which the gases, left after the action of chlorine on oil
and coal gas, bear to each other. This he accomplished by skilfully
availing himself of the property (recently discovered by Döbereiner),
in finely divided platinum, of causing gaseous combinations, and he
was thus enabled to prove the exact composition of the fire-damp
of mines. All the experiments of Dr. Henry which have been
previously alluded to bore upon äeriform bodies ; but although
these were his favourite studies, his acquaintance with general
chemistry is proved by his ' Elements of Experimental Chemistry,'
to have been both sound and extensive. This work was one of the
first on chemical science published in this country, which combined
great literary elegance with the highest standard of scientific accuracy. His comparative analysis of many varieties of British and
foreign salts were models of accurate analysis, and were important
in dispelling the prejudices then popular in favour of the latter for
economical purposes. His ' Memoir on the Theories of Galvanic
Decomposition' earned the cordial approval of Berzelius, as being

among the first maintaining that view which he himself so earnestly supported.

It is greatly to be regretted that Dr. Henry did not contribute more to the literature of science, as he appears to have been eminently fitted, both by natural tastes and by after culture, to excel in this particular respect; especially is it to be regretted that he did not live to carry out the great literary project for which he had collected materials—a history of chemical discovery from the middle of the last century. He could have made it one of the most popular books in our tongue.

In the general intercourse of society Dr. Henry was distinguished by a polished courtesy, by an intuitive propriety, and by a considerate forethought and respect for the feelings and opinions of others; qualities issuing out of the same high-toned sensibility, that guided his taste in letters, and that softened and elevated his whole moral frame and bearing. His comprehensive range of thought and knowledge, his proneness to general speculation in contradistinction to detail, his ready command of the refinements of language, and the liveliness of his feelings and imagination, rendered him a most instructive and engaging companion. To the young, and more especially to such as gave evidence of a taste for liberal studies, his manner was peculiarly kind and encouraging. In measuring the amount and importance of his contributions to chemical knowledge, it must be borne in mind, that in his season of greatest mental activity, he never enjoyed that uncontrolled command of time and that serene concentration of thought which are essential to the completion of great scientific designs. In more advanced life, when relieved from the duties of an extensive medical practice and other equally pressing avocations, growing infirmities and failing bodily power restrained him to studies not demanding personal exertion, and even abridged his season of purely mental labour. That amid circumstances so unfriendly to original and sustained achievements in science, he should have accomplished so much, bears testimony to that energy of resolve, that unsubdued ardour of spirit which ever glowed within him, urging him steadily onwards in the career of honourable ambition, and prompting exertions more than commensurate with the decaying forces of a frame that had never been vigorous. At intervals during his whole life, Dr. Henry suffered severely from the effect of the accident already mentioned. The paroxysms of intense neuralgic agony which attacked him, at length caused the whole nervous system to be so irritated as to deprive him of sleep, and cause his death in September, 1836, at the age of sixty-one.—*Biographical Account of the late Dr. Henry, by his son, William Charles Henry, M.D., F.R.S., &c.—Encyclopædia Britannica, Eighth Edition.*

SIR WILLIAM HERSCHEL, D.C.L., F.R.S., &c.

Born November 15, 1738.   Died August 23, 1822.

Authentic particulars respecting both the early and private life of this great astronomer are sadly deficient; his scientific works are, however, of a world-wide reputation, and it is with these that we are chiefly concerned.   William Herschel was born at Hanover, and was one of a numerous family, who supported themselves chiefly by their musical talents.   At the age of fourteen William was placed, it is said, in the band of the Hanoverian regiment of Guards, which he accompanied to England at a period variously stated from 1757 to 1759.   On his arrival he remained for some time at Durham, and was subsequently, for several years, organist at Halifax, where he was also employed in teaching music and studying languages.   At length, about the year 1766, he found himself in comparatively easy circumstances, as organist of the Octagon Chapel at Bath.   Here Herschel began to study earnestly the science of astronomy; and feeling the necessity of obtaining a good telescope, the purchase of which would be beyond his means, he determined to make one himself.   After many trials, he succeeded in 1774 in executing with his own hands a reflecting telescope, and soon acquired so much dexterity, as to construct instruments of ten and twenty feet in focal length.

In the year 1780 he contributed his first paper, 'On the Variable Star in Cetus,' to the Royal Society; and on the 13th of March, 1781, announced to the world his discovery of a supposed comet, which, on further examination, proved to be a planet exterior to Saturn, now named Uranus.*   This fortunate success was the first addition to the number of primary planets since a period of an immemorial antiquity, and it speedily made the name of Herschel famous.

George III. took the new astronomer under his protection, and attached him to his court, bestowing on him the title of astronomer to the king, with a salary of 400*l.* a year.   It is difficult to estimate the amount of benefit thus conferred on astronomy by the award of this pension; for nothing short of the entire devotion of a lifetime, could have produced such results as we owe to Herschel.   His contributions to the 'Philosophical Transactions' alone amount to sixty-nine in number, and may give some idea of the unwearied activity of the author; they range over a period of thirty-five years, commencing in 1780 and terminating in 1815.   The numerous bodies which he added to the solar system, make that number half as large again as he found it.   Including Halley's comet, and the four satellites of Jupiter and five of Saturn, the number previously known

---

* Called at first Georgium Sidus in honour of George the Third.

was eighteen, to which Herschel added nine—namely Uranus and six satellites, and two satellites of Saturn. His discovery of the rotation of Saturn's ring, his measurements of the rotation of Saturn and Venus, his observations of the belts of the former, and his conjectural theory—derived from observation—of the rotation of Jupiter's satellites, with a large number of minor observations, prove that no one individual ever added so much to the facts on which our knowledge of the solar system is founded. His leading discoveries in siderial astronomy include—the discovery of binary systems of stars, and the orbits of several revolving stars; the discovery and classification of a prodigious multitude of nebulæ; the law of grouping of the entire firmament, and its connection with the great nebula of the Milky Way; and lastly, the determination of the motion of our sun and system in space, and the direction of that motion.

Herschel's magnificent speculations on the Milky Way, the constitution of nebulæ, &c., first opened the road to the conception, that what was called the universe was, in all probability, but a detached and minute portion of that fathomless series of similar formations which ought to bear the name. Imagination roves with ease upon such subjects; but before Herschel's observations, even that daring faculty would have rejected ideas which afterwards proved to be but sober philosophy. These great and arduous enquiries occupied Herschel during nearly the whole of his scientific career, extending to almost half a century, and, excepting the continuation of his labours by his illustrious son, Sir John, little has been added to our knowledge of 'the constitution of the heavens' since his death.

As an optician, Herschel deserves equal notice for the wonderful improvements which he effected in the dimensions and magnifying power of telescopes, and by the skill with which he applied them to celestial observations. The reflecting telescope was the one to the improvement of which he so successfully devoted himself; and the real secret of his success in this, was his astonishing perseverance; his determination being to obtain telescopes of twenty feet focal length or more, and of a perfection equal or superior to the small ones then in use. He himself relates, that whilst at Bath he had constructed 200 specula of seven feet focus, 150 of ten feet, and about 80 of twenty feet; a proof of extraordinary resolution in a man of limited means, and at that time engaged in a laborious profession.

Herschel at last succeeded in constructing his enormous telescope of forty feet focal length, which he erected in the grounds of his house at Slough. This instrument was begun in 1785, and finally completed on August 28th, 1789, on which day Herschel discovered with it the sixth satellite of Saturn; the diameter of the tube was 4 feet 10 inches, the speculum having a useful area of 4 feet: the total cost was 4000*l.*, which was entirely defrayed by the liberality of George the Third.

After the award of the king's pension, Sir William Herschel fixed his residence at Slough, near Windsor, his family consisting at first of one of his brothers, and his sister, Miss Caroline Herschel, who was his coadjutor and assistant in his computations and reductions, and was also actively employed in astronomical observation, being the discoverer of more than one comet. Herschel married a widow lady, Mrs. Mary Pitt, and left one son, the present Sir John, whose name has long been known to the public as one of the most active and successful adherents of science that our day has produced.

Dr. J. D. Forbes thus sums up the philosophical character of Sir William Herschel:—

" He united, in a remarkable degree, the resolute industry which distinguishes the Germans, with the ardour and constancy which has been thought characteristic of the Anglo-Saxon. From his native country he brought with him the boldness of speculation which has long distinguished it, and it is probable that he had also a vigorous and even poetical imagination. Yet he was ever impatient until he had brought his conjectures to the test of experiment, and observation of the most uncompromising kind. He delighted to give his data a numerical character, and where this was (by their nature) impossible, he confirmed his descriptions by reiterated observation, in different states of weather, with different telescopes, apertures, and magnifying powers ; and with praiseworthy fidelity he enabled his readers to form their own judgment of the character of his results, by copious and literal transcripts from his journals."

Herschel died peacefully at Slough, at the advanced age of eighty-three, on the 23rd of August, 1822, only one year after the publication of his latest memoir in the ' Transactions' of the then recently formed Astronomical Society, of which he was the first president. — *Sixth Dissertation, by James David Forbes, D.C.L., F.R.S., &c., Encyclopædia Britt.,* eighth edition.—*English Cyclopædia.* London, 1856.—*Weld's Hist. of Roy. Society.*

EDWARD CHARLES HOWARD, F.R.S.

Born May 28, 1774. Died September 28, 1816.

Mr. Howard was born at Darnell, in the parish of Sheffield, and was the third brother of the twelfth Duke of Norfolk. His name has become intimately connected with the manufacture of sugar,

from the many improvements which he introduced into the old
processes for the refinement of this most important article of commerce, and especially by his invention of the vacuum-pan.

It is related, on the authority of the late Mr. C. Few, that Mr.
Howard's attention was drawn towards this subject by Mr. Charles
Ellis, who, on the occasion of an immense quantity of West India
sugar being in bond, and for which the revenue could find no
market, recommended Howard, whose talents as a practical chemist
Mr. Ellis was well acquainted with, to try and see if he could not
relieve the Government warehouses, by converting the raw sugar
into some kind of manure, and thus avoid the duty and render the
article saleable. While experimenting for this purpose, Mr. Howard
accidentally discovered his process of purifying sugar, for which, in
conjunction with certain sugar refiners, he took out patents, and
ultimately realized a considerable fortune.

Howard's vacuum-pan was patented in 1812; it depends for its
action on the principle that liquids boil at temperatures dependent
on the pressures they have to sustain. Thus water, under the
ordinary pressure of the atmosphere (30 inches barometer), boils at
212° F., whereas in vacuo it will boil at about 80°; consequently a
comparatively low temperature will effect the boiling of sugar-syrup
in vacuo, evaporation will proceed far more safely than in the old
process of heating the syrup in open pans, and the percentage of
waste will be greatly reduced, rendering the manufacture highly
profitable in a commercial point of view.

Mr. Howard died at the early age of forty-two, and was buried at
St. Pancras, Middlesex. He left one son, and a daughter, Julia, who
was married in the year 1829 to the Hon. Henry Stafford Jerning-
ham, afterwards Lord Stafford.

CAPTAIN J. HUDDART, F.R.S.

Born Jan. 11, 1740. Died August 19, 1816.

Joseph Huddart was born at Allonby in Cumberland. His
Father, who was a shoemaker and farmer, desiring to give his son
the best education in his power, sent him to a day-school kept by
Mr. Wilson, the clergyman of the village. Here young Huddart
acquired a knowledge of the elements of mathematics, including
astronomy, sciences in which he attained great proficiency in after
life. When quite a boy, Huddart gave indications of an original
mind, combined with great industry and unwearied patience. Having
fallen in with a treatise by Mungo Murray on ship building, he was

so pleased with its clear directions, that he set to work and succeeded, after immense labour and ingenuity, in making a model of a
seventy-four gun-ship, with ribs, planks, and bolts complete. When
engaged in herding his father's cows, he used to carry out into the
country a desk of his own manufacture, employing his time in
reading, and mathematical drawing and calculations.

As Huddart grew up he evinced a strong bias for a sea-faring
life, and an event occurred in 1756 which decided his future career.
In that year large shoals of herrings came into the Solway Frith,
and the elder Huddart took advantage of the circumstance to trade
in conjunction with a Herring Fishery Company, while his son took
his place with others in the boats, and soon displayed so much skill
and ability in their management that he became noted among his
fellows for superiority of knowledge in nautical matters. Young
Huddart continued more or less in this new employment until his
father's death, in 1762, when he succeeded to a share in the fishery,
and at once took the command of a sloop employed in carrying the
salted herrings to Cork and other parts of Ireland, for the supply of
the West India markets.

These voyages gave him a thorough knowledge of St. George's
Channel, convinced him of the insufficiency of the charts then in
use, and ultimately led to his making a complete survey of that
sea, and to the subsequent publication of his own most valuable
chart. In 1768 Huddart, with the assistance of his uncle, designed
and built a vessel for himself, and named it the Patience, every
timber in it having been moulded with his own hand. In this
vessel he made his first voyage to North America, and continued to
sail in her until the year 1771, when he was induced by Sir Richard
Hotham, with whom he had become acquainted, to enter the East
India Mercantile Marine, in which service he continued for many
years, and realized a considerable independency.

Captain Huddart's scientific knowledge and high character introduced him into the Trinity House as an Elder Brother, and also into
the Committee of the Ramsgate Harbour Trust, and into the London
and East India Dock Directions. At the Trinity House all inquiries
relating to lights, lighthouses and charts were chiefly referred to
him, while the lighthouses on Hurst Point were built under his
superintendence and immediate direction.

On retirement from the East India Company's service, Huddart
engaged again in his favourite pursuit of ship building, making
many practical experiments to determine the lines, which consistent
with stability and capacity for stowage would give to vessels the
greatest velocity through the water. But that which constitutes
Captain Huddart's chief claim on the gratitude of posterity are his
great improvements and inventions in the manufacture of Cordage;
before his time nothing worthy of the name of machinery had been
applied to rope-making, and to him was reserved the honour of

bringing the wonderful power of Watt's steam engine to bear upon this most important article of manufacture.

Captain Huddart's attention was first drawn towards the subject during a voyage from India to China through the Straits of Sunda, where the ship he commanded was frequently compelled to anchor. When the anchor was weighed, the outer yarns of the cable were often found to be broken, and on opening a piece of cable to find out the cause, Huddart's attention was forcibly drawn to the fact that rope as then manufactured, bore almost the entire strain on the outer yarns of the strands, from the yarns being originally of the same length, and the strand in the process of twisting becoming shortened. He determined to remedy this, and ultimately constructed a machine which, by means of what he called a register plate, gave to every yarn the same strain, and its proper position in the strand which was compressed through a tube into the desired form.

Government refusing to take up this valuable invention, a company was formed by Huddart's friends for the manufacture of rope upon his new principle. These gentlemen built a factory at Limehouse, which was established under the name of Huddart & Co.

Captain Huddart now devoted himself to the further development of his valuable invention; he contrived a registering machine whereby the yarns were formed as they came out of the tar-kettle' the tar being kept at the temperature (212-220° Fah.) he found by experiment to be sufficient for the required purpose, without injuring by too great heat the fibres of the rope.

He also constructed a laying machine, which gave the same length and twist to every strand, and an uniform angle and pressure to the rope or cable. These improvements involved the manufacture of much beautiful machinery, which was made after Huddart's design and under his own personal superintendance.*

Captain Huddart lived to an advanced old age, and even in his last illness his disposition to inquire into causes and effects did not forsake him, as his body gradually wasted away, he caused himself to be weighed from time to time, noting thereby the quantity of moisture which escaped by the breath and insensible perspiration. He died at Highbury Terrace, London, at the age of seventy-six, and was interred in a vault under St. Martin's Church, in the Strand.—*Memoir of Capt. Jos. Huddart, by Wm. Cotton, D.C.L.* London, 1855.

* This machinery was constructed by John Rennie.—*Mechanics' Magazine*, Sept. 20, 1861.

EDWARD JENNER, M.D., L.L.D., F.R.S., &c.

MEMBER OF THE INSTITUTE OF FRANCE.

Born May 17, 1749. Died January 26, 1823.

Edward Jenner, who by his discovery of vaccination has pre-eminently acquired a right to the title of the "Benefactor of Mankind," was born at the vicarage house of Berkeley, in Gloucestershire, and was the third son of the Rev. Stephen Jenner, rector of Rockhampton, and vicar of Berkeley. Jenner's father died when he was only five years old, leaving him to be brought up under the care of his uncle. At eight years of age he was put to school at Wotton-under-Edge, from whence he was removed shortly afterwards to the care of Dr. Washborn, at Cirencester. Jenner early displayed that taste for natural history which afterwards formed so marked a feature in his character. Before he was nine years old he had made a collection of the nests of the dormouse, and when at Cirencester used to spend his hours of recreation in searching for the fossils which abound in that district.

After the completion of his scholastic education, Jenner removed to Sudbury, near Bristol, where he acquired the elements of surgery and pharmacy under Mr. Ludlow, an eminent surgeon in the neighbourhood. Having completed his term with this gentleman, he went to London and became a pupil of the celebrated John Hunter, in whose family he resided for two years, laying the foundation of an intimate friendship only broken by Hunter's death. Under the tuition of this distinguished anatomist he acquired an almost unrivalled skill in minute dissections and delicate injections of parts; and when, in the year 1771, Captain Cook returned from his first voyage of discovery, the valuable specimens of Natural History, which had been collected by Sir Joseph Banks, were in a great measure arranged and prepared by Jenner, who was recommended by Mr. Hunter for that purpose. In executing this task, he evinced so much dexterity and intelligence, that he was offered the post of Naturalist in the next expedition, which sailed in 1772. Jenner, however, refused the offer, and determined to fix his abode at the place of his birth. He returned to Berkeley when about twenty-four years old, and at once commenced practice as a country surgeon. His first attempts were very successful; and as he added to his professional skill the manners of a thorough gentleman, and the information of a scholar, he became a welcome guest in the most distinguished families. He was in the habit at this time of cultivating the art of poetry, and used to send his compositions to his friends in the ordinary interchange of literary correspondence. He was likewise clever at an epigram or a ballad, and had a natural taste for music, being able to play on the flute and violin, and sing his own verses with considerable taste and feeling. Such was the attachment of Jenner's friends to him at this period of his career, and so highly did they value his amusing and interesting conversation, that, when he had called at their houses, either as a visitor or in his professional capacity, they would accompany him, on leaving, many miles on his way home, and this too, often at midnight, in order that they might prolong the pleasure derived from his company and conversation.

Although Jenner's time was chiefly occupied with his profess iona duties, he still kept up a constant and regular correspondence with his friend John Hunter on different scientific subjects. He managed also to find leisure to institute many experiments and observations in natural history, one of the results of which was his account of the Cuckoo, a most carefully elaborated essay, and which has always been considered as a model of accurate observation. This paper was read to the Royal Society on the 10th of March, 1788, and printed in their 'Transactions.' It explained the habits of this curious bird very satisfactorily, and its publication at once secured the author a considerable reputation as a Naturalist. As this paper appears not to be very generally known, the following account taken from it may be interesting :—

"The cuckoo furtively deposits her egg in the nest of another bird; it is done not that her offspring may be a sharer of the care of the foster-parent, but that it may engross it entirely to the total destruction of its own natural offspring. A perversion of all the maternal instincts is a most remarkable result of this vicarious incubation. The hedge-sparrow, or other birds whose nests have been visited by the cuckoo, actually sometimes eject their own eggs to make room for the new guest; but it occasionally happens that this is not done; the eggs are not disturbed, and the process of hatching is allowed to go on regularly, and the young sparrows and the cuckoo emerge from the shell about the same time. This event, when it is permitted to happen, does not at all improve the condition of the former; on the contrary, it only exposes them to greater sufferings. The size of the egg of the cuckoo does not vary much from that of the bird in whose nest it is deposited. When the young sparrow, therefore, and the intruder first come into life, they are pretty much on an equality; but unhappily for the foster-brethren, this equality does not last long: the cuckoo's growth rapidly outstrips that of his companions, and he immediately exercises his new powers with abundant selfishness and cruelty. By a singular configuration of his own body he contrives to lodge his companions, one by one, upon his back, and then scrambling up the sides of the nest, he suddenly throws them from their seat, and completely ejects them from their own home to become food for worms. There is reason to believe that the unnatural parent is often an unmoved witness of this atrocity. Her whole care and affection are absorbed by the intruder, and her own flesh and blood literally turned out to perish. It sometimes, though very rarely, happens that two cuckoo's eggs are deposited in the same nest. When this occurs, and they are both hatched together, a bitter feud arises, which is only terminated by the ejection of one or other from the nest."

All naturalists previous to Jenner were inclined to ascribe the peculiarity in the economy of the cuckoo to its structure; the largeness of the stomach, which is only protected by a thin covering, they asserted, rendered the pressure attendant upon incubation incompatible with health. This theory is incorrect, and was adopted without due examination.

Jenner observes, "May they not, be owing to the following circumstances?—namely, the short residence this bird is allowed to make in this country, where it is destined to propagate its species, and the call that nature has upon it, during that short residence, to produce a numerous progeny. The cuckoo's first appearance here is about the middle of April. Its egg is not ready for incubation till some weeks after its arrival. A fortnight is taken up by the sitting bird in hatching the egg. The young bird generally continues three weeks in the nest before it flies, and the foster-parents feed it more than five weeks after this period: so that even if a cuckoo should be ready with an egg much sooner than the time pointed out, not a single nestling, would be fit to provide for itself, before its parent would be instinctively directed to seek a new residence, and be thus compelled to abandon its young; for the old cuckoos take their final leave of this country the first week in July."

The domestic incidents of Jenner's life during this period, although important to himself and his future career, were not otherwise remarkable. Having experienced a disappointment in his affections early in life, he continued for many years unmarried. Ultimately, however, on the 6th of March, 1788, he was married to Catherine Kingscote, a descendant of an ancient Gloucestershire family.

In 1793 John Hunter died, and Jenner was deeply affected by the loss of his esteemed friend. Many years previous to this sad event, Jenner's anxious and affectionate attention to the symptoms of the disease, which as early as 1777 had begun to attack Hunter, had enabled him to detect the true nature of his illness (Angina pectoris), and the result of the examination after death fully established the correctness of Jenner's views.

In 1792, having determined to give up the general practice of his profession, and practice as a physician only, Jenner obtained the degree of Doctor of Medicine from St. Andrews; and three years afterwards, on finding that Berkeley by itself could never support a physician, commenced making professional visits to Cheltenham, a practice which he continued for many years.

We now come to the important epoch in the life of this eminent man. On the 14th of May, 1796 (commemorated in Berlin as an annual festival), he made his first successful vaccination on a boy of the name of Phipps, eight years old, and announced the event in a letter to a friend named Gardner, in the following words : "But listen to the most delightful part of my story. The boy has since been inoculated for the small-pox, which, as I ventured to predict, produced no effect. I shall now pursue my experiments with redoubled ardour." In the year 1798 he made public the result of his continued observations and experiments, published during this year his work entitled an 'Inquiry into the Causes and Effects of the Variolœ Vaccinœ,' and henceforth the imperishable name of Jenner was to be identified with vaccination. Although Jenner announced his discovery thus late in life, his attention had been drawn forcibly towards the subject when quite a youth, while pursuing his professional education in the house of his master at Sudbury. During that time, a young countrywoman having come to seek advice, the subject of small-pox was mentioned in her presence ; she immediately observed, "I cannot take that, for I have had the cow-pox." This incident rivetted the attention of Jenner, and he resolved to let no opportunity escape of procuring knowledge upon so interesting a subject. When, in 1770, he was prosecuting his studies in London, he mentioned the matter to Hunter, who told him not to *think* but *try*, and above all to be patient and accurate. Hunter, however, from the great number of original and important pursuits, which fully engrossed his attention, was never so greatly impressed, as Jenner, with the probable consequences of the successful elucidation of the subject of cow-pox ; while other surgeons and scientific men, to whom the subject was mentioned, ridiculed the idea ; and even when Jenner had drawn up his 'Inquiry,' he was recommended not to send it to the Royal Society, lest it should injure the scientific reputation which he had formerly acquired with that body by his paper on the 'Natural History of the Cuckoo.' Undeterred by this want of sympathy, Jenner, during the time of his practice at Berkeley, patiently continued his investigations as to the nature of cow-pox, and, gradually struggling through the difficulties which he had to encounter on his way, eliminated the following facts : that there were certain people to whom it was impossible to give the small-pox by inoculation, and that these had all had the cow-pox ; but that there were also others who had had cow-pox, and who yet received small-pox. This, after much labour, led him to the discovery that the cow was subject to a variety of eruptions, of which one only had the power of guarding from small-pox, and that this, the true cow-pox, as he called it, could, at only one period of its course, produce, by inoculation, such an influence upon the constitution as to render the individual safe from further contagion. This was the basis upon which the fundamental rules for the practice of vaccination were founded. The publication of his 'Inquiry' excited the greatest interest, for the evidence in it seemed conclusive; yet the practice of vaccination met with opposition, as severe as it was unfair, and its success seemed uncertain until a year had passed, when upwards of seventy of the principal physicians and surgeons in London signed a declaration of their entire confidence in it. An attempt was then made to deprive Jenner of the merit of his discovery, but it signally failed, and scientific honours began to be bestowed on him from all quarters. Nothing could, however, induce Jenner to leave his native village, and all his correspondence shows that the purest benevolence, rather than ambition, had been the motive which actuated his labours. In a letter to Mr. Clive, who instituted the first successful case of vaccination in London, he says: "Shall I, who, even in the morning of my life, sought the lowly and sequestered paths of life, the valley and not the mountain; shall I, now my evening is fast approaching, hold myself up as an object for fortune and for fame? Admitting it as a certainty that I obtain both, what stock should I add to my little fund of happiness? And as for fame, what is it?—a gilded butt for ever pierced with the arrows of malignancy." On the Continent Jenner's claims on the gratitude of mankind were quickly recognised, and the influence of his name and character was very great. On one occasion during the war he addressed a letter to Napoleon, requesting permission for two men of science and literature to return to England; and it is related that Napoleon, being about to reject the petition, heard Josephine utter the name of Jenner; on which the Emperor paused for an instant, and exclaimed, "Jenner! ah, we can refuse nothing to that man." He subsequently made other applications both to the French and other governments, which were uniformly attended with similar success. In fact his name became at length so potent, and his influence so well known, that persons left England with certificates signed by him, which had all the force and value of real passports. England, however, was more tardy in recognizing the claims of this great man. He once or twice applied to the British government on behalf of some French prisoners, but unhappily without success. Nor was he permitted to share in the least degree in the vast patronage at the disposal of the government, and all his attempts to obtain a living for one of his nephews failed, although he applied where he was quite justified in thinking he would meet with attention and success. On the occasion of the first parliamentary grant to Jenner in the year 1802, the Chancellor of the Exchequer stated that he thought the "approbation" of the House was the highest reward that could be given him, inasmuch as it would lead to an extended and very lucrative practice; and although it was proved in evidence that 40,000 men were annually preserved to the State, even at that time, by Dr. Jenner's discovery, the proposition of a grant for 10,000*l.* was carried only by a majority of

three. Jenner's feelings were deeply wounded by the manner in
which this grant was made, and he would gladly have repudiated
the whole affair. It remained unpaid for two years, and when at
length the money was paid to him, it was so loaded with taxes and
other expenses, as to be of little pecuniary benefit. Happily, however, both for Jenner and the credit of Great Britain, the Marquis
of Lansdowne (then Lord Henry Petty) was a principal mover in
his second parliamentary grant, and through the able advocacy of
this enlightened nobleman, together with Mr. Whitbread, Mr.
Windham, and Mr. Edward Morris and others, a more fitting recompense of 20,000l., free of all charges, was awarded him in July
1807.

Jenner had several attacks of severe illness during his life, but he
notwithstanding attained to a good old age. Till the last day of
his life he was occupied in the most anxious labours to diffuse the
advantages of his discovery both at home and abroad; and he had
the satisfaction of knowing that vaccination had even then shed
its blessing over every civilised nation of the world, prolonging life,
and preventing the ravages of one of the most terrible scourges to
which the human race was ever subject. He died suddenly from
an attack of paralysis in July 1823, having attained the seventy-
fifth year of his age.

Shortly after Jenner's death a statue was erected to his memory
in Gloucester Cathedral, chiefly through the exertions of his friend
and biographer, Dr. Baron; still more recently the statue in bronze,
by William Calder Marshall, R.A., was erected in Trafalgar Square,
and afterwards removed to Kensington Gardens, as a 'TRIBUTE
FROM ALL NATIONS' to the memory of this distinguished phi-
lanthropist. — *Life of Edward Jenner, by John Baron, M.D., &c.*
London, 1827.—*Memoir by Dr. Thos. Laycock, Encyclopædia Bri-*
tannica.

WILLIAM JESSOP.

Born 1745.   Died 1814.

This engineer forms the connecting link between the first and
second generations of civil engineers in this country. To the
former belong Smeaton and Brindsley, while the latter are headed
by the great names of Telford and Rennie.

The father of Mr. Jessop was engaged under Smeaton in superintending the erection of the Eddystone Lighthouse, and his son

William, the subject of this memoir, was born at Plymouth. When he had attained the age of sixteen his father died, leaving the guardianship of his family to Smeaton, who thenceforth adopted William as his pupil, determining to bring him up to his own profession. Young Jessop remained with Smeaton for a period of ten years, enjoying, during this the busiest part of Smeaton's active career, many opportunities of acquiring an extensive knowledge of the business of civil engineering. After leaving the service of Smeaton, Mr. Jessop was engaged for several years in improving the navigation of the rivers Aire and Calder, and of the Calder and Hebble in Yorkshire. He was also employed on the river Trent in Nottinghamshire, and he appears to have been principally occupied on these works for some time subsequent to his leaving Smeaton.

A few years before the retirement of the latter, which took place in 1791, his pupil began to obtain active employment, and we find him about the years 1788 and 1789, reporting on the navigation of the Sussex Ouse, and the drainage of Laughton Level in the same country, being called on, at the same time, by the Commissioners of the Thames and Isis, to advise on the works they had undertaken, and were about to execute, for the improvement of this important navigation.

In the three following years (1790-2) his professional employment greatly increased. He was now actively engaged in prosecuting various important canals in connection with the great central navigation of the Trent. Amongst these were the Cromford Canal, penetrating amongst the mountains of Derbyshire into the rich mineral districts of that wild and romantic country; the Nottingham Canal, which connects the Cromford with the Trent at Nottingham; the Loughborough and Leicester navigation, connecting the Ashby Coalfield with the navigable part of the Soar and with Nottingham, thus opening an important communication with the Trent on the one hand, and with Nottingham and the whole south of England on the other. In addition to this system in connection with the Trent, he projected and commenced at this time the Horncastle navigation, which, besides acting as a valuable drainage for this part of the fens, was productive of great benefit to a large district, by bringing it into communication with the river Witham, which is navigable to the sea in one direction, and in the other through Lincoln to the Trent.

But a larger and more important work than these last named, which Mr. Jessop was at this period engaged on, was the Grand Junction Canal, which, joining the Oxford Canal at Braunston, in Northamptonshire, connects the whole inland navigation with the metropolis, by means of a comparatively direct line ninety miles in length, traced in a diagonal direction across the two formidable ranges of hills peculiar to the secondary formations of England.

This canal communicates with the Thames by its main line at

Brentford, and by a branch starting five miles above at Bullbridge, stretching to Paddington, from whence the Regent's Canal proceeds round the north side of London to the Thames at Limehouse, thus completing the connection between the main line and the lower part of the river. The execution of this canal necessitated the construction of many heavy works, consisting of tunnels, deep cuttings, embankments, aqueducts, reservoirs, and weirs. Of these works one of the most famous is the Blisworth Tunnel, 3080 yards in length, cut through the inferior oolite and the shales of the lias. Its internal width is 16½ feet, the depth below the water-line to the inverted arch being 7 feet, while the soffit or crown of the arch is 11 feet above the same line. The cost of this great undertaking, with all its branches and attendant works, amounted to about two millions sterling.

During the execution of this work, Mr. Jessop was also called into Ireland, and was taking an active part in carrying on the public works which had been undertaken by the authority of Parliament in that country.

The year 1793 originated several great projects, in furtherance of which Mr. Jessop's aid was secured. Amongst these were the Grantham Canal, supplied by vast artificial reservoirs, and extending from the river Trent, through a rich pasture district of the new red sandstone, winding for many miles through the broad and fertile vale of Belvoir, up to Grantham at the base of the Lincolnshire hills, the furthest point to which it is possible to penetrate in this direction.

The Barnsley Canal, which opens up an immense amount of mineral wealth in the Yorkshire coalfield, and brings it into communication with the river Calder, and the Dearn and Dove Canal; and finally, the Great Ellesmere Canal, which completes a communication between the Severn and the Mersey, and ramifies in numerous directions amongst the rugged hills and valleys of North Wales.

In the carrying on of this last named undertaking, Mr. Telford was likewise engaged under Mr. Jessop. Two of its most important works are the great aqueducts of Chirk and Pont-y-cysylte, the former of which carries the canal over the river Ceriog, at an elevation of 70 feet, while the latter carries it across the Dee at an elevation of 127 feet. The grand peculiarity in these aqueducts consisted in constructing a water-tight trough of cast iron for carrying the canal across the arches, instead of an immense puddled clay trough, as was the practice until that time in use. The execution and management of the numerous works here mentioned occupied the greater part of Mr. Jessop's time during the next few years. But the commencement of the present century was the signal for another torrent of speculation, which, in addition to canals, began now to be directed towards docks and railroads. The promoters of the first great public dock establishment employed Mr. Jessop to conduct their works, and he had the honour of completing the great project of the West India Docks, with their numerous accompanying details, in a manner which alone entitles him to rank among our most eminent engineers.

On the completion of these docks his professional services were engaged by the citizens of Bristol, to effect a great and comprehensive measure of harbour improvement, designed to place the port of Bristol at once in the foremost position with respect to commercial advantages. This was the conversion of part of the river Avon into an immense floating dock, capable of accommodating 1400 vessels. Mr. Jessop was also at this time occupied in constructing the Surrey iron railways, which consisted of a double tramroad, from the Thames at Wandsworth to the town of Croydon, with an extension from Croydon to Godstone and Merstham; they are principally remarkable as being the first public railroads constructed in the south of England. The whole of these tramroads were afterwards bought and taken up by the Brighton Railway Company. Mr. Jessop was likewise connected with the Caledonian Canal, which he was specially called upon to survey before its commencement, and of which he continued to be the consulting engineer for many years.

In concluding this brief notice of Mr. Jessop's life, it remains only to be said that with him exclusively originated the idea of taking advantage of the immense floods to which certain districts are subject, by storing these waters up for the gradual and regular supply of his canals. In addition to this he shares with Mr. Telford the honour of first using iron in the construction of the troughs of aqueducts, and for the heads, heel-posts and ribs of lock-gates, as adopted on the Caledonian and Ellesmere canals.— *Memoir of William Jessop, by Samuel Hughes, C.E.*

CAPTAIN HENRY KATER, F.R.S., &c.

Born April 16, 1777. Died April 26, 1835.

Captain Henry Kater, distinguished by his mathematical and physical researches during the space of nearly half a century, was born at Bristol; his father was of a German family, and his mother was the daughter of an eminent architect; both were distinguished for their scientific attainments, and united in imbuing their son with a similar taste. Henry was, however, destined by his father for the law, and had with great reluctance to give up for a time his hitherto exclusive devotion to abstract science. Mr. Kater continued for two years to remain in a pleader's office, during which time he acquired a considerable portion of legal knowledge, on which he valued himself through life; but the death of his father, in 1794, permitted him to resume his favourite studies; and bidding adieu to the law, he obtained a commission in the 12th Regiment of Foot, at that time stationed in India.

During the following year, Mr. Kater was engaged in the trigonometrical survey of India under Colonel Lambton, contributing greatly, by his untiring labours, to the success of that vast undertaking. About the same period, he was also occupied in constructing a peculiarly sensible hygrometer, of which he published a description in the 'Asiatic Researches.' Mr. Kater remained in India seven years, during which time his unremitting study in a hot climate greatly injured his constitution, and was the cause of his falling into a state of ill health, from which he suffered more or less until the end of his life.

On his return to England, he qualified himself to serve on the general staff, and later in life retired on half-pay, from which period he devoted himself entirely to science. When Parliament, in the years 1818-19, determined on establishing an uniform system of weights and measures, Captain Kater, in conjunction with Sir Joseph Banks, Sir George Clerk, Davies Gilbert, and Drs. Wollaston and Young, was appointed to investigate this most important subject; and he instituted a series of experiments with a pendulum made of a bar of brass, $1\frac{1}{2}$ inches wide and $\frac{1}{8}$ of an inch thick, to which two knife-edges of a kind of steel prepared in India, and known by the name of wootz, were attached, playing upon agate plates. The knife-edges were placed in a parallel direction on the brass bar, facing opposite ways upon either of which it might be swung. They were so arranged, that when either was used as the point of suspension the other nearly represented the centre of oscillation, and by means of a small adjustable weight, this condition might be accurately fulfilled. These experiments were made in the house of Mr. H. Browne, F.R.S., which was situated in a part of Portland Place not likely to be disturbed by carriages. They occupied Captain Kater's close attention for several years; and he has permanently attached his name to the beautiful theorem of Huygens respecting the reciprocity of the centres of oscillation and suspension, and their consequent quality of convertibility. Although this was a property already known to belong to the centre of oscillation, it had never hitherto been practically applied to determine the exact length of a pendulum vibrating seconds; it was, therefore, highly creditable to his ingenuity, and claims the same order of merit as an original invention. In this, as well as in Kater's laborious inquiries respecting a standard of weights and measures, even where his conclusions have not escaped all the chances of error, he has led the way to the still more delicate researches which have followed.

Captain Kater also instituted a series of experiments as to the best kind of steel and shape for compass needles; it resulted in the adoption of the shear clock-spring steel, and the pierced rhombus form, in the proportion of five inches in length to two in width. In the year 1831 he received the gold medal of the Royal Astronomical Society, for the construction of his floating collimator, an instrument for ascertaining the accurate zero or level points of divided astronomical instruments. The optical principle upon which it depends is a very beautiful one, and the invention of Kater, with several improvements in point of form, has become the auxiliary of nearly every observatory in the world, being one of those small but happy improvements which affect materially the progress of science. Most of the learned societies in Great Britain and on the Continent testified at different times their sense of the value of his services, by enrolling him among their members. The Emperor of Russia employed him to construct standards for the weights and measures of his dominions, and was so pleased with the execution of them, that he presented Kater with the Order of St. Anne and a diamond snuff-box. The greater part of his publications appeared in the 'Philosophical Transactions' of the Royal Society, chiefly between the years 1813 and 1828.

Captain Kater died from a severe affection of the lungs, at his residence, York Gate, in the fifty-third year of his age.—*Athenæum*, May, 1835.—*Weld's History of the Royal Society.* London, 1848.—*Monthly Notices of the Royal Astronomical Society*, vol. 3, February, 1836.—*Sixth Dissertation Encyclopædia Britannica*, Eighth Edition.

SIR JOHN LESLIE, F.R.S.E., &c.

Born April 16, 1766. Died November 3, 1832.

Sir John Leslie, Professor of Natural Philosophy in the University of Edinburgh, the son of a poor joiner or cabinetmaker, was born at the village of Largo, in the county of Fife. Although both weak and sickly as a child, he soon acquired considerable knowledge of mathematical and physical science, and at the age of eleven attracted the notice of Mr. Oliphant, the minister of the parish, by his precocious attainments. This gentleman kindly lent young Leslie some scientific books, and strongly advised him to continue the study of Latin, for which he had a great aversion, although in after life he attained considerable proficiency in that language.

He also became known to Professors Robison and Stewart, of Edinburgh, and by their advice was sent, in his thirteenth year, to the University of St. Andrew's, to study mathematics under Professor Vilant. Here, at the end of the first session, his abilities procured him the second prize, and likewise attracted the notice of the Earl of Kinnoull, then Chancellor of the University, who undertook to defray the expenses of his education, provided that he would enter the Church. Leslie prosecuted his studies at this university during six sessions, and became about this time acquainted with Playfair and Dr. Small.

In 1783-4 he quitted St. Andrews and went to Edinburgh, where, though he formally entered the Divinity Hall, he contrived to devote his first session to the sciences, particularly chemistry; in fact, Leslie seems early to have relinquished all thoughts of the Church—a resolution hastened by the death of his patron, the Earl of Kinnoull, shortly after his removal to Edinburgh. While engaged at the university, he also acted as tutor to Mr. Douglas, afterwards Lord Reston, the nephew of Dr. Adam Smith, and he thus became known to that philosopher, who treated him kindly, and occasionally favoured him with directions as to his pursuits. Leslie's first essay, ' On the Resolution of Indeterminate Problems,' was composed about this time, and read to the Royal Society of Edinburgh by Mr. Playfair, in 1788, and published in their ' Transactions' for 1790.

In 1788, he became tutor to two young Americans of the name of Randolph, and accompanied them to Virginia, where he remained for about a twelvemonth, during which time he visited New York, Philadelphia, &c. In January 1790, carrying, among other letters of recommendation, one from Adam Smith, Leslie repaired to London, with the intention of delivering a course of lectures on natural philosophy; but finding, to use his own words, that "rational lectures would not succeed," he employed himself for some time in writing for the ' Monthly Review,' and in other literary occupations.

In April 1790, he became tutor to the younger Wedgewoods, of Etruria, in Staffordshire, who had been his former fellow-students, and with whom he remained until the close of 1792. Leslie was likewise employed during this period in experimental investigations, and in completing a translation of Buffon's ' Natural History of Birds,' published in 1793, in nine volumes, for which he received a considerable sum,—the foundation of that pecuniary competency which his industrious and prudent habits enabled him ultimately to acquire.

During the years 1794-5 he resided at Largo, occupied upon a long series of hygrometrical experiments, during the course of which he invented his differential thermometer, the parent, as it may be called, of his subsequent inventions—the hygroscope, photometer, pyroscope, æthrioscope, and atmometer. Although Leslie

has been accused of having plagiarized this invention either from
Van Helmont, who died in 1644, or from John Christopher Sturmius,
who died sixty years later, he at all events showed, by his skilful
and fruitful employment of the disputed invention, how much he
surpassed, and how little he needed the help of, him whom he is
ungenerously supposed to have robbed of his legitimate honours.

In 1800 he wrote several papers, on different branches of physics,
in Nicholson's ' Philosophical Journal,' which resulted in the publication at London, in 1804, of his ' Experimental Inquiry into the
Nature and Propagation of Heat.' The originality and boldness of
the peculiar doctrines contained in this work, and the number of
new and important facts disclosed by its ingenious experimental
combinations, rendered it an object of extraordinary interest in the
scientific world. The Royal Society of London unanimously ad-
judged to its author the Rumford medal; and although paradoxical
in many of its theories, defective in arrangement, and over ambitious
in style, this work is almost unrivalled in the entire range of physical
science, for its indication of vigorous and inventive genius.

Previous to this period of life, Leslie had appeared twice as a
candidate for an academical chair; first in the University of St.
Andrew's, afterwards in that of Glasgow; but on both occasions
without success. He now became a candidate for the Mathematical
chair at Edinburgh, vacant through the promotion of Professor
Playfair to the chair of Natural Philosophy. After a severe contest,
during which much party spirit was displayed, owing to his principal competitor, Dr. Thomas Macknight, one of the ministers of
Edinburgh, being supported by the majority of the city clergy,
Leslie was, in March, 1805, elected to the Mathematical chair. He
entered immediately upon his official duties, which he continued to
discharge with zeal and assiduity during the following fourteen
years.

Notwithstanding the labours which these duties entailed upon
him, Leslie continued his experimental inquiries, and in June, 1810,
discovered his beautiful process of artificial congelation, by which
he was enabled to produce ice, and even to freeze mercury at
pleasure. The process consists of a combination of the powers of
rarefaction and absorption, effected by placing a very strong ab-
sorbent under the receiver of an air-pump. This experiment was
performed in London in 1811, before a meeting of some members of
the Royal Society; and the discovery was announced in the same
year in the ' Memoirs' of the French Institute. He explained his
experiments and views on this subject in 1813, in a volume published at Edinburgh, entitled, ' A short Account of Experiments
and Instruments depending on the Relations of Air to Heat and
Moisture.' Closely connected with the subject of this treatise
was an ingenious paper, published in 1818, in the ' Transactions' of
the Royal Society of Edinburgh, under the title, ' On certain Im-

pressions of Cold transmitted from the Higher Atmosphere; with a Description of an Instrument to Measure them.' The æthrioscope was the instrument here alluded to.

In 1819, upon the death of Playfair, Leslie was called to the chair of Natural Philosophy, when his first care was directed to the extension of the apparatus required in the more enlarged series of experiments which he thought necessary for the illustration of the course. " This, indeed," says his biographer, Mr. Napier, " was an object of which he never lost sight; and it is due to him to state, that, through his exertions, the means of experimental illustration in the Natural Philosophy class were for the first time made worthy of the place."

In 1823 he published, chiefly for the use of this class, his ' Elements of Natural Philosophy,' a second edition of which was published in 1829, with corrections and additions. Besides the above-mentioned works, Leslie wrote the following:—' Elements of Geometry, Geometrical Analysis and Plane Trigonometry,' in 1809; ' Observations on Electrical Theories,' published in 1824, in the ' Edinburgh Philosophical Journal;' also many articles in the ' Edinburgh Review;' and the articles on Achromatic Glasses; Acoustics; Aeronautics; Andes; Angle and Trisection of Angle; Arithmetic; Atmometer; Barometer; Barometrical Measurements; Climate; Cold and Congelation; Dew; Interpolation; and Meteorology, in the seventh edition of the ' Encyclopædia Britannica.'

Early in the year 1832, on the recommendation of Lord Brougham, then Lord High Chancellor, Leslie was created, along with several other eminent men of science, a Knight of the Guelphic Order. He was also a member of the Royal Society of Edinburgh, and in 1820 had been elected a corresponding member of the French Institute. During the month of October, whilst engaged in superintending some improvements on his grounds, he caught a severe cold, which was followed by erysipelas in one of his legs, and his neglect of this, owing to a contempt for medicine, and great confidence in his own strength and durability, resulted in his death, at Coates, in the November following, at the age of sixty-six.

Sir John Leslie has been described as rivalling all his contemporaries in that creative faculty which discovers, often by an intuitive glimpse, the hidden secrets of nature ; but possessing in a less degree the powers of judgment and reason, being thus often led in his speculations to results glaringly inconsistent. His exquisite instruments, and his experimental combinations, will, however, ever test the utility, no less than the originality of his labours, and will continue to act as aids to farther discovery.—*Encyclopædia Britannica*, Eighth Edition.—*Abstract of Memoir of Sir John Leslie, by Macvey Napier, English Cyclopædia.* London, 1856.

NEVIL MASKELYNE, D.D., F.R.S.

MEMBER OF THE INSTITUTE OF FRANCE, ETC.

Born October 6, 1732.   Died February 9, 1811.

This most accurate and industrious astronomer was born in London, and was the son of Mr. Edmund Maskelyne, a gentleman of respectable family in Wiltshire. At the age of nine Maskelyne was sent to Westminster school, where he early began to distinguish himself, and to display a decided taste for the study of optics and astronomy.

The great solar eclipse, which occurred in 1748 was, however, the immediate cause of his directing his attention to these sciences, and from that period he devoted himself with ardour to the study of mathematics as subservient to that of astronomy. It is a curious fact that the same eclipse is said to have produced a similar effect upon the French astronomer Lalande, who was only three months older than his English contemporary.

Soon after this Maskelyne entered the University of Cambridge as a member of Catherine Hall, removing afterwards to Trinity, where he took the degree of Bachelor of Arts with great credit in 1754, and proceeded regularly through the succeeding stages of academical rank in divinity. In 1755 he was ordained to a curacy at Barnet, and in the following year obtained a fellowship at Trinity. In the year 1758 he was elected a fellow of the Royal Society, previous to which event he had become acquainted with Dr. Bradley, and had determined to make astronomy the principal pursuit of his life, feeling that it was perfectly compatible with an enlightened devotion to the duties of his own profession.

1761 marks the period when Maskelyne commenced his public career as an astronomer. During that year he was chosen by the Royal Society to undertake a voyage to the island of St. Helena, for the purpose of observing the transit of Venus; and in order to make the voyage as useful as possible, Maskelyne undertook to make observations upon the parallax of Sirius. He remained ten months at St. Helena, but the weather hindered his observing the transit to advantage, while the inaccuracy of his quadrant, which was of the same construction as was then usually employed, prevented his observations on the stars from being as conclusive as he had expected. His voyage was, however, of great service to navigation, by promoting the introduction of lunar observations for ascertaining the longitude; and he taught the officers of the ship in which he was in, the proper use of the instruments as well as the mode of making the computations.

On his return to England, Maskelyne published, in 1763, his

E 3

'British Mariner's Guide,' the earliest of his separate publications, in which he proposes the adoption of a Nautical Almanac according to the plan indicated by Lacaille, after his voyage to the Cape of Good Hope. In the same year he performed a second voyage to the island of Barbadoes, in order to determine the rates of Harrison's chronometers. In his report on the results of this voyage Maskelyne, while doing justice to the works of this eminent mechanician, decided in favour of the employment of lunar observations for determining the longitude, strongly supporting the cause of Professor Mayer, who had computed lunar tables for this purpose. The liberality of the British Government, however, bestowed on Harrison the whole reward that he claimed,* while Maskelyne, having been appointed to the situation of Astronomer Royal which likewise made him a member of the Board of Longitude, was instrumental in procuring a reward of 5,000l. for the family of Professor Mayer, and a compliment of 300l. for Euler, whose theorems had been employed in the investigation.

When the merits of Mayer's tables had been fully established, the Board of Longitude was induced to promote their application to practical purposes by the annual publication of the Nautical Almanac, which, during the remainder of his life, was arranged and conducted entirely under Maskelyne's direction.

Maskelyne held the situation of Astronomer Royal for forty-seven years, during which period he acquired the respect of all Europe, by the diligence and accuracy of his observations, which he always, if possible, conducted in person, requiring the aid of only one assistant.

Up to Maskelyne's time the observations of the Astronomers Royal had been considered as private property; Flamsted publishing his own, while Bradley's were very liberally bought of his family, and afterwards printed by the University of Oxford. Dr. Maskelyne, on the contrary, obtained leave from the British Government to have his observations printed at the public expense under the direction of the Royal Society, who are the legal visitors of the observatory, appointed by the royal sign manual; and by thus causing the observations of the Astronomer Royal to be recorded publicly, he supplied a great want which had hitherto existed both in the English and French establishments. He also made several improvements in the arrangement and employment of the instruments used in the observatory, particularly, by enlarging the slits through which the light was admitted; by making the eyeglass of his transit telescope moveable to the place of each of the wires of the micrometer; and above all, by marking the time to tenths of a second, a refinement which had never been attempted before.

---

* 20,000l., the reward offered for a chronometer sufficiently exact to correct the longitude within certain limits required by Act of Parliament.

Maskelyne received his doctor's degree in the year 1777, he also obtained the rare distinction of being made one of the eight foreign associates of the French Academy of Science. In consequence of an unsuccessful attempt made by Bouguer to measure the local attraction of a mountain in South America, Maskelyne determined, in 1772, to ascertain that of Schehallien in Scotland; and this latter undertaking, together with the determination of the lunar orbit from observation, and its application to navigation, may be considered as his most important contributions to the cause of science.

In character Dr. Maskelyne was modest and somewhat timid in receiving the visits of strangers, but his ordinary conversation was cheerful and often playful, with a fondness for point and classical allusion. He inherited a good paternal property, and obtained considerable preferment from his college; somewhat late in life he married the sister and co-heiress of Lady Booth of Northamptonshire; his sister was the wife of Robert Lord Clive, and the mother of the Earl of Powis. Dr. Maskelyne died on the ninth of February, 1811, in his seventy-ninth year, leaving a widow and an only daughter.—*Notice sur la vie et les travaux de M. Maskelyne par Delambre.* London, 1813.—*Memoir by Dr. T. Young, Encyclopædia Britannica.*

HENRY MAUDSLAY.

Born Aug. 22, 1771. Died Feb. 14, 1831.

This distinguished mechanical engineer was descended from an eminent Lancashire family, who trace back their origin as far as the year 1200. His father in early life enlisted in the Royal Artillery at Norwich, and afterwards became store-keeper at the Royal Dockyard of Woolwich, where his son Henry was born and spent his boyhood, acquiring in the dockyard the first rudiments of that mechanical knowledge which has since made him so justly celebrated.

After being employed for two years as a ' powder monkey' in the dockyard, that is, in making and filling cartridges, Maudslay was placed, at the age of fourteen, in the carpenter's shop. He however infinitely preferred the blacksmith's shop, availing himself of every opportunity to escape from his proper place, and steal off to the smithy. His propensity was in fact so strong that it was thought better to yield to it, and he was accordingly removed there in his fifteenth year. He now made rapid progress, and soon became so expert a smith and metal-worker as to attract considerable notice.

Even in after life, when at the head of the well-known firm which he founded, nothing pleased him more than to set to work upon a difficult piece of forging and to overcome the difficulties which it presented, which few could do so well as he. The reputation which Maudslay acquired here, led to his introduction and ultimate employment by Bramah, who was at that time engaged in constructing his celebrated lock.

One of the chief obstacles which Bramah had to contend with in getting his lock into general use, was, the difficulty he experienced in having it manufactured with sufficient precision and at such a price as to render it an article of successful commerce. Maudslay's* ability as a workman and sound mechanical knowledge was of great service to Bramah in this particular; the most difficult and delicate jobs were entrusted to him, and among others he constructed the identical lock, the picking of which so severely tested the skill and ability of Mr. Hobbs in the year 1851. He also, according to the testimony of Mr. J. Nasmyth, supplied Bramah with the key to the practical success of the hydraulic press, viz., the self-tightening leather collar.†

About the year 1797 Maudslay commenced business on his own account in Wells Street, Oxford Street, removing a few years afterwards to Margaret Street, Cavendish Square. Here he matured and carried out many improvements in tools connected with the mechanical arts, bringing into general notice and use planing machines and the slide rest. So great was the prejudice felt against this last named important adjunct of a lathe, that on the first introduction of the slide rest to the engineers of the period, it was received with great disfavour, and called by one in derision the 'Go Cart.' Maudslay also directed his attention to the subject of screw cutting. Previous to his time the tools used for making screws were of the most rude and inexact kind: each manufacturing establishment made them after their own fashion, and no system was observed as to the pitch. Every bolt and nut was a speciality in itself; and to such an extent was this carried that all bolts and their corresponding nuts had to be marked, any mixing of them together causing endless trouble and confusion. Maudslay changed all this—he brought screw-cutting into a proper system, and laid the foundation of all that has since been done in this important branch of machine-construction, and many of those who afterwards became eminent in this particular branch of manufacture, acquired their first knowledge of the subject in his employ.‡ While residing in Margaret Street he became acquainted with Sir Isambard (then Mr.) Brunel, who was in the habit of bringing drawings of small pieces of machinery

---

* A very interesting account of Maudslay's introduction, &c., to Bramah is given by Mr. Smiles in his 'Industrial Biography.' London 1863. P. 201-3.
† See 'Memoir of Bramah.'
‡ In particular may be mentioned Joseph Clement and Joseph Whitworth.

for him to construct: this attracted Maudslay's attention, and at last he one day exclaimed to Sir Isambard, "Ah! I see what you are thinking of—you want machinery for making blocks:" this so pleased Brunel, that he became more open of communication, and in the subsequent completion of the beautiful block machinery afterwards erected at Portsmouth Dockyard, Mr. Brunel derived great advantage from the sound mechanical knowledge of Maudslay. The friendship commenced thus was never afterwards shaken, and when Brunel began the Thames Tunnel, he consulted his old friend relative to the construction of the shield, as it was termed, under shelter of which the excavation beneath the bed of the river, and the brickwork for forming the Tunnel were proceeded with.

In the year 1807 Maudslay took out a patent for improvements in the steam-engine, by which he much simplified its parts and secured greater directness of action. His new engine was called the Pyramidal, from its form, and was the first move towards direct acting engines. In 1810, finding his business getting too extensive for his premises in Margaret Street, he removed to the more capacious ones in Westminster Road, Lambeth. Here he for many years carried on a large business, embracing the manufacture of all kinds of machinery, but more particularly of marine engines, to the construction and improvement of which he early directed his attention, foreseeing how important a branch of industry they would eventually become; and it may be interesting to record, that the engines (24 H. P.) of the 'Regent,' the first steamboat which ran between London and Margate, were made at this yard in the year 1816.

Mr. Maudslay held for several years the contract for supplying the Royal Navy with ship tanks, and this led to his making improved machinery for punching and shearing the iron plates used in their manufacture, reducing the cost of preparing the plates for receiving the rivets from seven shillings, to ninepence, per Tank.

Mr. Maudslay has been described by his friend Mr. James Nasmyth as the very beau-ideal of an honest, upright, straightforward, hardworking intelligent Englishman: he died in his 60th year from a severe cold which he had caught on his way home from a visit to France, and was buried in Woolwich churchyard, in a vault he had caused to be constructed there; the monument and tablet erected to his memory were of cast iron, and were made from a design of his own. Maudslay married when twenty years old Sarah Tindel, by whom he had four sons and three daughters, of whom now survive only one daughter, and one son Thomas Henry Maudslay.— *From particulars communicated by members of the present firm of Maudslay, Sons and Field.—Smile's Industrial Biography.* London, 1863.

PATRICK MILLER.

Born in Scotland 1730.
Died at Dalswinton House, near Dumfries, 1815.

Patrick Miller, of Dalswinton, was originally a banker, and ultimately became possessed of considerable independent property. At different periods of his life he embarked in many schemes of great public utility. He made considerable improvements in artillery and naval architecture, and during the course of his various experiments expended upwards of thirty thousand pounds. One of the immediate results of his experiments in the first-named science was the invention of the well-known carronade ; while in the course of his experiments in naval architecture, he constructed double and triple vessels, and was the first to practically apply the present form of the paddle-wheels now in ordinary use to their propulsion. Having satisfied himself of the usefulness of his researches in this respect, by many costly experiments undertaken at his own expense, Mr. Miller published at Edinburgh, in 1787, a book in English and French, containing a full account of them, and sent a copy of his work to every sovereign in Europe, and also to the American States, inasmuch as he considered that his inventions ought to be the property of the human kind.* The paddle-wheels in these experiments (undertaken in the years 1786-7) were turned by manual labour, and on the occasion of a severe contest between one of his double boats and a Custom-house boat, reckoned to be a fast sailer, the want of a more powerful force to turn the wheels was greatly felt. Mr. James Taylor, at that time a tutor in Mr. Miller's family, suggested steam power, and ultimately introduced Miller to Wm. Symington, with whose aid Mr. Miller commenced and carried out those experiments (in the years 1788-89) which have justly entitled him to the honour of being the first to originate the present system of steam navigation.†

It is much to be regretted that since the deaths of Mr. Miller and Mr. Symington, statements have been made in which the *entire* merit of first establishing steam navigation is claimed, on the one hand, for Miller, by his eldest son, in a paper published in the 'Edinburgh Philosophical Journal' for July 1825 ; and on the other for Symington, by Richard Bowie, in his pamphlet published in 1833; whereas these two gentlemen appear to be inseparably connected with the first introduction of this grand application of steam. As far as it is possible to reconcile the conflicting statements, the

* See 'Memorials of Great Britain and Ireland,' by Sir John Dalrymple, Bart.
† For fuller account of Miller and Symington's experiments see ' Memoir of Symington.'

facts may be briefly stated thus. Patrick Miller was the first to successfully propel vessels by paddle-wheels moved by manual labour. He then, in conjunction with William Symington, applied steam to move these paddle-wheels, and constructed two steam-boats, which were publicly tried, on the Forth and Clyde Canal, in the years 1788-89. Although these trials triumphantly proved the practicability of steam navigation, further improvements were required before a really successful steam-boat could be said to have been constructed. At this point, unfortunately, Mr. Miller, having already spent large sums of money in his experiments, let the matter drop; but Symington, about ten years afterwards, under the patronage of Lord Dundas, succeeding in constructing 'The Charlotte Dundas,' a steam-boat which, for the first time, combined together those improvements which constitute the present system of steam navigation. In the narrative written by Patrick Miller, Jun., a good deal of praise, in regard to this matter, is given to James Taylor, before referred to, who is considered by some as having a just claim to participate in the honour awarded to Miller and Symington. Mr. Taylor's merits, however, appear chiefly to consist in having suggested, upon the occasion of a race between one of Miller's boats and a Custom House boat, that they only re-quired the help of a steam-engine to beat their antagonists; also, in having introduced Symington, whose steam-carriage had ren-dered him famous, to the notice of Mr. Miller; and although Taylor assisted in the subsequent experiments, he seems to have con-tributed little to their practical success.—*Narrative of Facts relative to Invention and Practice of Steam Navigation, &c., by Patrick Miller, Jun., 'Edinburgh Philosophical Journal,' Vol. 13, July 1825.— Narrative by R. Bowie, proving William Symington the Inventor of Steam Land Carriage Locomotion and of Steam Navigation. London, 1833.—Stuart's Anecdotes of the Steam Engine. London, 1829.— Descriptive Catalogue of the Museum of the Commissioners of Patents.*

WILLIAM MURDOCK.

Born 1754. Died November 15, 1839.

William Murdock was born at Bellow Mill, near Old Cumnock, Ayrshire, where his father carried on the business of a millwright and miller, and likewise possessed a farm on the estate of the Bos-well family of Auchinleck. His mother's maiden name was Bruce, and she used to boast of being lineally descended from Robert Bruce, of Scottish History. Little is known of Murdock's life prior

to his coming to England, and joining, in the year 1777, Boulton
and Watt's establishment at Soho, at that time in its infancy. He
must, however, have had some celebrity in his native country, as
he was employed to build a bridge over the river Nith, in Dum-
frieshire, a very handsome structure, and still in existence. His
talents were soon appreciated at Soho, particularly by James Watt,
with whom he continued on terms of the closest friendship until
Mr. Watt's death in 1819. After remaining two years at Soho,
Murdock was appointed by Messrs. Boulton and Watt to superintend
the erection, and undertake the general charge, of their new steam-
engines in Cornwall, where he erected the first engine, in that part
of the country, with a separate condenser. He continued to live in
the district for the space of nineteen years, giving great satisfaction
to the mining interest; so much so, that when it became known
that he was about to return to Soho, 1000l. a-year was offered him
to remain in Cornwall. During his residence there Murdock contrived and executed a model locomotive, which, as early as the year
1784, he was in the habit of showing to his friends in working
order, and drawing a small waggon round a room in his house at
Redruth. He used to tell a story, that while making experiments
with this engine, he one night determined to test its powers on a
level road leading from his house to the church, which was situated
about a mile distant from the town; this road was bounded on each
side by high edges, and well suited for the purpose. Murdock accordingly sallied out, and placing his engine on the ground, lit
the fire, or rather lamp, under the boiler; after a few minutes off
started the locomotive with the inventor full chase after it; after
continuing the pursuit for a short distance, he heard cries as of a
person in great distress; the night was too dark to perceive objects
afar off, but on going on, he found that the sounds proceeded from
the clergyman of the parish, who had set out for the town on business, and being met on this lonely road by the fiery monster, had
taken it for the Evil One in person. This model locomotive was
exhibited before a meeting of the Institution of Mechanical Engineers in 1850, sixty-six years after the date of its construction.

Mr. Murdock is, however, better known to the public by his application of the light of coal gas to general purposes. Although
this gas had been well known, and obtained both naturally and
artificially more than half a century before his time, no attempt had
as yet been made to turn the discovery to any useful account. In
the year 1792 Murdock first employed coal gas for the purpose of
lighting his house and offices at Redruth; he made it serve also as
a lantern, by attaching a bladder with a tube mouthpiece under the
bottom of a glass shade, which contrivance used to light him across
the moors when returning home at night from the mining engines
he was erecting in different parts of the district. After various
experiments which proved the economy and convenience of light

so obtained, he perfected his apparatus and made a public exhibition of it by lighting up the front of Boulton and Watt's manufactory at Soho, on the occasion of the general illumination for the peace of Amiens, in 1802. He subsequently lighted up some cotton mills at Manchester, beginning with Messrs. Phillips and Lee's, and published a paper on the subject in the 'Philosophical Transactions' of 1808, for which the Royal Society presented him with the Rumford gold medal.

In 1798 Murdock returned to take up his permanent residence at Soho, superintending the machinery there, and occasionally the erection of engines at a distance, among which may be mentioned those of the New River Head, Lambeth, Chelsea, Southwark, East London, West Middlesex, and other waterworks. In the following year he took out a patent for improvements in boring cylinders and in the manufacture of steam casings; this patent also included the double D slide valve and a rotary engine. Amongst other inventions and discoveries of Murdock's are: a plan for boring stone pipes for water, and cutting columns out of solid blocks of stone (for which he took a patent in 1810); a pneumatic lift working by compressed air; and a cast iron cement, which he was led to discover by the accidental observance of some iron borings and sal-ammoniac, which had got mixed in his tool-chest and rusted a sword blade nearly through. He also made use of compressed air to ring the bells in his house; a plan which so pleased Sir Walter Scott, to whom it had been described, that he had his house at Abbotsford fitted up in a similar manner. Murdock likewise discovered a substitute for isinglass, and when in London for the purpose of explaining to the brewers the nature of his discovery, occupied very handsome apartments. Being, however, at all times absorbed in whatever subject he had in hand, he little respected the splendour of his drawing-room, but proceeded with his experiments as if in the laboratory at Soho, quite unconscious of the mischief he was doing. This resulted in his abrupt dismissal from the apartments by the enraged landlady, who one morning, on calling in to receive orders, was horrified at seeing all her magnificent paper-hangings covered with wet fish skins hung up to dry, and actually caught him in the act of pinning up a cod's skin to undergo the same process.

In the year 1815, while Mr. Murdock was fitting up an apparatus of his own invention for heating the water of the baths at Leamington, a ponderous cast-iron plate fell upon his leg above the ankle, nearly severing it in two. This severe accident laid him up for a long time, and he never entirely recovered from the effects of it. During the latter years of his life Murdock's faculties, both corpereal and mental, experienced a gradual decay, causing him to live in complete retirement. He died in 1839, aged eighty-five years, and his remains were buried in Handsworth Church, near to those of Boulton and James Watt.

Mr. Murdock married in the year 1785 the daughter of Captain Paynter, of Redruth, Cornwall, who died at the early age of twenty-four, having had four children.—*From a Paper read by Mr. William Buckle, of Soho, before a meeting of the Institution of Mechanical Engineers*, October 23, 1850.

ROBERT MYLNE.

Born January 4, 1733. Died May 5, 1811.

Robert Mylne, the architect of Blackfriars Bridge, was born at Edinburgh. His father was an architect, and magistrate of the city; and his family, it has been ascertained, held the office of Master Masons to the Kings of Scotland for a period of five hundred years, until the union of the crowns of England and Scotland.

On arriving at man's estate, Mylne travelled for improvement; and his enthusiastic prosecution of his art soon brought him into notice. In 1758 he became a candidate for the honours of the Academy of St. Luke at Rome, and the chief prize in the highest class of architecture was awarded to him; being the first instance of a native of Great Britain obtaining that honour.

Mylne resided at Rome during a space of five years, and on his return to England executed a design for Blackfriars Bridge, which was selected from among twenty others. This bridge was commenced in 1760; and on the occasion of the laying of the foundation-stone by the Lord Mayor, among other medals deposited in the stone was a silver one, the memorial of the young architect's first triumph, viz., the medal (one of two) given him by the Academy at Rome. The bridge was completed in 1769; the arches are elliptical in shape, and were the first instances in England in which the form of an ellipse was substituted for a semicircle. The total cost of the bridge itself, exclusive of the approaches, amounted to 152,840*l.*

Mylne's reputation was now established, and his services were employed in the erection or improvement of many edifices throughout the United Kingdom. He received at the hands of the Archbishop of Canterbury, the Bishop of London, and the Lord Mayor, the office of Surveyor of St. Paul's Cathedral; and while holding this appointment, suggested the famous inscription to Sir Christopher Wren—' *Si monumentum quæris circumspice.*' He also held the office of Clerk of the Works at Greenwich Hospital for fifteen years, and was Engineer to the New River Water Works from the year 1762 until his death, in 1811, when he was succeeded by his son.

Towards the close of the eighteenth century, he became acquainted with Mr. John Rennie, whose celebrity as an engineer was then approaching its height; and the two became from that time inseparable friends.* Mr. Mylne was also an intimate friend of Dr. Johnson, their acquaintance having originated out of a controversy as to the form of the arch for Blackfriars Bridge.

Mylne was buried in St. Paul's Cathedral, by the side of his illustrious predecessor, Sir Christopher Wren.—*Gateshead Observer*, October 20, 1860.—*Encyclopædia Britannica.*

ALEXANDER NASMYTH.

Born September 7, 1758.   Died April 10, 1840.

Alexander Nasmyth, the distinguished Scotch landscape painter, and known also as a man of science, was born at Edinburgh. He came early in life to London, where he was for some time the pupil of Allen Ramsay, painter to George III. He resided afterwards in Rome for several years, during which time he studied portrait, history, and landscape painting.

From Rome, Nasmyth returned to Edinburgh, where he settled as a portrait painter, and executed his well-known painting of Robert Burns—the most authentic likeness of this great poet. Having, however, a decided taste for landscape painting, he ultimately confined himself to this branch of art; but much of his time was occupied in teaching, in which he was very successful. His landscapes, which are very numerous, were, many of them, reminiscences of Italian scenery, and although wanting in originality and vigour, possess so much beauty and grace as to have caused their author to acquire the name of the ' Scottish Claude.'

Mr. Nasmyth was a favourite in society, and was the leading teacher in art of the highest classes in Scotland; during his later years being commonly looked up to as the patriarch of Scottish art. He not only took much interest in the proceedings of the artistic societies of Edinburgh, but often raised an influential voice in respect to the alterations making in that city; and was one of the three successful competitors between whom the first prize offered for the best plan for laying out and building the New Town of Edinburgh was equally divided.

Mr. Nasmyth spent much of his time in scientific experiments, and was the inventor of ' bow and string bridges,' and of a method of driving the screw-propellers of vessels by direct action, in front of the rudder. Much of his leisure time was spent in a workshop

* *Mechanics' Magazine*, September 20, 1861.

which he had fitted up for himself, and which proved the nursery of the early mechanical genius of the present James Nasmyth, the celebrated engineer.

Soon after his return from Italy, Alexander Nasmyth married the sister of Sir James Foulis of Woodhall Colinton, by whom he had a family of three sons and five daughters, all of whom inherited more or less their father's talents, while the eldest, Patrick, has acquired a separate renown of no inconsiderable extent, for the beauty of his landscapes.

Alexander Nasmyth died in York Place, Edinburgh, at the age of eighty-three, and was interred in the West Church burying-ground of that city.—*English Cyclopædia.* London, 1857.—*Catalogue of Gallery of Portraits of Inventors, &c., in the South Kensington Museum.*

JOHN PLAYFAIR, F.R.S. L. and E.

PROFESSOR OF MATHEMATICS AT THE UNIVERSITY OF EDINBURGH.

Born March 10, 1748.   Died July 19, 1819.

John Playfair, a mathematician and philosopher of great eminence and celebrity, was born at Benvie in Forfarshire, and was the eldest son of the Rev. James Playfair, the minister of that place. Playfair resided at home, under the domestic tuition of his father, until the age of fourteen, when he entered the University of St. Andrew's, where he became almost immediately distinguished, not merely for his singular proficiency in mathematical learning, but also for the extent of his general knowledge, the clearness of his judgment, and the dignity and propriety of his conduct. A strong proof of his capabilities at this time is given by the fact, that when Dr. Wilkie, the professor of natural philosophy, was prevented by indisposition from delivering the regular lectures, he used generally to delegate the task of instruction to his youthful pupil, Playfair.

In 1769 Playfair removed to Edinburgh, and while residing there became acquainted with Adam Smith, Drs. Robertson, Matthew Stewart, Black, and Hutton, with all of whom he continued on terms of the utmost cordiality during the whole period of their lives.

During the course of the year 1772, the death of his father suddenly devolved upon Playfair the burden of supporting his family, and compelled him in a measure to seek a livelihood by entering the Church. Although he had been educated with a view to his entering this profession, for which he was in every way qualified, his decided predilection for science had hitherto made him hesitate about engaging in a vocation, the duties of which, he felt, if conscientiously discharged, would necessarily interfere greatly with the studies he was loath to abandon. In this emergency, however, he considered himself no longer entitled to indulge in these predilections, and therefore made an application, which proved successful, to Lord Gray, the patron, for a presentation to the livings of Liff and Benvie, which had been previously held by his father. From this period until 1782, he was constantly resident at Liff, occupied almost exclusively with the pastoral duties of his office, and with the education of his younger brothers.

In the year 1779 Playfair contributed to the 'Transactions' of the Royal Society of London a paper on the 'Arithmetic of Impossible Quantities,' which exhibits, within a very small compass, a striking example of the rare and admirable talent of detaching the sound spirit of science from what may be termed its mysticism. In the year 1782 he was induced by very advantageous offers to resign his charge, and to superintend the education of Ferguson of Raith, and his brother Sir Ronald; an arrangement which restored him in a great measure to the literary and scientific society of Edinburgh, and enabled him to visit London, where he was gratified by a personal introduction to several of the most eminent cultivators of science in that city.

Playfair was received into the University of Edinburgh during the course of the year 1785, and, in consequence of an arrangement made between Dr. Adam Ferguson and Mr. Dugald Stewart, was appointed joint-professor of mathematics with Dr. Ferguson, whose delicate state of health prevented him from discharging the active duties of the professorship; Mr. Stewart filling the chair of moral philosophy, previously held by Dr. Ferguson.

Previous to this, like Leslie, Playfair had been twice a candidate for a similar honour, but unsuccessfully. On the first occasion, when only eighteen years old, he had offered himself, with the approbation of his instructors at St. Andrew's, as candidate for the professorship of mathematics in Marischal College, Aberdeen, and had sustained with much credit a competitive examination which lasted eleven days, and embraced nearly the whole range of the exact sciences. Out of six competitors, two only were judged to have surpassed him—the Rev. Dr. Trail, who was appointed to the office, and Dr. Hamilton, who afterwards succeeded to and long filled it with much reputation.

In 1788, Playfair published, in the 'Transactions' of the Royal Society of Edinburgh, a biographical account of Dr. Matthew Stewart, which also contains a singularly clear and interesting account of the labours of Dr. Simson in the restoration of ancient geometry. In this year likewise appeared his paper 'On the Causes which affect the accuracy of Barometrical Measurements,' which is

written with all the perspicuity, caution, and sagacity, that constitute the great excellence and the great difficulty of such disquisitions, where scientific principles are employed to give precision to
physical observations. In 1790 appeared, in the same 'Transactions,'
a paper of still greater interest and delicacy, 'On the Astronomy of
the Brahmins,' the publication of which attracted very general
attention, both in Europe and in Asia, and gave rise to much discussion and research. This was followed in 1794 by a learned and
very beautiful treatise on the 'Origin and Investigation of Porisms,'
in which the obscure nature of the very comprehensive and indefinite theorems to which this name was applied by the ancient
geometers, is explained with the most lucid simplicity.

In 1797 he composed a sequel to his first paper on the Indian
astronomy, in the shape of 'Observations on the Trigonometrical
Tables of the Brahmins,' and also a masterly collection of 'Theorems
on the Figure of the Earth.' During the course of the last-mentioned year, his friend Dr. James Hutton died; and Playfair, having
undertaken to draw up a biographical account of him for the Royal
Society, was led to study the doctor's ingenious but crude speculations on the 'Theory of the Earth,' and afterwards to lend them the
assistance of his own powerful pen, in his 'Illustrations of the Huttonian Theory.' This work, upon which he bestowed more time
and labour than on any of his other productions, did not appear
until 1802; and whatever opinion may be formed of the truth or
soundness of Dr. Hutton's speculations, it is impossible to doubt
that Playfair's illustration of that theory must always be ranked
amongst the most brilliant and powerful productions of philosophical genius. Its merits have been universally acknowledged, even
by those not convinced by its reasonings, and have extorted, even
from the fastidious critics of France, the acknowledgment that
"Mr. Playfair writes as well as Buffon, and reasons incomparably
better."

In 1805 he quitted the chair of mathematics to succeed Professor
Robison in that of natural philosophy. In the contest which ensued
upon the appointment of Leslie as his successor in this chair, he
took a very active part; and amongst the heaviest blows which
Leslie's opponents had to sustain, were those that parted from the
hand of Mr. Playfair. In 1807 he was elected a Fellow of the Royal
Society, to which learned body he very soon afterwards presented
his 'Account of the Lithological Survey of Schehallien;' this was
the result of his investigations during the period of Dr. Maskelyne's
visit to Schehallien, to measure the attraction of that mountain, on
which occasion Playfair shared the shelter of this distinguished
astronomer's tent on the side of the mountain, and contracted with
him a friendship which lasted during the remainder of their lives.

In 1809 he contributed to the 'Edinburgh Transactions' an excellent paper on 'Solids of the Greatest Attraction,' and in 1812, another, on the 'Progress of Heat in Spherical Bodies.' In 1814 he published, in two volumes octavo, for the use of his class, an elementary work of great value, under the title of 'Outlines of Natural Philosophy.' About the same time he drew up for the 'Encyclopædia Britannica' an introductory 'Dissertation on the Progress of Mathematical and Physical Science,' a treatise distinguished for the soundness of judgment, beauty of writing, and extent of knowledge displayed in it. In 1815, Playfair wrote for the Royal Society of Edinburgh a very interesting memoir of his distinguished predecessor, Dr. Robison. In the course of the same year he undertook, at the age of sixty-eight, a long journey through France and Switzerland into Italy, and did not return for a period of nearly eighteen months, during which time his principal attention was directed to the mineralogical and geological phenomena of the different regions which he visited. On his return from this expedition, he was occupied in drawing up a memoir on the 'Naval Tactics of Clerk of Eldin,' which was published after his death in the 'Philosophical Transactions.'

Playfair had for several years suffered from a recurrence at different times of a painful affection of the bladder, which appeared with increased severity in the early part of 1819, but was so far got under as to enable him to complete his course of lectures in the spring. It returned, however, in a still more distressing form in the summer, and at last put a period to his life on the 19th of July. Though suffering great pain during the last part of his confinement, he retained not only his intellectual faculties quite unimpaired, but also the serenity and mildness of his spirit, occupying himself until within a few days of his death in correcting the proof-sheets of the 'Dissertation' before noticed.

Besides the previously mentioned works, Playfair was a frequent contributor to the 'Edinburgh Review,' and also wrote the articles 'Æpinus' and 'Physical Astronomy,' in the 'Encyclopædia Britannica.' Francis Jeffrey, of whose elaborate and elegant memoir the above is but a brief summary, speaks of Playfair as being "one of the most learned mathematicians of the age, and among the first, if not the very first, who introduced the beautiful discoveries of the later Continental geometers to the knowledge of his countrymen, and gave their just value and true place in the scheme of European knowledge, to those important improvements by which the whole aspect of abstract science has been renovated since the days of our illustrious Newton;" also, "as possessing in the highest degree all the characteristics both of a fine and powerful understanding, at once penetrating and vigilant, but more distinguished perhaps for the caution and sureness of its march than for the brilliancy or rapidity of its movements; and guided and adorned through all its progress by the most genuine enthusiasm for all that is grand, and the justest taste for all that is beautiful."—*Memoir of John Playfair, by Lord Jeffrey.—Encyclopædia Britannica.*

JOHN RENNIE, F.R.S. L. and E., &c.

Born June 7, 1761.   Died October 4, 1821.

John Rennie was born at Phantassie, in the parish of Prestonkirk, in the county of East Lothian.   His father was a highly respectable farmer, who died in 1766, leaving a widow and nine children, of whom John was the youngest.   He acquired the first rudiments of his education at the village school, which was situated on the opposite side of a brook.   To cross this at certain seasons of the year it was necessary to make use of a boat, which was kept at the workshop of Andrew Meikle, an ingenious mechanic well known in Scotland as the inventor of the threshing machine.   Young Rennie, having thus frequent occasion to pass through Meikle's workshop, became deeply interested in the various mechanical operations that were in progress, and a great part of his leisure and holiday time was spent therein.   During the evening he employed himself in imitating the machines which had particularly attracted his attention, and when only ten years old succeeded in constructing a model of a steam-engine, a windmill, and a pile-driving machine.   At twelve years of age he left the Preston school and entered the service of Mr. Meikle for a space of two years, at the end of which time, finding that a constant application to manual labour retarded the progress of his intellectual faculties, he determined to place himself under the tuition of Mr. Gibson, an eminent mathematical master at Dunbar.   Here Young Rennie attained such proficiency in his studies, that when, two or three years afterwards, Mr. Gibson was appointed master to the public academy at Perth, he was able to undertake the temporary management of the Dunbar school. While at this school he attracted the especial notice of Mr. David Lock, who, in describing a visit to Dunbar, makes particular mention of him as one likely to prove an honour to his country.*   On leaving Mr. Gibson, Rennie returned to Mr. Meikle, continuing more or less with that ingenious man for the next two or three years.†   His first essay in practical mechanics was the repairing of a corn mill in his native village, and he erected two or three others before he had reached the age of eighteen.   While occupied in these works Rennie took care at the same time to attend to his other studies, managing occasionally to visit Edinburgh, where he entered himself as a student at the University, and attended the lectures of

---

* *Lock's Essays on the Trade and Commerce, Manufactories and Fisheries, of Scotland,* 1779.   3 vols.

† According to an article published in the *Mechanics' Magazine,* Sept. 20, 1861, Mr. Rennie appears likewise to have attended the collegiate academy at Perth.   The above brief account of his early life is given on the authority of a Memoir furnished by Mr. George Rennie, F.R.S., and published in the *Encyclopædia Britannica.*

Professors Robison and Black. With the former gentleman he gradually formed an intimate acquaintance, and was by him introduced to Messrs. Boulton and Watt, of Soho, with whom he remained during the space of twelve months; it being their wish to have engaged his services for a longer period, but Rennie, conscious of his own powers, determined to make the capital the theatre of his future efforts. His first practical essay at millwright work in England was the rolling mills at Soho, which were entirely remodelled and rebuilt under his direction.

In 1784 he established himself in London, and commenced work by the erection of the Albion Mills near Blackfriars Bridge, Boulton and Watt, who had the direction of the steam-engines, having, in accordance with the advice of Professors Robison and Black, entrusted to him the execution of the millwork. Mr. Watt, in his notes to Professor Robison's account of the steam-engine, says that " in the construction of the millwork and machinery, they derived most valuable assistance from that able mechanician and engineer, Mr. John Rennie, then just entering into business, who assisted in placing them, and under whose direction they were executed." He also adds that the machinery, which used to be made of wood, was here made of cast iron, and considers that this was the commencement of that system of millwork which has proved so beneficial to this country. After executing this undertaking, Rennie was employed on the flour mills at Wandsworth, and the rolling and triturating mills at the Mint. His mills, and particularly his water wheels, were regarded as models of perfection, while in all hydraulic works he was the worthy successor of Smeaton. From this time until his comparatively early death in 1821, Rennie was constantly employed on various large and splendid undertakings, among which his bridges occupy an important place. Of these structures the finest is the Waterloo Bridge over the Thames, begun in 1809 and finished in 1817. It is built of Aberdeen granite, and consists of nine equal semi-elliptical arches of 20 feet span, with a level roadway 45 feet wide from outside to outside of parapet, which adds greatly to its beauty. This bridge was opened to the public by the Prince Regent, who offered at the time to confer upon Mr. Rennie the honour of knighthood; this offer, however, he declined. London Bridge, which he designed but did not live to execute, was finished by his sons, Mr. George and Sir John Rennie. It is built of the finest blue and white granite from Scotland and Devonshire, and consists of five semi-elliptical arches, two of 130, two of 140, and the centre one of 152½ ft. span, being perhaps the largest elliptical arch ever attempted. The beautiful stone bridge over the Tweed at Kelso, and those at Musselburgh and New Galloway, were also designed by him. When speaking of the first-named of these bridges, Mr. Rennie used often playfully to declare, that he considered himself a benefactor to his country, inasmuch as one of his earliest

F

public works was to build a bridge across the Tweed! The iron bridges which he executed are, the one at Boston, over the Witham, with a span of 100 feet; and the noble bridge at Southwark, over the Thames, begun in 1815 and opened in 1819. The latter consists of three circular arches of equal curvature, the centre one having a span of 240, and the other two of 210 feet. The total weight of iron in the structure was 5780 tons, and the entire cost, including approaches, &c., 800,000*l.*

The improvement of harbours and the construction of docks occupied much of Mr. Rennie's attention, and in these operations his diving-bell apparatus was of peculiar value. Smeaton was the first who used the diving-bell effectually for building with stone under water; the machine he employed for that purpose was, however, very defective, and could only be used in certain situations. But Rennie, by improvements in the instrument itself, and in the machinery by which its movements could be regulated,* was enabled to carry on masonry, and the foundations of sea-walls, piers, and quays, as well under water as above it. He first employed his apparatus in 1813, in building the East Pierhead at Ramsgate, the foundations of which were 17 feet below low water at spring tides. It was afterwards used in founding the pierheads and outer walls of the harbours at Holyhead, Howth, and Sheerness, and other works under his direction. Amongst the numerous wet docks introduced at Liverpool in 1716, and since constructed at almost all the principal sea-ports in the kingdom, Mr. Rennie executed the London Docks, and those at Leith, Dublin, Hull, and Greenock, and also the East and West India Docks, in conjunction with Jessop and Ralph Walker. He also constructed the harbours of Queensferry, Berwick, Howth, Holyhead, and that at Kingston, the largest attempted in this country. At the low water of spring tide, the depth of this harbour was 26 feet, while the area enclosed amounted to 250 acres. The breakwater at Plymouth for protecting the Sound from the swell of the sea was likewise designed by him and Mr. Whitby, and was the first and largest example of a detached breakwater in this country. One of the most useful works executed by Mr. Rennie was the drainage of the great Fen district bordering upon the rivers Trent, Witham, New Welland, and Ouse, and extending 60 miles in length by 25 in breadth. In the carrying out of this great work, by which many hundreds of square miles were rendered productive, and the salubrity of the district improved, he was assisted by Mr. Telford and his son, Sir John Rennie. The chief canals of which he was engineer are the Kennet, Avon, Crinan, Rochdale, and Lancaster. The naval dockyards at Portsmouth, Plymouth, Chatham, and Sheerness, also attest his skill as an engi-

---

* By the invention and employment of what is now well known as the travelling-crane.

neer. The latter was a mere quicksand 40 feet deep, mixed with mud and the wrecks of old ships; the whole of which was excavated, and a magnificent basin constructed with a surrounding wall of granite, with which three large and commodious dry docks communicated. Several magnificent works of great public utility were proposed to the government by Mr. Rennie but never executed. The most remarkable of these is his design for a great naval arsenal on the Thames at Northfleet, intended as a substitute for the imperfect naval establishments on the river. It was to consist of six capacious basins, with an area of 600 acres within the walls, and to comprehend machinery for every operation connected with the naval science. The estimated cost of this noble plan was eight millions, which might have amounted to ten or eleven millions, but would even then have been a measure of economy compared with the vast sums expended on the old establishments on the Thames and Medway.

Before closing the present brief account of this celebrated engineer's life and works, his lighthouse on the Bell Rock must not be passed by without notice. Like the Eddystone, it was built of stone; commenced in 1806, and finished in 1811, it still remains an enduring monument of the skill of its architect.

Until within a few years of his death Mr. Rennie enjoyed robust health, but he was cut off in the sixty-first year of his age after a few days' illness. He was buried in St. Paul's Cathedral, his remains being interred near to those of Sir Christopher Wren.—*Encyclopædia Britannica.*—*North British Review*, Feb., 1861.—*Mechanics' Magazine*, September 20 and November 22, 1861.

FRANCIS RONALDS, F.R.S.

Francis Ronalds was born in London, in the year 1788. From a very early period in life he devoted himself to the advancement of electrical science, a course he has consistently pursued during a large portion of his life, which has not yet we are glad to be able to state drawn to its close. He is the inventor of an electric telegraph, electrical machine, electrometer, a new mode of electrical insulation, a pendulum doubler, an electric clock, several meteorological and magnetical instruments and other mechanical contrivances. The year 1816, however, marked Mr. Ronald's great achievement in the advancement of electric telegraphs. During that year he was the first to demonstrate that they could be practically and unerringly applied to the passage of messages through a long distance. Well

aware of the difficulties arising from imperfect insulation, which
had baffled his predecessors, Mr. Ronalds secured the success of his
apparatus both by employing better means of insulation than had
hitherto been adopted, and also by making use of a form of apparatus
which should of itself be capable of supplying any loss of electricity
which might arise from defects in the insulation.* Mr. Ronalds
placed his telegraph wire in glass tubes surrounded by wooden
troughs lined with pitch, which were placed in a trench dug in his
garden at Hammersmith. He also suspended eight miles of wire
by silken cords from a wooden frame erected on his lawn, through
which he was enabled to successfully pass messages except in wet
weather, the cords not being protected from the wet.

Mr. Ronald's peculiar form of apparatus may be thus briefly described:—At two stations were placed two clocks, with a dial with
20 letters placed on the arbour of the second-hand; in front of each
of these dials was placed a screen with a small orifice cut in it so
that, as the dial revolved, only one letter could be seen at a time.
The clocks were made to go *isochronously*, and were started at the
same instant with the same letter appearing on the dial through
the orifices of each of the screens, both dials, therefore, as they
revolved, would of course continue to show similar letters. This
formed the readable index of his telegraph; means of communication between the two stations were produced in the following
manner:—connected with each end of the telegraph wire, and placed
in front of the clocks, were two pith ball electrometers, upon which
a constant stream of electricity, produced from an ordinary frictional
machine, operated and consequently kept in a state of divergence,
except when a letter on the dial was to be denoted; the electricity
was then partially discharged by breaking the connection, the pith
balls in a measure collapsed, and the distant observer was thereby informed to note down the letter then visible through the orifice on the
screen. In this way letter after letter might be denoted and intel-
legence of any kind conveyed. All that was absolutely required for
the success of Mr. Ronald's telegraph was, that the clocks should
go isochronously *during the time* intelligence was being transmitted,
for, by a preconcerted arrangement, both clocks might be easily
started at the same letter upon a given signal. The attention of
the distant observer was called by the explosion of gas by means of
an electric spark. In 1823, Mr. Ronalds published a full description
of his telegraph, in a work entitled, ' Descriptions of an Electrical
Telegraph, and of some other Electrical Apparatus.'

In 1825, Mr. Ronalds invented a perspective tracing instrument,
to facilitate drawing from nature or from plans and elevations, an
account of which he published in 1828 in a work entitled, ' Mecha-

* This peculiarity of Mr. Ronalds' apparatus is stated in full by Mr. Highton,
C.E., in his work on the ' Telegraph,' page 50. London, John Weale.

nical Perspective.' With this machine he was enabled some years afterwards (in 1835), assisted by Dr. Blair, to procure exact perspective projections taken from given noted stations, of the Celtic remains at Carnac in Brittany. The result of these researches was published by Mr. Ronalds and Dr. Blair in 1836, and was entitled, 'Sketches at Carnac; or, Notes concerning the present state of the Celtic Antiquities in that and some of the adjoining Communes.' In connection with this tracing apparatus, he likewise contrived a hexipod staff used for a support, and which has been much employed for the support of instruments requiring great steadiness, such as telescopes, theodolites, cameras, &c. In the year 1843 he became the first and honorary director of the Kew Observatory, and while occupying this office he supplied the observatory with various new contrivances, for which he received a government reward from the special service fund, and a small pension from the civil list. The most considerable of these contrivances were his atmospheric electrical conductor and its appendages, adopted at the Greenwich, the Madrid, and the Bombay magnetic observatories; his photo-barograph, and two photo-thermographs, adopted at the Radcliff observatory, Oxford; his photo-electrograph, and three photo-magnetographs. Besides the writings above-mentioned, Mr. Ronalds is the author of an article in the *Philosophical Magazine* of 1814, entitled, 'On Electro-galvanic Agency, employed as a moving power, with descriptions of a Galvanic Clock;' and other articles in the same journal, detailing his original experiments to illustrate the relations of *quantity* and *intensity* in the electric pile. He also wrote four Reports on the Kew observatory, which were fully illustrated and printed in the reports of the British Association for the years 1845-50-51 and 52; and one paper in the Philosophical Transactions on 'Photographic Self-registering Meteorological and Magnetical Instruments,' written in 1846 and printed in the year following. In 1856 Mr. Ronalds published in French, at Paris, a summary of these reports, with some additions, entitled, 'Descriptions de quelques Instruments Meteorologiques et Magnetiques,' intended to explain his instruments at the French exhibition.

Mr. Ronalds is now (April 1864) residing at Battle in Sussex, and during the latter years of life has spent much time and part of his small pension, in collecting and collating an electric library, which might be conveniently available for the advancement of his favourite science, and prove worthy of presentation or bequest to some British public institution, so as to form the nucleus of one which might approximate possibly to a complete electrical library.— *From particulars derived from authentic sources.*

COUNT RUMFORD (SIR BENJAMIN THOMPSON), LL.D., V.P.R.S.,

MEMBER OF THE ROYAL INSTITUTE OF FRANCE, ETC.

Born March 26, 1753.   Died Aug. 21, 1814.

Benjamin Thompson, the founder of the Royal Institution, and more generally known by the title of Count Rumford, which he afterwards acquired, was born at Woburn in Massachussets. His ancestors appear to have been among the earliest colonists of this district, and in all probability came originally from England.

Thompson's father died while his son was a mere infant, and two or three years afterwards his mother married a second husband, Josiah Pierce, also a resident at Woburn. As soon as young Thompson was able to learn his letters he was sent to the school of his native town, kept by a Mr. John Fowle, where he remained until his eleventh year, when he joined the school of a Mr. Hill at Medford. Here Thompson made such advances in mathematics and astronomy as to be able to calculate eclipses. At the age of thirteen he was bound apprentice to Mr. John Appleby, a respectable merchant in Salem, the second town in point of size in Massachussets. His occupations with Mr. Appleby were principally those of a clerk in the counting house, but he appears to have had sufficient leisure to extend his reading in scientific subjects, and also to indulge a taste, he began to exhibit, for designing and engraving. At this time he was likewise occupied with a contrivance for solving the famous problem of perpetual motion, but was ultimately made to see the fallacy of his expectations, by the arguments of an old friend and schoolfellow, Loammi Baldwin, who induced him to attempt something more practicable though less magnificent.

At this period, 1767, the differences between Great Britain and her American colonies were beginning to assume a serious aspect, and there ensued such a stagnation of trade at Salem and other towns, that Mr. Appleby, having no further occasion for the services of a clerk, was glad to give up to young Thompson his indentures, and allow him to return to Woburn. For the next two or three years Thompson's course of life seems to have been wavering and undecided. At one time he appears to have had thoughts of entering the medical profession, for he remained during some months under the tuition of Dr. Hay, a physician in Woburn, and entered zealously upon the study of anatomy and physiology.

In 1770, however, he resumed his mercantile avocations in the capacity of a clerk at a dry goods store at Boston, kept by a Mr. Capen, and was thus engaged during the famous riots which took place in that town, on the attempt to land a cargo of tea from a British vessel, contrary to a resolution of the colonists against admitting British goods. These disturbances caused Mr. Capen's business to decline as Mr. Appleby's had formerly done, and Thompson was again obliged to return to Woburn. He now seriously turned his attention to the acquisition of scientific knowledge, and in company with his friend Baldwin attended a course of lectures on experimental philosophy delivered at Harvard College, instituting at the same time many experiments of his own, some of which proved the germs of valuable conclusions published in after life. In particular may be mentioned a course of experiments which he began in order to ascertain and measure the projectile force of gunpowder.

Thompson, though still only in his seventeenth year, had now acquired a certain amount of reputation; he was also endowed with much natural grace and many personal advantages, which subsequently proved the means of gaining him access to the first circles in Europe.

Towards the close of the year 1770 he was invited by Colonel Timothy Walker, one of the most important residents in the village of Rumford, now Concord, in New Hampshire, to take charge of an Academy in that place. Two years later, at the age of twenty, he married Mrs. Rolfe, a colonel's widow possessed of a considerable fortune. After his marriage Thompson took his place as one of the wealthiest inhabitants of the district in which he resided, mixing with the best society the colony afforded. Among others he made the acquaintance of the governor John Wentworth, who, wishing to attach to the British party so influential a colonist, gave Thompson the commission of major in a regiment of the New Hampshire Militia, in which a vacancy had occurred. This act of attention, while gratifying to Thompson, procured him much ill-will from the officers already in the service, and over whose head he had been promoted.

From this period he began to be unpopular in his native country. He was represented as a friend of Great Britain, and an enemy to the interests of the colonies. The public hatred of him at length rose to such a height, that he only escaped by flight from the ignominy of being tarred and feathered in the open streets. Leaving his wife and an infant daughter, Thomas first took refuge in his native town of Woburn, and then proceeded to Charlestown where he remained for several months. From Charlestown he went to Boston, at which place he was well received by General Gage and the officers of the British army at that time in garrison at Boston. Returning in the spring of 1775 to Woburn, he again ran the risk of being tarred and feathered, but was saved by the interference of his friend Baldwin.

The commencement of open hostilities between the Colonists and the British troops in May, 1775, made Thompson's position still more critical, and finding that he could not overcome the prejudice felt against him, he came to the desperate resolution of quitting his native country, and leaving his wife and child. To effect this he first escaped to Boston, where he remained, with his friend General Gage, until the evacuation of the town by the British troops, when he embarked on board the Scarborough, and 'set sail for England, with despatches from General Gage to Lord George Germain, the British Secretary of State for Colonial Affairs.

Although Thompson arrived in England the bearer of gloomy tidings, and sustaining the equivocal character of a deserter from the American cause, he soon showed that he was a man capable of commanding his fortune anywhere. The capacity in which he had come over introduced him to various public men who were both struck by his abilities and charmed by his manners. But a short time elapsed after his arrival before he was offered a post in the Colonial Office, and four years after, in 1780, was raised by his patron Lord Germain to the post of under secretary for the colonies, an instance of rapid promotion which, considering the circumstances in which the subject of it stood, is almost unexampled.

The income and consequence which Thompson derived from this office gave him admission to the highest metropolitan circles, and he had thus opportunities not only of becoming known, but also of exercising his inventive mind in many pursuits not immediately connected with his official duties. Fertility of resources, and a disposition to propose improvements in all departments, appear to have been his most striking characteristics, and it was probably this ready genius for practical reform in everything which came under his notice, that recommended him so much to public men. While engaged generally in a variety of matters, Thompson was at the same time following out certain specific lines of scientific investigation. His experiments on the heat caused by friction, deduced from the boring of cannon, are among the best we possess.

In 1777 he made some curious and interesting experiments on the strength of solid bodies, which were, however, never published. In 1778 he employed himself in further experiments on the strength of gunpowder and the velocity of military projectiles; and these were followed up by a cruise of some months in the Channel fleet, where he proposed to repeat his experiments on a larger scale. He communicated the result of his researches on this subject, in several papers, to the 'Philosophical Transactions' of the Royal Society, of which he became a member in the last-mentioned year.

On the retirement of Lord George Germain from office, Thompson was sent out to New York in the year 1781, with the royal commission of major, afterwards changed to that of lieutenant-colonel, charged with the task of organizing an efficient regiment of dragoons out of the broken and disjointed native cavalry regiments which had been fighting on the royalist side. This regiment was, however, of no avail; peace was concluded between Great Britain and the United States, and Colonel Thompson on his return to England obtained leave of absence to travel on the Continent. In crossing from England to France, it happened that he had as a fellow-traveller the celebrated historian Gibbon, who, in some subsequent correspondence, spoke of him as "the soldier, philosopher, statesman—Thompson."

While on his way to Vienna, Thompson attended a review of the garrison of Strasbourg, and, attracting general attention by his superb English horse and uniform of colonel of dragoons, became introduced to the notice of Prince Maximilian, nephew and presumptive heir of the Elector of Bavaria. This prince was agreeably impressed by the manners and address of Thompson, and furnished him with letters of introduction to his uncle, the Bavarian Elector. When Thompson arrived at Munich (so great seems to have been his power of conciliating favour), he was offered, on his first interview with the elector, an important situation at court, if he would take up his residence there. After a little delay, Thompson accepted this offer, conditional upon receiving permission from his Britannic Majesty. Proceeding to London to obtain the required consent, he was very favourably received by George III., who conferred on him the honour of knighthood, and allowed him to retain his title of lieutenant-colonel, together with the half-pay attached to it.

Towards the close of the year 1784, Sir Benjamin Thompson, at the age of thirty-one, took up his residence at Munich, and filled the posts of aide-de-camp and chamberlain to the Elector; being thus connected both with the military and civil service of the Bavarian dominions. Into these twin branches of government he soon introduced many important and salutary reforms; he reorganized the Bavarian army, and introduced many improvements into the art of agriculture as practised in that part of Europe; he also took wise and effectual measures for the suppression of mendicancy, and for the ameliorization of the condition of the poor at Munich, introducing among them some excellent plans for the economization of food and fuel.

While investigating this latter subject, Sir Benjamin paid particular attention to the construction of grates and fireplaces, and to the scientific properties of light and heat. He so improved the methods of heating apartments and of cooking food, as to produce a saving in the precious element of heat varying from one-half to seven-eighths of the fuel previously consumed; so that it was wittily said, that he would never rest satisfied until he had cooked his dinner with his neighbours' smoke. To him also is the honour due of being the first to explain the manner in which heat is propagated in fluids. In requital of these important services to the Bavarian state, Thompson was decorated with two orders of Polish knighthood; he also received the appointments of member of the Council of State and lieutenant-general in the army, was created com-

mander-in-chief of the general staff, minister of war, and superintendent of the police of the electorate, and was finally, in 1790,
raised to the dignity of Count of the Holy Roman Empire, by the
title of Count Rumford, in memory of the American village where
he had formerly officiated as schoolmaster. The scientific part of
the community also showed their esteem for him, by electing him a
member of the Academies of Munich and Manheim; and in 1787,
when on a visit to Prussia, he was chosen a member of the Academy
of Sciences at Berlin.

When the advance of the French army under Moreau compelled
the Elector to quit his capital, Count Rumford was for a short time
placed at the head of the Regency, and in this capacity succeeded
in the arduous task of freeing the Bavarian state from foreign in-
vasion. This important service increased Rumford's reputation
with the Elector and the people, and he was permitted to settle
one-half of the pension which he enjoyed on his daughter, to be
paid during her lifetime.

In the year 1798, the Elector appointed him his ambassador to
the court of Great Britain; but on arriving in London, Rumford,
much to his mortification, found that, as a British subject he could
not hold that office. Shortly after this, in 1799, his friend and
patron the Elector Charles Theodore died. Deeply grieved by the
loss he had sustained, Rumford contemplated returning to his native
country, in compliance with a formal invitation which he had received from the United States government. He was, however, led
to change this design, and remain for several years in London,
during which period he devoted the greatest portion of his time to
the interests of the Royal Institution, of which he may be considered
the founder. The objects of this institution, now one of the recognised scientific establishments of the world, and which can boast of
having given employment to such men as Young, Davy, Brande,
and Faraday, were "to diffuse the knowledge and facilitate the
general introduction of useful mechanical inventions and improvements, and to teach by courses of philosophical lectures and experiments the application of science to the useful purposes of life."
Such an institution was precisely the one which Rumford was qualified to superintend; and in its early history, the influence of his
peculiar habits of thought is discernible, in the choice of subjects
for investigation by the members. Rumford's name will ever be
connected with the progress of science in England, from the establishment of this institution, and also from the foundation by him of
a perpetual medal and prize in the gift of the Royal Society, for the
reward of discoveries connected with light and heat.

During the latter portion of his life, Count Rumford, retaining an
income of 1200*l.* a year from the Bavarian court, resided chiefly at
Auteuil, a small villa near Paris. Here he was married again to
the widow of the eminent French chemist Lavoisier, his former wife

having died in 1792. Rumford's death took place at Auteuil, on the 21st of August, 1814, in the sixty-second year of his age. His only daughter by his first wife inherited the title of Countess of Rumford, with the continuation of her father's Bavarian pension. She married Cuvier the naturalist, and survived until a few years ago, forming a link between the age of Lavoisier and those of the middle of the nineteenth century.—*Chambers' Miscellany*, No. 161. —*Encyclopædia Britannica*, eighth edition.—*Voyage de trois mois en Angleterre, en Ecosse, &c., par Marc-Auguste Pictet, F.R.S., &c.* Geneva, 1802.

DANIEL RUTHERFORD, M.D.

Born November 3, 1749.   Died November 15, 1819.

Daniel Rutherford was born at Edinburgh and educated at the University of his native city. He took his degree of M.D. in 1772, and in the Thesis which he published upon this occasion, entitled 'De Aëre Fixo,' he pointed out for the first time a new gaseous substance, since distinguished by the name of Azote or Nitrogen. On the 6th of May, 1777, he was admitted a Fellow of the Royal College of Physicians, and in a paper on Nitre, read before the Philosophical Society in 1778, he described, under the name of Vital Air, what is now called Oxygen gas.

On the death of Dr. John Hope in 1786, Rutherford was elected Professor of Botany and Keeper of the Botanical Gardens at Edinburgh, a duty which he discharged until the time of his death, in 1819, at the age of seventy.—*Edinburgh Philosophical Journal*, vol. 3. May 1820.

WILLIAM SMITH, LL.D.

Born March 23, 1769.   Died August 28, 1839.

William Smith, the 'Father of English Geology,' was born at Churchill, a village in Oxfordshire. His father died when he was eight years old, and his mother marrying again, William was brought up under the care of his uncle, to part of whose property he was heir. From this kinsman, who had little sympathy with his nephew's early displayed taste for collecting specimens of the various stones in the neighbourhood, young Smith with difficulty obtained money for the purchase of a few books fit to instruct a boy in the rudiments of geometry and surveying. He, however, continued to prosecute these studies without instruction or sympathy, but still with ardour and success until the year 1787, when, having attained the age of eighteen, and being tolerably versed in the geometry and calculations at that time thought sufficient for engineers and surveyors, he became assistant to Mr. Edward Webb, of Stow-on-the-Wold, who had been appointed to make a complete survey of the parish of Churchill. Being speedily entrusted with the management of all the ordinary business of a surveyor, Mr. Smith traversed in continual activity the counties of Oxfordshire, Gloucestershire, and Warwickshire, carefully noticing all the varieties of soil over which he passed, and comparing them with the general aspect and character of the country. Between the years 1791 and 1793, he also made minute subterraneous surveys of the High Littleton collieries, which afforded him an opportunity of confirming views previously conceived as to the regularity in formation of the different strata composing the earth's crust. At this period the services of civil engineers were in great request, and the duties entrusted to them were such as Mr. Smith was well qualified to perform. Several gentlemen in the neighbourhood interested themselves in forwarding his professional career, and he obtained an engagement to make surveys and levels for a proposed line of canal in Somersetshire. In the course of these operations, Smith discovered that the strata lying above coal were not laid horizontally, but inclined in one direction—viz., to the eastward; resembling on a large scale the ordinary appearance of superposed slices of bread and butter. This fact he had previously imagined to be the case, and it was now proved to be true.

In 1794 the Canal Bill on which he was engaged received the sanction of Parliament, and one of the first steps taken by the committee of management was to depute two of their members to accompany Mr. Smith, their engineer, on a tour of investigation as to the construction and management of other navigations in England and Wales. This journey extended altogether through 900 miles of country, and occupied the space of one or two months; the party reached Newcastle by one route, and returned by another, through Shropshire and Wales to Bath. During the whole tour Mr. Smith seized every opportunity of observing all local peculiarities as to the aspect and structure of the country passed through, and was able to verify on a large scale his pre-conceived generalizations regarding a settled order of succession, continuity of range at the surface, and general declination eastward of the different strata. During the next six years he was engaged in setting out and superintending the works on the Somersetshire coal canal; being able, from the knowledge he had acquired, to inform the contractors what would be the nature of the ground to be cut through, and what parts of the canal would require particular care to be kept water-tight. He also discovered, during the formation of this work, that each stratum contained organised fossils peculiar to itself, by examination of which, it might in cases otherwise doubtful be recognised and discriminated from others like it, but in a different part of the series. This fact was subsequently still further investigated by him, and he proved that whatever stratum was found in any part of England, the same remains would be found in it and no other.

Mr. Smith was now (1795) twenty-six years old, and at this period removed from the village of High Littleton to Bath, in the vicinity of which city he shortly afterwards purchased a small but beautiful estate. In the following year he first contemplated publishing his discoveries in geology, but it was not until the year 1799, after his engagement with the Coal Canal Company had ceased, that he made public his intention of publishing a work on the Stratification of Britain, and prosecuting an actual survey of the Geological structure of England and Wales. About this time he became acquainted with the Rev. Benjamin Richardson and the Rev. Jos. Townsend, two gentlemen thoroughly competent to estimate the truth and value of his views, and who, in conjunction with him, drew up a tabular statement of the order of the strata, with their imbedded organic remains, in the vicinity of Bath. Copies of this document were extensively distributed, and it remained for a long period the type and authority for the descriptions and order of the superposition of the strata near Bath. The original document, in Mr. Richardson's handwriting, drawn up from Smith's dictation, was presented to the Geological Society in 1831. Mr. Smith now turned all his energies to the prosecution of his profession, and the tracing out the courses of the strata through districts as remote from Bath as his means would permit. In 1799 an unusual amount of rain prevailed, producing in the neighbourhood of Bath an extraordinary phenomenon. Vast mounds of earth, displaced by the augmented force of the springs and the direction of water into new channels below the surface, were sliding down the sides of the hills, bearing away with them houses, trees, lawns, and fields. To remedy such disasters and prevent their recurrence was exactly what Smith had learnt from Geology, and many operations of this kind were placed under his care and successfully accomplished. His reputation for success in draining on new principles became established, carrying him into Gloucestershire, the Isle of Purbeck, Wiltshire, &c., and for the next few years he was almost daily occupied in various parts of the country, first in draining land, and secondly in irrigating it when drained. In 1801 he accomplished the effectual drainage of Prisley Bog, a work which had often been attempted before, but without success. Mr. Smith thoroughly deprived the bog of its

stagnant water, and converted this hitherto worthless waste into
valuable meadows, by conducting a running stream over its surface.
For the performance of this undertaking he received in 1805 the
medal of the Society of Arts. Another great work, on which he
was engaged more or less during the space of nine years (1800-1809),
was the draining of the marsh lands in East Norfolk, between
Yarmouth and Happisburgh. These lands were continually liable
to be flooded by inundations from the German Ocean, which poured
in through breaches in the sand-hills lining the coast, and forming a
natural barrier against these inroads. Mr. Smith at once saw that the
first thing to be done, to prove an effectual remedy, must be the stop-
ping out the sea from the whole region of marsh land. This he accomplished by filling up the vast breaches (amounting altogether to one
mile in length) with artificial embankments made of pebbles and
sand as like as possible to the natural barriers thrown up by the
sea. This simple and effective plan, requiring almost nothing but
labour for its accomplishment, entirely succeeded; and the sea now
being effectually kept out, he was able to suggest to the proprietors
proper methods for draining and improving the marshes.

In 1806 Mr. Smith's first published work appeared, being entitled,
'A Treatise on the Construction and Management of Watermeadows.'
Several years previous to this he had been repeatedly urged by his
friends (among whom he now counted Francis, Duke of Bedford,
Sir Joseph Banks, Mr. Crawshaw, Thomas W. Coke, of Norfolk, and
the Rev. B. Richardson, before mentioned) to put in force his intention of publishing his discoveries. Many difficulties had, however,
occurred; his means were continually exhausted by his scientific
investigations; and an attempt, first made in 1801, to publish by
subscription a work on the natural order of the strata of England
and Wales, failed, partially from the deaths of his patrons the Duke
of Bedford and Mr. Crawshaw, and ultimately from his proposed
publisher, Debrett, falling into difficulties.

From this period until late in life, Mr. Smith continued unceasingly his professional occupations. In 1809 he began to execute the
Ouse navigation in Sussex; in 1810 he restored the hot springs of
Bath, which had failed; in 1811 he examined into the causes of
leakage on the Kennet and Avon Canal, and reported on trials for
coals in Buckinghamshire; and in 1812-1814 executed the Minsmere
drainage in Suffolk. During these and a hundred other engagements
of a like nature, which furnished him with the means and occasion
for incessant travelling, Mr. Smith lost no opportunity of committing to paper the result of the day's observations on the direction,
dip, and aspect of the rocks he passed over during his various
journies. In 1812, receiving proposals from Mr. Cary to publish his
map of the strata of England and Wales, Mr. Smith recommenced
his efforts to produce the great work on which he had been occupied
for the space of twenty years. This map was at length published

on the 1st of August, 1815, being dedicated to Sir Joseph Banks, and he received from the Society of Arts the premium of 50*l.*, which had long been offered for a work of this description. The fame of its author as a great original discoverer in English geology was now secured, but it brought Mr. Smith little pecuniary benefit. Geology had kept him poor all his life by consuming his professional gains; and an unfortunate speculation, which he at this time entered into, entirely failed, and compelled him to sell the property at Bath which he had purchased in 1798. A load of debt still remained to be discharged, and in order to liquidate this he proposed selling the valuable geological collection he had been making during his past life. This collection, of which the number of species was 693, and of specimens 2657, was purchased by Government for the British Museum for a total sum of 700*l.* In 1818 Mr. Smith's claims on public notice were fairly and fully advocated by Dr. Fitton, and it was chiefly from the favourable light in which this gentleman placed his long and solitary labours, that public interest for him was stimulated, and the Geological Society, who had hitherto passed him over, was at length roused to an impartial estimate of the value of his works. This resulted in the passing of a resolution in February, 1831, "That the first Wollaston medal be given to Mr. William Smith, in consideration of his being a great original discoverer in English Geology; and especially for his having been the first in this country to discover and to teach the identification of strata, and to determine their succession by means of their imbedded fossils." The following year he received from the Crown a pension of 100*l.* a-year. Previous to this, however, the state of Mr. Smith's finances compelled him to be unceasingly occupied in various professional engagements; and on one of these occasions, being engaged by Colonel Braddyll to make a general mining survey of some estates belonging to that gentleman, he drew the Colonel's attention to the great probability of there being coal at an attainable depth on part of his property situated at Haswell, in Durham. This ultimately led to the foundation of the magnificent works, called the South Hetton Colliery, which rival the greatest establishments of the Lambtons, Vanes, and Russels.

During the last few years of his life Mr. Smith lived principally at Scarborough, where, unfettered by any but temporary engagements, he devoted his mind to a review of the circumstances of his life, and the arrangement of his observations and opinions. In 1835 he received the degree of LL.D., which was conferred on him by the members of Trinity College, Dublin. Between the years 1837 and 1838 he was appointed by Government to join Sir Charles Barry and Sir Henry De la Beche in making a tour through a great part of England and Wales, to select the most suitable stone for building the Houses of Parliament. The stone ultimately selected for this purpose was the firm yellow granular magnesian limestone,

of Bolsover Moor, in Derbyshire. This was the last scientific work
on which Dr. Smith was engaged; a cold caught the following
year brought on diarrhœa, which terminated fatally. He died on
the 28th of August, in his seventy-first year, and was buried at
Northampton, at the west end of the church of All Saints, in which,
at the suggestion of Dr. Buckland, a tablet was erected to his
memory, the expense of which was defrayed by a subscription
among geologists.—*Memoirs of William Smith, LL.D., by his nephew,
John Phillips, F.R.S., F.G.S.* London, 1844.

EARL STANHOPE, F.R.S.

Born August 3, 1753. Died December 17, 1816.

Charles Stanhope, third earl of that name, was born at Chevening
in Kent, and was sent at a very early period to Eton; but at the
age of ten he removed with his family to Geneva, where he was
placed under the tuition of M. Le Sage, a well-known man of letters
in that place. There can be but little doubt that the whole political
career of Earl Stanhope was deeply influenced by the circumstance
of his receiving his early education in this republican city; and to
this may be ascribed the extreme views which he entertained in
after life respecting civil liberty and other points affecting the welfare of great communities.

While acquiring these sentiments, Lord Stanhope was at the
same time pursuing a course of training which subsequently made
him so remarkable, as a man of science and letters. Natural philosophy was his chief study; and the knowledge which he acquired
of this subject was decisively shewn by his gaining, at the early
age of eighteen, a prize offered by the Stockholm Society of Arts
for the best essay, written in French, on the pendulum; and this
essay was the more remarkable, as being the fruit not only of mere
reading, but of numerous original experiments, performed by him in
person.

Shortly after attaining his majority, Lord Stanhope, together
with his family, left Geneva amidst the regrets of the whole popu-
lation, while crowds of poor people assembled to take a last look on
the noble English residents who had long been their generous benefactors. On reaching England, the family rank and influence of the
young nobleman speedily procured him a seat in the House of
Commons, which he occupied until his succession to the Stanhope
title called him to the Upper House of Parliament. Here it was
that he became famous as a politician. Honesty and straight-

forwardness were the grand features of his statesmanship; his views, however, although now entertained by even moderate politicians, were at that time considered extreme, and subsequently led to a separation of the earl from his family.

But it is chiefly as a man of science, and as an inventor in the field of practical mechanics, that Earl Stanhope has rendered himself celebrated. Shortly after leaving the Continent, about the year 1775, he turned his attention to devising some means whereby forgeries in coins and bank-notes might be prevented; this resulted in his publishing a pamphlet on that subject, in which various processes calculated to prevent forgeries on the mint are recommended.

In the 'Philosophical Transactions' for 1778, Lord Stanhope gives a full account of experiments performed by him, on a large scale, in presence of the Lord Mayor and members of the Royal Society, showing that wood could be rendered fireproof, by coating it with a species of stucco or plaster of his own invention. The practical efficiency of this was still more decisively shown by a fire which broke out in the earl's mansion at Chevening. Having had occasion to rebuild this some time previously, Earl Stanhope had taken care to make use of his new discovery; a portion of the offices, however, remained unsecured, and here the fire originated; but on reaching the protected portion, it was at once arrested, and the mansion saved from destruction.

Among other works of Lord Stanhope which attracted most attention at that time are his experiments on electricity, his improvements in shipbuilding and navigation, a calculating machine, and the Stanhope printing-press, which to this day bears his name. He has also been called the inventor of stereotype printing, and had at all events the merit of greatly improving this most important process, and of introducing it into general use. The application of steam to navigation was another favourite study of Earl Stanhope; and, in concert with him, Fulton the American entered into an extensive series of experiments to prove its practicability. Although unsuccessful in this last pursuit, canal navigation owes much to the earl; the value of his improvements in canal-locks being felt to this day throughout the whole land. He lived in constant pursuit of these philosophical enquiries till the age of sixty-three, when he died of dropsy, at his seat in Kent.

Lord Stanhope was essentially a practical man, of a firm, upright, and independent character; and it is related of him, that when advising his children to pursue some useful calling, he remarked of himself, that "Charles Stanhope, as a carpenter, blacksmith, or millwright, could in any country, or at any time, preserve his independence, and bring up his family to honest and industrious courses, without soliciting either the bounty of friends or the charity of strangers." He merits the grateful remembrance of posterity, not only for the practical results of his genius, but for the indirect influence of his noble example exerted on others, and for the generous patronage he bestowed on many poorer fellow-labourers in the same great field.—*Chambers' Edinburgh Journal,* No. 392, August 3, 1839. —*Stuart's Anecdotes of the Steam-Engine.* London, 1829.

WILLIAM SYMINGTON.*

Born in 1763. Died March 22, 1831.

William Symington, claimant conjointly with Patrick Miller to the honour of originating the present system of steam navigation, was a native of Leadhills, in the county of Lanark, Scotland. He was originally destined for the church, but an early predilection for mechanical philosophy led him to abandon his theological studies, and pursue with ardour those connected with his favourite science. His genius soon attracted the notice, and secured the patronage of Gilbert Meason, a gentleman at that time connected with the Wanlock Head lead mines. Before completing his twenty-first year, Mr. Symington made several improvements on the steam-engine, for which he took out patents, and continued for some time to construct and introduce engines on his principle, in various parts of England and Scotland.

In the year 1784, the idea first occurred to him that steam might be advantageously employed for the propulsion of carriages; and in 1786 he succeeded in producing a working model of a steam-carriage, which he submitted to the inspection of the professors and other scientific gentlemen in Edinburgh. Although this steam-carriage afforded proofs of considerable capability, it was never proceeded further with, on account of the state of the roads in Scotland at that period, and the difficulty of procuring fuel and water.

In the meanwhile Patrick Miller, a gentleman of property residing on his estate at Dalswinton, Dumfriesshire, had for some time been engaged in making various experiments for the improvement of naval architecture, and had constructed a double or twin-boat, with paddle-wheels, to be moved by manual labour. At this point Miller was informed by Mr. James Taylor, a tutor in his family, of Symington's model steam-carriage, and they both called at Mr. Meason's house in Edinburgh to see it. During the course of conversation with Symington, the practicability of advantageously employing steam for the purposes of navigation was talked about, and it was ultimately arranged that Symington should endeavour to construct

* See also Patrick Miller.

a steam-engine to be fitted on board Miller's twin-boat, and capable of moving the paddle-wheels. This was accomplished in the autumn of 1788, when a trial was made, in the presence of Mr. Miller and various others, of so satisfactory a nature, that it was immediately determined to commence another experiment, upon a larger scale. It may, however, be satisfactory to state here, that this, the parent engine of steam navigation, after enduring many vicissitudes, was ultimately rescued from destruction by Mr. Bennet Woodcroft, and contributed by him for exhibition in the South Kensington Museum.

In the month of October 1789, a second exemplification of the practicability of steam navigation was afforded by Miller and Symington, on the Forth and Clyde Inland Navigation Canal, in the presence of many hundreds of spectators; the boat proceeding along at the rate of nearly six miles an hour. In this instance the machinery was constructed at the Carron Works, under the direction of Symington, and placed on board a boat which had been used in Miller's previous experiments. Unfortunately, Mr. Miller now withdrew from the concern; he had already expended nearly thirty thousand pounds on various experiments, and he determined to devote his time to the improvement of the Dalswinton estate.

Symington's pecuniary resources were insufficient to enable him unaided to pursue his experiments, and he was compelled to desist, and turn his attention to the fulfilment of engagements with the Wanlock Head company, for constructing machinery on a large scale. An interval of ten years thus elapsed, at the end of which time Mr. Symington secured the patronage of Thomas, Lord Dundas of Kerse, under whose auspices another series of experiments were commenced, in January 1801, at the cost of 7000*l.*; but they placed beyond the possibility of doubt the practicability of steam navigation. Symington had availed himself of the improvements made in the steam-engine by Watt and others, and he now constructed an improved marine engine, with boat and paddle-wheel after the plan at present adopted. This boat, called the 'Charlotte Dundas,'* was the first practical steamboat; and for the novel combination of the parts, Symington obtained a patent on the 14th October, 1801. The vessel made her first voyage in March 1803, on the Forth and Clyde Canal, and proceeded upwards of nineteen miles, drawing after her two laden vessels, each of seventy tons burden, although it blew so strong a gale right ahead, that no other vessel in the canal attempted to move to windward during that day. There were on board on this occasion Lord Dundas, the Hon. Captain George Dundas, R.N., and Archibald Spiers of Elderslee, together with several other gentlemen of their acquaintance.

Miller's boat had proved a practical steam-boat, but in the 'Charlotte Dundas' Symington had the undoubted merit of having

* Named in honour of Lord Dundas's daughter, Lady Milton.

combined together for the first time those improvements which constitute the present system of steam navigation. Although Henry Bell and Fulton the American are both claimants for the above honour, their inventions did not appear until some years afterwards, Fulton establishing his steamboat at New York in 1807, and Bell establishing one on the Clyde in 1811;* undoubted proof also exists that both these gentlemen were well acquainted with the result of Miller of Dalswinton's experiments, the 'Charlotte Dundas,' and must have derived considerable advantage from such knowledge.

After the successful experiment with the 'Charlotte Dundas,' a proposal was made to the canal proprietors to substitute steam-tugs in place of horses, but it was rejected on the ground that the undulation created in the water by the paddle-wheels might wash away the banks. Lord Dundas then introduced Symington to the notice of the Duke of Bridgewater, who, although at first averse to the project, ultimately gave Symington an order to build eight boats on his principle. On this Mr. Symington returned to Scotland full of hopes for the future, but these were suddenly frustrated by the death of the Duke. His resources were now exhausted, and, unable any longer to struggle against his misfortunes, Mr. Symington was obliged, although with great reluctance, to lay up his boat in a creek of the canal near Barnsford draw-bridge, where it remained for many years exposed to the view of the public.

Shortly after Bell's steamboat, the 'Comet,' had begun plying upon the Clyde, notice was sent by Symington, not only to Bell, but to all other proprietors following his example, that by so doing they were invading his right; and legal advice having been taken,† an action for damages was commenced. Before, however, the cause was settled, Mr. Symington's patent expired; and although he had given directions to institute an application to have it renewed, this was most unaccountably neglected to be done, and he saw his hopes expire, being reduced to much and severe distress through want of money—a state in which he continued more or less during the remainder of his life.

When in his last illness, the ruling passion of his life was strongly exhibited. At one time the irregular form of his bedroom occasioned him so much uneasiness, that, being slightly delirious, he requested his son to reduce it to a square; while his last act was an imitation of winding-up and adjusting a newly-invented chronometer, which he had lately completed.—*Stuart's Anecdotes of the Steam-Engine.* London, 1829.—*Narrative by R. Bowie, proving W. Symington the Inventor of Steam Land-Carriage Locomotion and of Steam Navigation.* London, 1833.—*Descriptive Catalogue of the Museum of the Commissioners of Patents.*

* The 'Comet.'
† John Clerk (Lord Eldin) pronounced the patent to be correctly drawn up, and that no doubt existed of Mr. Symington's right to recover damages from its invaders.

THOMAS TELFORD, F.R.S., L. and E., &c.

Born August 9, 1757.   Died September 2, 1834.

The life of Thomas Telford adds another striking instance to those on record of men who, from the force of natural talent, un-aided save by uprightness and persevering industry, have raised themselves from the low estate in which they were born, and taken their stand among the master-spirits of their age. Telford was born in the parish of Westerkirk, in the pastoral district of Esk-dale in Dumfriesshire. His father, who followed the occupation of a shepherd, died while his son was yet an infant, and the orphan boy was thus left to the care of his mother, whose maiden name was Janet Jackson, and for whom her son always cherished an affectionate regard, being in the habit, in after life, of writing letters to her in printed characters, in order that she might be able to read them without assistance.

Young Telford received the rudiments of education at the parish school of Westerkirk, and during the summer season was employed by his uncle as a shepherd boy. This occupation left him abundant leisure, of which he made diligent use in studying the books fur-nished by his village friends. At the age of fourteen he was appren-ticed to a stone mason in the neighbouring town of Langholm, and for several years was employed, chiefly in his native district, in the construction of plain bridges, farm buildings, simple village churches and manses, and other works of a similar nature, such as are usually performed by a country mason in a district where there is little occasion for the higher departments of his art.

These operations afforded, however, good opportunities for obtain-ing practical knowledge, and Telford himself has expressed his sense of the value of this humble training, observing, that " as there is not sufficient employment to produce a division of labour in building, the young practitioner is under the necessity of making himself acquainted with every detail in procuring, preparing, and employing every kind of material, whether it be the produce of the forest, the quarry, or the forge; and this necessity, although un-favourable to the dexterity of the individual workman, who earns his livelihood by expertness in one operation, is of singular advan-tage to the future architect and engineer, whose professional excel-lence must rest on the adaptation of materials, and a confirmed habit of discrimination and judicious superintendance."

When Telford had completed his apprenticeship as a stonemason, he remained for some time at Langholm working as a journeyman, his wages being *eighteenpence* per diem.*   The first bridge masonry

---

* Smiles's ' Lives of the Engineers.'   London, 1861.

on which he was engaged was the erection of a structure over the
Esk at Langholm to connect the old with the new town. Mr. Smiles,
in his 'Lives of the Engineers,' tells a good story in connection
with this bridge. Telford's master, one Thompson, was bound by
contract to maintain it for a period of seven years. Not long after
the completion of the structure an unusually high flood swept along
the valley, and Thompson's wife, Tibby, knowing the terms of her
husband's contract, was in a state of great alarm lest the fabric
should be carried away by the torrent. In her distress she thought
of Telford, and calling out, " Oh, we'll be ruined—we'll be ruined!
where's Tammy Telfer—where's Tammy? send in search of him."
When he came running up, Tibby exclaimed, " Oh, Tammy,
they're been on the brig and they say it's shaking! It'll be doon."
" Never you heed them, Tibby," said Telford, clapping her on the
shoulder, " there's nae fear o' the brig—I like it a' the better that it
shakes; it proves it's weel put thegither." Tibby's fears were not,
however, so easily allayed, and asserting that she heard the brig
" rumlin," she ran up and set her back against it to keep it from
falling. Whether Tibby's zealous support to the bridge in this
instance was of any avail or no, Telford's opinion of the soundness
of the structure has been proved by its withstanding the storms of
nearly a century.

At this early period of his life, Telford was remarkable for his
elastic spirits and good humour, and in his native district of Eskdale
was long remembered as 'laughing Tam.' His favourite pursuits
were not as yet scientific but literary, and he acquired some distinction as a poet. He wrote in the homely style of Ramsay and
Ferguson, and used to contribute small pieces to Ruddiman's
'Weekly Magazine,' under the signature of 'Eskdale Tam.' One
of his compositions, entitled ' Eskdale,' a short poem descriptive of
the scenes of his early years, appeared in a provincial miscellany,
and was subsequently reprinted at Shrewsbury, at the request of
his friends, and ultimately inserted in the appendix to his life.
Another pleasing fragment of his composition is given at the end of
the first volume of Dr. Currie's ' Life and Works of Burns,' published at Liverpool in 1800; it is an extract from a poetical epistle
sent by Telford, when at Shrewsbury, to the Ayreshire poet, recommending him to take up other subjects of a serious nature, similar
to the 'Cottar's Saturday Night.'

At the age of twenty-three Telford at length quitted Eskdale,
and visited Edinburgh with a view to obtain better employment.
The splendid improvements then in progress in that city enlarged
his field of observation, and enabled him to contemplate architecture
as applied to the object of magnificence as well as utility; and he
seems at this time to have devoted much attention both to the
scientific study of architecture and to drawing.

After remaining in Edinburgh two years, he removed to London, where he obtained employment upon the quadrangle of Somerset House, then erecting by Sir William Chambers, an engagement in which he states that he obtained much practical information.

After this, in 1784, he was engaged to superintend the erection of a house for the resident commissioner at Portsmouth Dockyard, and for the next three years was occupied upon various buildings in this dockyard, which gave him good opportunities of becoming well acquainted with the construction of graving-docks, wharf walls, and other similar engineering works. Two or three years previous to this, Telford's good character and promising talent had secured for him the friendship of two families resident in his native district,—the Pasleys and the Johnstones,—and to their influence his early employment on important works is in some measure to be attributed.

In 1787, having completed his engagements at Portsmouth, he was invited by Sir William Pulteney (a member of the Johnstone family) to take the superintendence of some alterations to be made in Shrewsbury Castle. Telford consequently removed to Shrewsbury, where he was employed to erect a new jail, completed in 1793, and was afterwards appointed county surveyor, in which office (retained by him until death) he had to design, and oversee the construction of, bridges and similar works. The first bridge which he designed and built was that over the Severn at Mont-fort, consisting of three elliptical stone arches, one of fifty-eight, and the others of fifty-five feet span. His next was the iron bridge over the Severn at Buildwas, which was the third iron bridge ever erected in Great Britain, the first being the Colebrookdale in Shropshire, built in the years 1777-9, and the second the Wearmouth,* erected between the years 1793-6. Telford's bridge over the Severn was erected in 1796, and consisted of a single arch of 130 feet span, formed of five cast iron ribs, and having a rise of only 14 feet; the width of the platform is 18 feet, and the total weight of iron in the bridge about 174 tons; it was constructed by the Coalbrookdale Ironmasters at a cost of 6,034*l.* Forty smaller bridges were erected in Shropshire under Telford's direction.

The first great undertaking, upon which Mr. Telford (in conjunction with Mr. Jessop) was engaged, was the Ellesmere Canal, a series of navigations intended to unite the Severn, the Dee, and the Mersey, and extending altogether to a length of nearly one hundred and twenty miles. From the date of this engagement, about 1793, Telford directed his attention almost entirely to civil engineering. In the execution of the immense aqueducts, required on this work, which cross the valleys of the Ceroig or Chirk, and of the Dee, at an elevation of 70 and 120 feet respectively, cast iron was first introduced as a material for forming the water-troughs of the canal,

* Originally designed by Thomas Paine.

in place of the usual puddled clay confined in masonry, a practice
which involved great expense, and some danger in times of frost,
from the expansion of the moist clay.   In the locks of this canal
Telford also introduced cast iron framing in place of timber; and in
one instance, where the lock was formed in a quicksand, he made
every part of the above material.

The Caledonial Canal, of which Mr. Jessop was consulting engineer, was another of Mr. Telford's principal works.   This canal
was opened throughout its course in the year 1823, and it forms a
noble monument of the skill of the engineer.   The locks are stated
by Telford to be the largest ever constructed at that time, being
40 feet wide, and from 170 to 180 feet long.   Of other canals constructed wholly or partially under his superintendance, it is sufficient to mention the Glasgow, Paisley, and Androssan; the Maccles-
field; the Birmingham and Liverpool Junction; the Gloucester and
Berkeley; the Birmingham, which was completely remodelled by
him and adapted to the conduct of a very extensive traffic, and the
Weaver navigation in Cheshire.   On the Continent he likewise
superintended the construction of the Gotha Canal in Sweden, a
navigation of about 125 English miles, of which 55 are artificial
canal.   From the Lake Wener at one extremity, this navigation
rises 162 feet to the summit level, and falls 370 feet to the Baltic at
the other; the rise and fall are effected by fifty-six locks, and the
canal is 42 feet wide at the bottom and 10 feet deep.   Upon its
completion Telford received a Swedish order of knighthood, and as
a farther mark of the royal approbation, received the King of
Sweden's portrait set in diamonds.

The works executed by Telford under the Commissioners *of
Highland Roads and Bridges are of great importance.   The practical
operations under this commission, appointed in 1803, embraced
about a thousand miles of new road, with nearly 1,200 new bridges,
which caused the whole of Scotland, from its southern boundary
near Carlisle, to the northern extremity of Caithness, and from
Aberdeenshire on the east, to the Argyleshire islands on the west,
to be intersected by roads; and its largest rivers and even inferior
streams to be crossed by bridges.   The execution of this undertaking occupied a period of twenty-five years, and all was done
under the sole direction of Telford.   The great road from London to
Holyhead remains, perhaps, one of the most perfect specimens of
his skill as an engineer; the improvements in it were executed by
him, under another Parliamentary Commission appointed in 1815,
and Telford himself appears to have regarded this work with peculiar satisfaction.

The Menai suspension bridge is, however, unquestionably one of
the noblest monuments of Mr. Telford's fame, and it may be said to
have inaugurated the era of the extensive introduction of wrought

iron into great permanent structures exposed to heavy strains.*
This bridge was commenced in 1819, and opened for traffic in 1826.
The distance between the two piers is 550 feet, and the whole roadway, which is carried over four arches on the one side, and three on
the other, has a length of 1000 feet, and a breadth of 30 feet. The
total cost of the work was 120,000*l.*

Mr. Telford also built many other bridges of considerable size,
and executed some important harbour works at Aberdeen and
Dundee; but his most striking performance of this latter class is
the St. Katharine Docks, London. One of his latest engagements
was the survey of Dover harbour, undertaken in January, 1834, at
the request of the Duke of Wellington, (as Warden of the Cinque
Ports,) with a view to the adoption of measures to check the accumulation of shingle at the entrance.

During the course of his life Mr. Telford taught himself Latin,
French, and German, so as to be able to read those languages with
fluency, and to be able to converse freely in French. He is likewise
said to have been well acquainted with algebra, but to have placed
more reliance upon experiment, than on mathematical investigation.
He contributed to the 'Edinburgh Encyclopædia' the articles—
'Architecture,' 'Bridge Building,' and 'Canal Making.' Besides the
above, he wrote an account of his own life, giving elaborate descriptions of his various professional undertakings. (Life of Thomas
Telford, written by himself. Edited by John Rickman. London,
1833, 4to.)

Although Telford was not connected with the Institution of Civil
Engineers at its formation, he accepted their invitation in 1820, and
became their President; and from that time he was unremitting in
his attention to the duties of the office, having become by his
partial retirement from business, a pretty regular resident in the
metropolis.

Telford was possessed of a robust frame, and till he had reached
the age of seventy, had never been visited with any serious illness.
While at Cambridge, in the year 1827, he was afflicted with a severe
and dangerous disorder; and although he gradually recovered a
certain degree of health, he never regained his former vigour. He
died a few years afterwards at his house in Abingdon Street, Westminster, having completed the seventy-seventh year of his age.
His remains were deposited in Westminster Abbey, where there is
a statue erected to his memory.—*Encyclopædia Britannica.—English
Cyclopædia.*

* Sixth Dissertation, by Dr. J. D. Forbes, F.R.S.—*Encyclopædia Britannica.*
Eighth Edition.

CHARLES TENNANT.

Born May 3, 1768. Died October 1, 1838.

Charles Tennant, the founder of the celebrated chemical works at St. Rollox, Glasgow, was born at Ochiltree, Ayrshire. His father, John Tennant, was factor or steward to the Countess of Glencairn, and also rented a farm on her estate, in the culture of which he displayed great practical and scientific ability. John Tennant married twice; after the death of his first wife, by whom he had two sons and one daughter, he married, in the year 1757, Margaret McLure, who, in the course of time, brought him a numerous family of six sons and seven daughters. John Tennant's second wife possessed very superior abilities, which she earnestly directed to the education and advancement of her family, ultimately having the satisfaction of seeing all her children turn out men of energy and success in life. Charles Tennant, the subject of our memoir, was the fifth son; he received his early education at home, afterwards attending the parish school of Ochiltree. When still very young, Charles left home and went to Kilbarhan, with the intention of learning the manufacture of silk. After remaining at this place a short time, Tennant removed to Wellmeadow bleachfield, where he studied the methods of bleaching at that time in use, and ultimately went to Darnly (the place from which the unfortunate husband of Mary, Queen of Scots, took his title), and established there an extensive bleachfield, taking into partnership with him Mr. Cochrane of Paisley. Mr. Tennant now devoted himself to the study of chemistry, feeling that the process of bleaching could only be effected by true chemical agency, whatever might be the particular method or operation, and that, therefore, the bleacher must in the first case look to the chemist for the discovery of more potent agents to effect his object. Before Mr. Tennant's time the operation of bleaching was of a very tedious and expensive nature. The cloth was steeped in alkaline lye, which was called 'bucking.' The subsequent process of bleaching was done by exposure on the grass, called 'crofting;' these operations were repeated five or six times, and extended over a period of eight or ten weeks. In the year 1787 an important change took place, in consequence of the discovery, by Mr. Scheele, of Sweden, of chlorine, which was used as a substitute for exposure to the atmosphere. The repeated experiments of Berthollet added considerably to the facts already known, while the practical effects of these discoveries were still more fully shown by Mr. Watt, and Dr. Henry of Manchester. In 1798 Mr. Tennant made his first great discovery, viz., a method of making saturated chloride of lime, an article which was found to answer perfectly all the purposes required by the bleacher. This invention, for which he took out a patent, consisted in the substitution of lime for potash. His patent right was, however, resisted by certain of the bleachers of Lancashire, and was set aside by the verdict of a jury, on the grounds that the patent included a mode of 'bucking' with quicklime and water, which was not a new invention; and because one part of the patent was not new, the whole of the claim must be set aside. By this decision the use of liquid chloride of lime in bleaching was thrown open to all; and through an unfortunate error of expression in describing his process, Mr. Tennant was deprived of the fruits of a laborious investigation extending over a period of several years. This subsequently caused a strong feeling of sympathy to be manifested for him by many of the bleachers of Lancashire, who, as an expression of their grateful acknowledgment, presented him with a service of plate, which he accepted. Mr. Tennant, however, in accordance with the character of his original design, determined to press onward with his discoveries, and to bring, if possible, his first invention to a still more practical issue. He therefore adopted a new method, and at length completed and secured by patent a process for impregnating quicklime in a dry state with chlorine, which proved perfectly successful; this, his second patent, remained uncontested, and he lived to secure a large pecuniary reward.

Mr. Tennant's discoveries, together with the introduction of soda-ash or 'British soda,' in place of potash, greatly facilitated and cheapened the process of bleaching, while the introduction of mechanical appliances and the power of the steam-engine superseded the previous laborious operations by hand. The result has been that the same amount of bleaching is now performed in as many days as was formerly performed in weeks, while the price has been reduced from 7s. 6d. (1803) to 6d. (1861) for a piece of cloth of 28 yards.

In the year 1800 Mr. Tennant removed from Darnly to St. Rollox, Glasgow, where he commenced business as a large manufacturing chemist, taking into partnership Mr. Charles Mackintosh, Mr. William Cowper, and Mr. James Knox. During the remainder of his life Mr. Tennant devoted himself with energy to the forwarding of his business, and ultimately caused his manufactory to become the largest and most extensive of its kind in Europe. He also took considerable interest in the politics of the day. His principles were those of an intelligent and liberal-minded reformer, and he was long looked up to as one of the leading men of his party, although the least tainted by mere party spirit or selfishness. Mr. Tennant was likewise conspicuous in his promotion of many public undertakings. He took a deep interest in the furtherance of the railway system; the Garnkirk and Glasgow Railway may be said to owe its origin and completion almost entirely to him, while his invincible industry and perseverance contributed greatly towards the establishment of the Edinburgh and Glasgow Railway. He was a great friend of George Stephenson's, and was present with him at the opening of the Liverpool and Manchester Railroad when the unfortunate accident occurred which resulted in the melancholy death of Mr. Huskisson.

Mr. Tennant died rather suddenly, in his seventy-first year, at his house in Abercrombie Place, Glasgow. He was possessed of a constitutional nervousness, rather remarkable in one of a large and healthy frame, allied to a peculiar sensitiveness to the beautiful. In after life he would often talk with pleasure of his youthful reminiscences of the poet Burns, who was at 'that time on terms of considerable intimacy with his family. Mr. Tennant was an earnest and indefatigable promoter of economical and educational improvement; an uncompromising friend of civil and religious liberty; while his own inborn energy of character and clear intellect placed him among the foremost of those men who, by uniting science to manufactures, have at once extended their fields of action, and entitled their occupations to be classed among the ranks of the liberal professions.—*The Progress of Science and Art as developed in the Bleaching of Cotton, by Henry Ashworth, Paper read before the British Association at Manchester*, September 5, 1861; *and, Particulars communicated by the Family.*

THOMAS THOMSON, M.D., F.R.S.

Born April 12, 1773.   Died July 2, 1852.

Dr. Thomas Thomson, Regius Professor of Chemistry in the University of Glasgow, who exercised a remarkable influence in the development and extension of the science of chemistry during the present age, was born at Crieff, in Perthshire. He received his early education at the parish school of that place, and after remaining for a time under the care of Dr. Doig, of Stirling, went to the University of St. Andrews, where he remained for a period of three years.

Thomson entered upon his medical studies at the University of Edinburgh, and during the session of 1795–96 attended the lectures of the celebrated Dr. Black, who first awoke in him the latent taste for that science of which he was destined to become so bright an ornament. In 1796 he became connected with the *Encyclopædia Britannica,* for an early edition of which he wrote the articles— Chemistry, Mineralogy, Vegetable Substances, Animal Substances, and Dyeing Substances, &c. These articles formed the basis of his system of chemistry, which he published at Edinburgh in the year 1804, in four volumes, and afterwards greatly enlarged and improved as the demand for the book increased. Dr. Thomson commenced delivering a series of lectures on chemistry at Edinburgh in 1800, which were continued with increasing popularity until 1810. Meanwhile he invented the system of chemical symbols now generally adopted by all men of science (with variations as the time demands), and without which chemical language would be unintelligible. He was also the first to open a laboratory in Great Britain for practical manipulation in chemistry. In 1810 he published his 'Elements of Chemistry,' and in 1812 visited Sweden, and on his return wrote a description of that country. The following year to this Dr. Thomson started in London the 'Annals of Philosophy,' a scientific journal, which he continued to edit until the year 1822, and which a few years afterwards was merged in the 'Philosophical Magazine.' He also about this time conducted for the Board of Excise a series of investigations on brewing, which formed the basis of Scottish legislation on that subject.

In the year 1817 Thomson was elected lecturer on chemistry in the University of Glasgow, and in the following year received the title of Professor. This chair he held until his death, being assisted in his latter years by his nephew and son-in-law, Dr. R. D. Thomson. When Dalton had worked out his grand discovery of the Atomic Theory, he communicated the result of his researches to Thomson, who at once perceived the value and importance of the discovery, and in the year 1807 was the first to publish it to the world. He gave a sketch of this grand theory in the third edition of his 'System of Chemistry;' and we are chiefly indebted to the labours of Professor Thomson, conjointly with Dr. Henry of Manchester, and Dr. Wollaston, for luminous views on this important subject. In 1825 Dr. Thomson wrote, in two volumes, 'An Attempt to Establish the First Principles of Chemistry by Experiment.' In 1830-31 he published his 'History of Chemistry,' a work which has been described as a masterpiece of learning and research. In 1836 appeared his 'Outlines of Mineralogy and Geology;' and in 1849 he issued his last work, 'On Brewing and Distillation.'

Thomson performed in science, and its history and literature, a very great amount of valuable labour, and acquired a distinguished reputation both as an original discoverer, and as a practical teacher of his favourite science. He died in 1852, at the age of seventy-nine, and has left behind him a son who bears his name, now (1860) superintendent of the East India Company's Botanic Gardens at Calcutta, and one of the most distinguished scientific botanists of the day.—*Encyclopædia Britannica*, Eighth Edition.—*English Cyclopædia*. London, 1858.

RICHARD TREVITHICK.

Born April 13, 1771.   Died April 22, 1833.

Richard Trevithick, inventor of the first high pressure steam-engine, and the first steam-carriage used in England, was born in the parish of Illogan, in Cornwall.   He was the son of a purser of the mines in the district, and although he received but little early education, his talents were great in his own special subject, mechanics.   When a boy he had no taste for school exercises, and being an only son, was allowed by his parents to do much as he pleased; so that most of his time was passed either in strolling over the mines amidst which he lived, or in working out schemes which had already begun to fill his youthful imagination, seated under a hedge, with a slate in his hand.   Trevithick was a pupil of William Bull, an engineer practising at that time in Cornwall, employed in erecting Watt's engines, and who afterwards accompanied Trevithick to South America.   When he had attained the age of twenty-one, Trevithick was appointed engineer to several mines, a more responsible situation than the one held by his father, who, on hearing of his son's appointment, expressed great surprise, and even considered it his duty to remonstrate with the gentlemen who had proposed the appointment.   About this period (in 1792) he was also employed to test one of Hornblower's engines, and even before this, had, with the assistance of William Bull, constructed several engines which did not come under Watt's patent.   Trevithick's duties, as engineer, at this time, frequently required him to visit Mr. Harvey's iron foundry at Hayle, who was in the habit of inviting him to his house; this ultimately resulted in his becoming attached to Mr. Harvey's daughter, to whom he was married on the 7th of November, 1797.   After his marriage Trevithick lived at Plane-an-quary in Redruth for a few months, then at Camborne for ten years. From about 1808 to 1810 he resided in London; but after his unfortunate failure in attempting to tunnel the Thames, returned to Penponds in the parish of Camborne, where he lived for five or six years, at the house of his mother, afterwards living at Penzance, from which town he sailed for Peru on the 20th October, 1816. While residing at Camborne, Trevithick influenced perhaps by the success of Murdock's model steam-carriage, determined to build one adapted to ordinary road traffic.   One Andrew Vivian supplied the pecuniary means and joined him in the project, for which, on its completion, a patent was taken out in 1802, and in the same year a small one was erected at Marazion, which was worked by steam of at least thirty pounds on the square inch above atmospheric pressure.*   Their steam-carriage presented the appearance of an ordi-

* The specification of this patent gives likewise the first mention (we believe)

nary stage-coach on four wheels, having one horizontal cylinder, which, together with the boiler and fire-box, were placed at the back of the hind axle. Mr. Michael Williams, late M.P. for Cornwall, in a letter to Mr. E. Watkins, dated the 5th of January, 1853, mentions having been present at the first trial of Trevithick's locomotive, and says "the experiments made on the public road close by Camborne were perfectly successful, and although many improvements in the details of such description of engines have been since effected, the leading principles of construction and arrangement are continued, I believe, with little alteration in the magnificent railroad engines of the present day." After making several satisfactory trials in the neighbourhood of Plymouth, Trevithick and Vivian exhibited their invention publicly in London, first at Lord's Cricket-ground, and afterwards on the spot of ground now occupied by Euston Square.* At this latter place, however, Trevithick, influenced by some curious whim, suddenly closed the exhibition on the second day, leaving hundreds waiting outside in a state of great wrath. Mrs. Humblestone, an old inhabitant of London, who at that period used to keep a shop near to the present Pantheon, Oxford Street, relates that she well remembers witnessing a public trial of Trevithick's steam-carriage. On this occasion the shops were shut, no horses or carriages were allowed in the streets, and the roofs of the houses in the neighbourhood were crowded with people, who hurraed and waived their handkerchiefs as the 'steam monster' was seen coming along Oxford Street at a rapid pace.†

Two years afterwards Trevithick constructed the first successful railway locomotive, which was used on the Merthyr Tydvil Railway in the year 1804. This engine had an eight-inch cylinder, of four feet six inches stroke, placed horizontally as at present, and working on a cranked axle; while, in order to secure a continuous rotatory motion, a fly-wheel was placed on the end of the axle. When we add to this, that the fly-wheel was furnished with a break, that the boiler had a safety-valve or a fusible plug beyond the reach of the engineer, and that the patent includes the production of a more equable rotatory motion—"by causing the piston rods of *two* cylinders to work on the said axis by means of cranks at a quarter of a turn asunder"—it is scarcely too much to say that nothing material was added to the design of the locomotive until the invention of the

on record of oscillating engines. Sir John Rennie, F.R.S., in his address to the Institution of Civil Engineers, in 1846, mentions the following passage:—"Even the objection of extra friction, however, if tenable, is obviated *by the vibrating cylinder described in Trevithick and Vivian's patent, in* 1802; patented by Whitty in 1813, and by Manby in 1821, by whom the first engines of the kind were constructed."

* An eye-witness, who is still living, relates that on one of these trials he saw Trevithick's steam-carriage proceeding at the rate of twelve miles an hour.

† Mrs. Humblestone (1861) is now eighty-one years of age, and is residing in the neighbourhood of Edgware Road.

tubular boiler in 1829.*   On the occasion of its first trial, on the
21st of February, 1804, this engine drew carriages containing ten
tons of bar iron for a distance of nine miles, at the rate of five miles
an hour.   The specification of the patent for Trevithick's steam-
carriage mentions a plan for causing the wheels, *in certain cases*, to
take a stronger hold of the ground by means of sundry rough projections, but it also adds that, *in general, the ordinary structure or
figure of the external surface of these wheels will be found to answer the
intended purpose*, which appears to have been the case in the above-
mentioned engine.†   After making a few experiments with his
engine, Trevithick forsook the locomotive for other projects of his
versatile genius, and this great invention was left to be perfected
and carried into general use by George Stephenson.

    In the year 1809 Trevithick commenced an attempt at tunnelling
under the Thames.   It was the second time that this difficult undertaking had been tried, Ralph Dodd having been the first of the
unsuccessful borers.   When a large sum of money had been raised
by subscriptions Trevithick commenced boring at Rotherhithe, and
in order to save both labour and expense, kept very near to the
bottom of the river; but notwithstanding the increased difficulties
which he had to encounter on this account, he actually carried the
tunnel through a distance of 1011 feet, and within 100 feet of the
proposed terminus.   At this point an unfortunate dispute arose
between him and the surveyor appointed to verify his work, the
surveyor asserting that the tunnel had been run a foot or two on
one side.   This reflection on his skill as an engineer excited Trevithick's Cornish blood, and he is said to have adopted the absurd
expedient of making a hole in the roof of the tunnel at low water,
and thrusting through a series of jointed rods, which were to be
received by a man in a boat, and then observed from the shore.   In
the execution of this scheme, delays ensued in fitting the rods together, and at length so much water made its way through the gulley
formed by the opening in the roof, that retreat became necessary;
Trevithick, with an inborn courage, refused to go first, but sent the
men before him, and his life nearly fell a sacrifice to his devotion:
as he made his escape on the other side, the water rose with him
to his neck, owing to the tunnel following the curve of the bed of
the river, which necessarily caused the water to congregate towards
one part.   The work was thus ended almost at the point of its suc-

* Sixth Dissertation, *Encyclopædia Britannica*, Eighth Edition.
† See *Practical Treatise on Railroads, &c.*, by Luke Hebert, London, 1837.
Pages 21-4.—Mr. Francis Trevithick, who has spent considerable time in ascertaining the facts regarding his father's first locomotive, states that he has no
doubt the wheels of this engine were not in any way roughed: that he has often
conversed with those who made and worked the engine; that he has their copies
of the original drawings; and that in all these cases he never heard or saw anything which indicated that the wheels were roughed.

cessful completion, being at once a melancholy monument of his folly and his skill.

After this unfortunate failure, Trevithick commenced many schemes; among others, his attention was directed towards the introduction of iron tanks and buoys into the Royal Navy. On first representing the importance of this to the Admiralty, the objection was raised, that perhaps, in the case of the tanks, iron would be prejudicial to the water, and consequently to the health of the crews; Trevithick was therefore requested to consult Abernethy upon the subject, which he accordingly did, and received for his answer the following characteristic reply: "That the Admiralty ought to have known better than to have sent you to me with such a question." He likewise, about this period, contributed largely to the improvement and better working of the Cornish engines, and to him the merit is due of introducing into these engines the system of high-pressure steam, and of inventing in the year 1804 the cylindrical wrought iron boiler, (now known as the Cornish boiler,) in which he placed the fire inside instead of outside, as had been the practice before his time.

Trevithick also appears to have been among, if not the very first to employ the expansive principle of steam. In the year 1811–12 he erected a single-acting engine of 25 inches cylinder at Hull-Prosper in Gwithian, with a cylindrical boiler, in which the steam was more than 40 lbs. on the square inch above atmospheric pressure; and the engine was so loaded that it worked full seven-eighths of the stroke expansively. In this he seems to have preceded Woolf by several years. It is also stated by Mr. Gordon in his 'Treatise on Elementary Locomotion,' that Trevithick was the first to turn the eduction-pipe into the chimney of the locomotive to increase the draught.*

We now come to the most romantic and stirring period of Trevithick's career. In 1811 M. Uvillé, a Swiss gentleman at that time living in Lima, came to England to see if he could procure machinery for clearing the silver mines, in the Peruvian mountains, of water. Watt's condensing engines were, however, of too ponderous a nature to be transported over the Cordilleras on the backs of the feeble llamas, and Uvillé was about to give the matter up in despair, when, on the eve of his departure from this country, he chanced to see a small working model of Trevithick's engine in a shop window near Fitzroy Square. This model he carried out with him to Lima, and had the satisfaction of seeing it work successfully on the high ridge of the Sierra de Pasco. Uvillé now returned to England to procure more engines of the same kind, but he was a second time almost forced to give the matter up; for Boulton and Watt, the

* *Phil. Mag. and Annals of Philosophy,* August, 1831, in a letter to Richard Taylor, F.S.A., by W. Jory Henwood, F.G.S.

most distinguished engineers of their time, assured him that it was
impossible to make engines of sufficient power and yet small enough
to be carried over the Andes. Fortunately, however, Uvillé at this
point met with Trevithick himself, and was enabled to make such
arrangements with him as resulted in the embarkation, during September 1814, of three engineers and nine of Trevithick's engines.
On landing at Peru, Uvillé and his charge were received with a
royal salute, and in due time the engines, which had been simplified
to the greatest extent, and so divided as to form adequate loads for
the weakly llama, were safely carried over precipices where a stone
may be thrown for a league. An engine was soon erected at Lauri-
cocha, in the province of Tarma, which successfully drained the
shaft of the Santa Rosa mine, and enabled working operations to be
recommenced. During the year 1816 Trevithick, hearing of this
success, gave up family and fortune and embarked for South America. On landing he was received with the highest honours; all
Lima was in a state of excitement, which rose to a still greater
pitch, when it was found that his engines, by clearing the mines of
water, had doubled their produce and increased the coining machinery sixfold. Trevithick was created a marquis and grandee of
old Spain, and the lord warden of the mines proposed to raise a
silver statue in his honour. All went well until the revolution
broke out, when the Cornish engineer found himself placed in a very
disagreeable position between the two parties. The patriots kept
him in the mountains in a kind of honourable captivity, while the
royalists ruined his property and mutilated his engines. Trevithick,
never very patient, soon determined to end this, and, after incurring
many hardships and dangers, succeeded in making his escape from
the oppressive love and veneration of the mountain patriots. On
their way back Trevithick and his companions encountered many
perils; they had to shoot monkeys for subsistence, their clothes
were almost always wet through owing to it being the rainy
season of the year; they had also to ford rivers, and in many
cases make their own roads by cutting down the underwood and
other obstacles which impeded their progress. On one occasion
Trevithick nearly lost his life; in attempting to swim across a river
he became involved in a kind of whirlpool caused by some sunken
rocks, and notwithstanding all his efforts he was utterly unable to
swim beyond its influence, which kept carrying him round and
round; fortunately just as his strength was giving way a companion,
who had cut down a tall sappling, succeeded in stretching it out to
his assistance, and thus drew him to land. Ultimately, after a long
interval, Trevithick arrived at Cartagena, on the gulf of Darien,
almost in a state of utter destitution. Here he was met by the late
Robert Stephenson, who, having just received a remittance from
home, lent half to his brother engineer to help him on his way to
England, where he arrived on the 9th of October, 1827, bringing

back a pair of spurs and a few old coins, the sole remnants of the colossal fortune made, 'but not realized,' in the Peruvian mines. Before this occurred, however, Trevithick had visited various parts of the West coast of South America; part of this time he was in the company of Earl Dundonald (then Lord Cochrane), but the last four years of this period were spent by him at Costa Rica, in the countries now so well known as the route of the Nicaraguan transit and the scene of General Walker's filibuster warfare, where he projected mines and devised many magnificent schemes, but realized no permanent good for himself. Among other things, having discovered some valuable mineral deposits, he obtained from the government a grant of the land which contained them, and on his return to England succeeded, by his representations (which were confirmed by a Scotchman of the name of Gerard, who had been his companion), in organizing a company for sinking the necessary mines. Before, however, active operations were commenced, Trevithick one day entered the new company's offices to arrange finally about his own interest in the concern. A cheque for 7000*l.* was at once offered him as purchase-money for his land in Southern America. This however was not what he had wanted, and without giving a thought to the largeness of the sum offered, he indignantly threw back the cheque across the table and walked out of the office.* After this the company broke up, and Trevithick never realized a penny-piece from his really valuable possessions in that country.

After his return from America but little is known of Trevithick; late in life he commenced a petition to Parliament, in which he asks for some grant or remuneration for his services to the country, by reason of the superiority of his machinery, stating that from the use of his engines the saving to the Cornish mines alone amounted to 100,000*l.* per annum; but before presenting this petition, he met with a monied partner, who supplied him with the means of perfecting his never-ceasing inventions. This was all Trevithick wanted, and the petition was consequently laid aside. Thus assisted he obtained a patent in 1831 for an improved steam engine; and another in the same year for a method or apparatus for heating apartments; and a third on the 22nd of September, 1832, for improvements on the steam engine, and in the application of steam power to navigation and locomotion. This was the last patent he took out; he died at Dartford in Kent during the following year, at the age of sixty-two.

Trevithick, by his marriage with Miss Jane Harvey, had four sons and two daughters, all of whom are still living. His manners were

---

* The late Michael Williams, M.P. for West Cornwall, was present during this transaction, and afterwards remonstrated with Trevithick on his folly.— The cheque offered to him has been stated by one gentleman to have been for a far larger sum.

blunt and unassuming, but yet possessed a certain kind of fascina-
tion which generally secured for him, in whatever society he might
be, an eager and attentive auditory. In person he was tall and
strongly made, being six feet two inches in height, and broad in
proportion, and to this day stories of his extraordinary feats of
strength are told among the miners of Cornwall. His life remains
a record of constant but brilliant failures, and that from no inherent
defect in his inventions, but solely from the absence in his character
of that perseverance and worldly prudence necessary to bring every
new undertaking to a successful commercial issue.—*Contributions to
the Biography of R. Trevithick, by R. Edmunds, Jun., Edinburgh New
Philosophical Journal,* October, 1859.—*The Land's End District, &c.,
with Brief Memoir of Ric. Trevithick, by R. Edmunds.* London and
Penzance, 1862.—*All the Year Round,* August 4, 1860.—And other
particulars taken from original and authentic sources.

EDWARD TROUGHTON, F.R.A.S.

Born October, 1753.   Died June 12, 1835.

Edward Troughton, the first astronomical instrument maker of
our day, was born in the parish of Corney, on the south-west coast
of Cumberland, and was the third son of a small farmer. An uncle
of the same name, and his eldest brother John were settled in London
as mathematical instrument makers; and as his second brother was
apprenticed to the same business, Edward was designed to be a
farmer, continuing to be his father's assistant till the age of seventeen.

The death of his younger brother, however, altered Edward's
destination, and caused him to be placed with his brother John, at
that time a chamber master, employed chiefly in dividing and engraving for the trade, and the higher branches of the art. Under
the instruction of John, who was an excellent workman, Troughton
made very rapid progress, and at the end of his time was taken into
partnership.

About the year 1782 the Troughtons established themselves in
Fleet Street, where they commenced an independant business and
soon rose into eminence. After the death of his brother John,
Edward alone continued the business until the year 1826, when
increasing age and dislike to routine employment, induced him to
take Mr. William Simms as his partner and successor.

The instruments which facilitate navigation were peculiarly ob-

jects of interest to Mr. Troughton, and long after his infirmities
were an effectual bar to the applications of his most esteemed
friends, he exerted himself to supply the seamen with well adjusted
and accurate sextants. " Your fancies," he would say, " may wait;
their necessities cannot."

In 1778 he took out a patent for the double framed sextant, a
construction which, combining firmness and lightness, yet admitted
of a considerable radius in this invaluable instrument. After trying
and rejecting the repeating reflecting circle of Borda, Mr. Troughton,
in 1796, hit upon one of his happiest constructions, the British reflecting circle, as he delighted to call it, an instrument which in
right hands is capable of wonderful accuracy. It is a characteristic
trait of Mr. Troughton, that in order to bring his favourite circle
into general use, he reduced its price far below the usual profits of
trade; and if he had succeeded in his attempt, he might have been
ruined by his success, for his sextants were by far the most gainful
article of his business.

With the same earnestness to promote the interests of navigation,
he invented the dip sector (afterwards re-invented by Dr. Wollaston),
and expended time, money, and ingenuity to no inconsiderable
amount, in attempting to perfect the marine top for producing a
true horizontal reflecting surface at sea. The marine barometer,
the snuff-box sextant, and the portable universal dial, owe to him
all their elegance, and much of their accuracy. Where others invented or sketched he perfected.

In the ordinary physical apparatus Troughton made considerable
improvement in the construction of the balance, and of the mountain barometer. In the same class may be mentioned the form
given to the compensated mercurial pendulum; his pyrometer, by
which some very valuable expansions have been determined; the
apparatus by which Sir George Shuckburgh attempted to ascertain
the standard of weight and measure; and that apparatus which, in
the hands of Francis Baily, has given an invariable simple seconds
pendulum. In the ordinary geodesical instruments Mr. Troughton
greatly improved the surveying level and staff, and reduced them
both in weight and price, with increased convenience and accuracy.
It is, however, in the construction of astronomical instruments that
this great mechanician particularly excelled; here he reigned without a rival. His portable astronomical quadrants are models of
strength and lightness, while the repeating circle of Borda, an
instrument which he disliked, first received its beauty and accuracy
from his hands.

The ordinary reading micrometer, and the position micrometer,
commonly employed in the measurement of double stars, were
greatly improved by him in simplicity and brought to perfection;
and he first applied the former to dividing, though in circles and
scales it had already been used in reading off.

Mr. Troughton's larger works, such as his equatorial instruments, circles, transits, &c., are as well known in the astronomical world as those of Wren in the architectural; they are too numerous to mention here, and are distributed in various parts of the world. The gigantic zenith tube at Greenwich was about the last work on which he was engaged, and he had just time to finish it before his strength failed. The only astronomical instrument which is not greatly indebted to Mr. Troughton is the telescope, and he was deterred from making any attempt in this branch of his art by the curious physical defect of colour blindness, which existed in many members of his family. Like Dalton he could not distinguish colours, and had little idea of them, except generally as they conveyed the impression of greater or less light. The ripe cherry and its leaf were to him of one hue, only to be distinguished by their form. With this defect in his vision he never attempted any experiments in which colour was concerned; and it is difficult to see how he could have done so with success.

The most remarkable of Troughton's writings are, 'An account of a method of dividing astronomical and other instruments by ocular inspection,' &c.—Phil. Trans., 1809, which was awarded with the Copley medal; 'A comparison of the repeating circle of Borda, with the altitude and Azimuth Circle'—Memoirs R. Ast. Soc.; and several articles in Brewster's 'Edinburgh Cyclopædia,' such as 'Circle,' 'Graduations,' &c.

In the year 1825 Mr. Troughton paid a visit to Paris, and in 1830 he received an honorary gold medal from the King of Denmark. During the latter portion of his life he became almost entirely deaf, only hearing by the aid of a powerful trumpet. He died at his house in Fleet Street, June 12, 1835, in the eighty-second year of his age, and was buried at the Cemetery, Kensal Green.—*Monthly Notices of the Royal Astronomical Society*, vol. 3, February, 1836.

RICHARD WATSON, BISHOP OF LLANDAFF,
D.D., F.R.S., &c.

Born August, 1737.   Died June 4, 1816.

Richard Watson, celebrated both as an able theologian, and as a professor of chemistry, was born at Haversham, near Kendal in Westmoreland. His ancestors had been farmers of their own estates for several generations, and his father, a younger son, was for forty years the head master of the Grammar-school at Haversham, but had resigned his duties about the period of the birth of his son Richard. Young Watson received his education at this school, and about a year after his father's death, in 1753, was sent on an exhibition of 50*l.* belonging to the school, to Trinity College, Cambridge, where he was admitted as a sizar on the 3rd of November, 1754. All he had, besides his exhibition, to carry him through college, was a sum of 300*l.* which his father had left him, but he set bravely to work, to make his way to independence by hard study and hard living; his dress is said at first to have been a coarse mottled Westmoreland coat, and blue yarn stockings.

In May, 1757, he obtained a scholarship, and in the September following, while still only a junior soph, he began to take pupils, continuing to be employed, first as private, then as a college tutor, until in October, 1767, he became one of the head tutors of Trinity College. Meanwhile Watson had taken his degree of B.A. in January, 1759, being classed as second wrangler, which he seems to have considered, and not without reason, as the place of honour for the year; the senior wrangler, who was a member of St. John's, having, as it was generally believed, been unfairly preferred to him.

In October, 1760, he was elected a fellow of his college, and in November, 1764, on the death of Dr. Hadley, he was unanimously elected by the senate to the professorship of chemistry, although at that time he knew nothing of the science. Watson did not, however, disappoint the confidence that was placed by others in his abilities. With the assistance of an operator, whom he immediately sent for from Paris, and by shutting himself up in his laboratory, he acquired such an acquaintance with his new subject, as to enable him in about fourteen months to read his first course of lectures, which were honoured with a numerous attendance, and proved highly successful. Other courses followed which were equally well received; and, in 1768, he printed a synopsis of the principles of the science, under the title of 'Institutiones Metallurgicæ.'

Watson was elected a Fellow of the Royal Society in 1769, and for some years afterwards contributed many chemical papers to the 'Philosophical Transactions.' In 1771 he published 'An Essay on the Subjects of Chemistry, and their General Divisions.' In 1781 he published two volumes 12mo. of 'Chemical Essays;' a third appeared in 1782; and a fourth in 1786 completed the work, which has often been reprinted, and was long very popular. In connection with his chemical professorship, Watson obtained from Government, by proper representations, a salary of 100*l.* for himself, and for all future professors. He also paid some attention to theoretical and practical anatomy, as having a certain relation to the science of chemistry.

In October, 1771, on the death of Dr. Rutherforth, he unexpectedly obtained the lucrative and important office of Regius Professor of Divinity, and in that capacity, held the Rectory of Somersham in

Huntingdonshire. At this time he had neither taken his degree of B.D. or D.D., and by his own account, seems to have known little more of theological learning than he did of chemistry seven years before. Yet such was his good fortune, or the reputation that he had established, for carrying an object whenever he took it in hand, that no other candidate appeared for the professorship, while his eloquence and ingenuity supplied the want of deeper erudition, and attracted as numerous audiences to the exercises in the schools at which he presided, as had ever attended his chemical lectures.

Watson himself, in the anecdotes of his life, gives the following account of this circumstance:—" I was not, when Dr. Rutherforth died, either Bachelor or Doctor in Divinity, and without being one of them I could not become a candidate for the Professorship. This puzzled me for a moment, I had only seven days to transact the business in, but by hard travelling, and some adroitness, I accomplished my purpose, obtained the King's mandate for a Doctor's degree, and was created Doctor on the day previous to that appointed for the examination of the candidates. Thus did I, by hard and incessant labour for seventeen years, attain at the age of thirty-four, the first office for honour in the University; and, exclusive of the mastership of Trinity College, I have made it the first for profit; I found the Professorship not worth quite 330*l.*, and it is now worth 1000*l.* at least."

Watson's clerical preferment after this was very rapid. In 1773, through the influence of the Duke of Grafton, he obtained possession of a sinecure rectory in North Wales, which he was enabled to exchange during the course of the following year for a prebend in the Church of Ely. In 1780 he succeeded Dr. Plumtree as archdeacon of that diocese; the same year he was presented to the Rectory of Northwold in Norfolk, and in the beginning of the year following, received another much more valuable living, the Rectory of Knaptoft in Leicestershire, from the hands of the Duke of Rutland, who had been his pupil at the University. Lastly, in July, 1782, he was promoted to the bishopric of Llandaff, by the Prime Minister of that period Lord Shelburne, who hoped thereby both to gratify the Duke of Rutland, and also to secure an active partisan.

Watson, however, proved a very unmanageable bishop, and during the course of his political career was singularly free and independent in his sentiments. One of his first acts was to publish in 1783, ' A Letter to Archbishop Cornwallis on the Church Revenues, recommending an equalization of the Bishoprics.' This he did in spite of all that could be said to make him see that it would embarrass the Government, and at the same time do nothing to forward his own object. And so he continued to take his own way, and was very soon left to do so, without any party or person seeking either to guide or stop him.

In 1783 Bishop Watson had married the eldest daughter of Edward

Wilson of Dalham Tower in Westmoreland. In the year 1789 he retired from politics and betook himself to an estate which he had at Calgarth, on the banks of Winandermere, occupying himself in educating his family, and in agricultural improvements, especially planting, for which he received a medal from the Society of Arts in 1789.

Previous to this, in 1786, his friend and former pupil, Mr. Luther, of Ongar in Essex, had left him an estate which he sold for more than 20,000*l.* Bishop Watson died on the 4th of June, 1816, in his seventy-ninth year. His writings are very numerous and miscellaneous in their character; some of the more well known are:—an 'Apology for Christianity,' written in 1776 in answer to Gibbon; a 'Collection of Theological Tracts, selected from various Authors, for the use of the Younger Students in the University,' in six volumes 8vo., 1785; 'Apology for the Bible, in a series of Letters addressed to Thomas Paine,' 1796; and, 'An Address to the People of Great Britain,' which went through fourteen editions, 1798.

One of the best practical results of his chemical studies was the suggestion which he made to the Duke of Richmond, at that time Master of the Ordnance, respecting the preparation of charcoal for gunpowder, by burning the wood in close vessels, a process very materially improving the quality of the powder, and which is now generally adopted.—*Anecdotes of the Life of Richard Watson, Bishop of Llandaff, written by himself.* London, 1817.—*Memoir by Dr. Thomas Young, Encyclopædia Britannica.—English Cyclopædia.*

JAMES WATT, LL.D., F.R.S. L. and E., &c.

MEMBER OF THE FRENCH INSTITUTE.

Born at Greenock on the Clyde, 1736. Died August 25, 1819.

To James Watt, philosopher, mechanician, and civil engineer, whose genius perfected the control of one of the greatest revealed powers yet given to man, may well be applied the saying of Wellington, "That which makes a great general makes a great artist, the power and the determination to overcome difficulties." Born with a sickly temperament, and prevented thereby from attending school, or indulging in the usual healthy play of children, Watt, unassisted by others, devoted his time to study, and in retirement and reflection laid the foundation of knowledge destined to bear such ample fruit. In addition to mere book knowledge, he early exhibited a partiality for mechanical contrivances and operations, and this determined him to commence his career as a mathematical instrument maker. For this purpose he set out for Glasgow in 1754, but owing to the limited resources of the town at that period, he finally decided on going to London, where, after great difficulty, he was apprenticed for a twelvemonth to an instrument maker in Finch Lane. At the end of his apprenticeship Watt, having become enfeebled from over attention to work,. repaired to Greenock to recruit his health, and ultimately returned to Glasgow, where he was established by the authorities, within the precincts of the college as mathematical instrument maker to the University. In process of time Watt's shop became a favourite resort for professors as well as students, and he counted among his visitors Professor Simson, Drs. Black, Dick, and Moor;* but his most intimate friend, and the one most closely connected with his after life, was John Robison, a student at Glasgow, afterwards Professor of Natural Philosophy at Edinburgh University, to whom the honour is due of having first directed Watt's attention to the steam-engine. The event which actually led to the commencement of his invaluable discoveries on this subject, was the entrusting to him the repair of a small model of Newcomen's engine, which the college possessed. In his endeavours to put this engine into working order, Watt was led to investigate thoroughly the properties of steam upon which its action depended; and ultimately in the spring of 1765, after many trials and untiring perseverance, he arrived at the great and simple idea of a separate condenser, into which the steam expanded; thereby preventing that wasteful expenditure of heat, which was the necessary result of the old plan of condensing the steam in the working cylinder, by admitting a jet of cold water directly under the piston. In addition to this Watt surrounded the cylinder with a second casing to be filled with the surplus steam, for the purpose of preventing radiation of heat, and closed in the top (which in Newcomen's engine had been left open for the sake of the pressure of the atmosphere upon the piston) by putting a cover on, with a hole and stuffing box for the piston rod to slide through; a plan which enabled steam pressure to be used in place of atmospheric. Newcomen's

---

* During his residence at Glasgow, a Mason's Lodge were desirous of possessing an organ, and Watt was asked to build it. He was totally destitute of a musical ear, and could not distinguish one note from the other, but he nevertheless accepted the offer; for having studied the philosophical theory of music, he found that science would be a substitute for want of ear. He commenced by building a small one for Dr. Black, and then proceeded to the large one, in the building of which he devised a number of novel expedients, such as indicators and regulators of the strength of the blast, with various contrivances for improving the efficiency of the stops. The qualities of this organ when finished are said to have elicited the surprise and admiration of musicians. During this period of his life Watt used likewise to construct and repair guitars, flutes, and violins, and had the same success as with his organ.—*Quarterly Review*, October, 1858.

engine, at this time used only for pumping out water in mines, thus became a true steam-engine of immense power, capable of being worked with economy, and of being turned to the various uses to which science has since applied it. For these great improvements a patent, dated January 5, 1769, was taken out by Watt and Dr. Roebuck, the founder of the Carron iron works, with whom Watt had become acquainted. Little, however, was done for some years in manufacturing engines on a large scale; Roebuck fell into difficulties, while Watt, harassed, depressed in spirits, and in want of money, was forced to obtain employment as a civil engineer and land-surveyor. Among the many works that he was engaged on in this capacity may be mentioned: the Crinan Canal, afterwards completed by Rennie; the deepening of the river Clyde; improvements in the harbours of Ayr, Port Glasgow, and Greenock; the building of bridges at Hamilton and Rutherglen; and lastly, surveying and estimating a line of canal between Fort William and Inverness, which was subsequently executed by Telford on a larger scale than was then proposed, under the name of the Caledonian Canal. In the latter half of the year 1773 Roebuck's affairs came to a crisis; and Watt, through the agency of Dr. Small, having been brought into relation with Mr. Boulton, a man possessing an intimate knowledge of business, with extended views and a liberal spirit of enterprise, an arrangement was entered into between them, and the firm of Boulton and Watt established at Soho. This was the turning point in Watt's fortunes; under the vigorous management of Boulton, his great invention at length began to be appreciated, and the saving of fuel was found to be nearly three-fourths of the quantity consumed by Newcomen's engine. In 1775 an extension of the original patent until the year 1800 was obtained. This gave a fresh stimulus to Watt's fertile brain, and resulted in patents being taken out, between the years 1781–1785, for the rotatory motion of the sun and planet wheels (the crank having been pirated by Wasbrough), *the expansive principle of working steam; the double engine; the parallel motion; the smokeless furnace; the float to regulate the supply of water into the boiler;* and *the governor*. At a later period Watt also invented the indicator, by means of which the actual horse power of an engine could be ascertained. This beautiful series of inventions in a measure may be said to have perfected the machine, and at the present time the condensing steam engine differs in no material respect from the engine as Watt left it.

While residing at Birmingham, Mr. Watt's house became the resort of many learned men. In the meetings of the Lunar Society, held at Soho House, originated his experiments on water, and between him and Cavendish is the honour divided of having first promulgated the theory of its composition. During the dispute which arose upon this subject, Watt's reply, on a friend regretting that another should have carried off this honour, is worth recording, as showing the modest dignity of his character: "It matters not," said he, "whether Cavendish discovered this or I, it is discovered." In the year 1800 Mr. Watt, having acquired an ample competency, ceased to take an active part in the business of the firm, and the remainder of his life was spent in retirement; but his active mind, still unwearied, continued to follow its natural bent. On two occasions afterwards, in 1811 and 1812, he gave proofs of the undiminished powers of his inventive genius. In the one instance he was induced, by his grateful recollections of his residence in Glasgow, to assist the proprietors of the waterworks there with a plan for supplying the town with better water, by means of a suction pipe laid across the Clyde to reach to the other side, where water of a very superior quality might be procured. This pipe was formed of cast iron, with flexible joints, after the manner of a lobster's tail, so as to accommodate itself to the bed of the river, and fully answered the purpose for which it was designed. In the other instance he was prevailed upon, by the earnest solicitation of the Lords Commissioners of the Admiralty, to attend a deputation of the Navy Board, and to give, with his friend Captain Huddart and Mr. J. Jessop, an opinion upon the works then carrying on at Sheerness Dockyard, and the further ones projected by Messrs. Rennie and Whitby. On this occasion he no less gratified the gentlemen associated with him by the clearness of his general views, than by his knowledge of the details; and he received the thanks of the Admiralty for his services. In 1814 he yielded to the wishes of his friends, of Dr. Brewster especially, and undertook a revision of Professor Robison's articles on steam and steam-engines for an early edition of the *Encyclopædia Britannica*, which he enriched with valuable notes, containing his own experiments on steam, and a short history of his principal improvements upon the engine itself. Among other mechanical contrivances of Mr. Watt's may be mentioned: a machine for copying letters; an instrument for measuring the specific gravity of fluids; a regulator lamp; a plan for heating buildings by steam; and a contrivance for drying linen. In his eighty-third year, Mr. Watt was still occupied in inventing a machine for copying statues, but this remained unfinished, death arrested his hand; he died in the year 1819, at Heathfield, in Staffordshire; and thus, full of years and honours, ended the life of a man who, though born in a secluded village town, and reared in comparative poverty, was yet enabled, by persevering industry and the happy gifts of nature) to contribute so greatly to the commercial prosperity of the world.

Mr. Watt was elected a member of the Royal Society of Edinburgh in 1784, of the Royal Society of London in 1785, and a corresponding member of the Batavian Society in 1787. In 1806 the honorary degree of LL.D. was conferred upon him by the spontaneous and unanimous vote of the Senate of the University of

Glasgow; and in 1808 he was elected, first a corresponding, and afterwards a foreign member of the Institute of France. A few years before his death it was intimated to him, by a message from Sir Joseph Banks, that, to use the words of Mr. Muirhead, the highest honour usually conferred in England on men of literature and science—namely a baronetcy, was open to him, should he desire it; but, although Watt felt flattered by this intimation, he determined, after consulting with his son, to decline the honour.

Five statues have been erected to the memory of this illustrious man, of which number the one in Westminster Abbey, by Chantrey, bears on its pedestal the famous inscription by Lord Brougham:—

NOT TO PERPETUATE A NAME

WHICH MUST ENDURE WHILE THE PEACEFUL ARTS FLOURISH

BUT TO SHEW

THAT MANKIND HAVE LEARNT TO HONOUR THOSE

WHO BEST DESERVE THEIR GRATITUDE

THE KING

HIS MINISTERS AND MANY OF THE NOBLES

AND COMMONERS OF THIS REALM

RAISED THIS MONUMENT TO

JAMES WATT

WHO DIRECTING THE FORCE OF AN ORIGINAL GENIUS

EARLY EXERCISED IN PHILOSOPHIC RESEARCH

TO THE IMPROVEMENT OF

THE STEAM ENGINE

ENLARGED THE RESOURCES OF HIS COUNTRY

INCREASED THE POWER OF MAN

AND ROSE TO AN EMINENT PLACE

AMONG THE MOST ILLUSTRIOUS FOLLOWERS OF SCIENCE

AND THE REAL BENEFACTORS OF THE WORLD

BORN AT GREENOCK MDCCXXXVI

DIED AT HEATHFIELD IN STAFFORDSHIRE MDCCCXIX.

—Muirhead's Translation of Arago's Historical Eloge of James Watt. London, 1839.—*Memoir, by his son J. Watt, Encyclopædia Britannica.—Quarterly Review,* October, 1858.

WILLIAM H. WOLLASTON, M.D., P.R.S. &c.

Born August 6, 1766.   Died December 22, 1828.

William Hyde Wollaston was born at East Dereham, a village sixteen miles from Norwich. His father was an astronomer of some eminence, who in the year 1800 published an extensive catalogue of the northern circumpolar stars.   After a preparatory education, Wollaston entered at Caius College, Cambridge, where he took the degree of M.B. in 1787, and that of M.D. in 1793; soon afterwards he became a Tancred Fellow.   During his residence at Cambridge, he devoted himself more to the study of astronomy than any other science.

On leaving Cambridge in 1789, he settled at Bury St. Edmunds, and began to practise as a physician, but met with so little success, that he soon removed to London.   Shortly after his arrival, he became a candidate for the office of Physician to St. George's Hospital, but was defeated by the election of his principal opponent, Dr. Pemberton.   It is stated that this circumstance had such an effect on Wollaston, that he declared, in a moment of pique, he would abandon the profession, and never more write a prescription, were it for his own father.   This statement is, however, contradicted in a biographical notice of him, contained in the reports of the Astronomical Society, where it is affirmed that he continued to practise physic in London to the end of the year 1800, when an accession of fortune determined him to relinquish a profession he never liked, and to devote himself entirely to science,

On the 9th of May, 1793, Wollaston was elected a Fellow of the Royal Society; and in June, 1797, appeared his first contribution to the 'Philosophical Transactions,' being a paper 'On Gouty and Urinary Concretions.'   From this period until his decease, Wollaston was a constant contributor to the 'Transactions,' as well as to various scientific journals.   His papers in the 'Philosophical Transactions' amount to thirty-nine, and, in addition to strictly chemical subjects, include memoirs in astronomy, optics, mechanics, acoustics, mineralogy, crystallography, physiology, and botany.

On the 30th of November, 1804, he was elected Junior Secretary to the Royal Society; and on the death of Sir Joseph Banks, in June, 1820, succeeded him in the President's chair, until the anniversary, November 30th of the same year, when he retired in favour of Sir Humphry Davy, to whom, at the election, he gave the whole weight of his influence.

In the years 1804–5 Wollaston first made known to the world the existence of the two metals, palladium and rhodium, which he found were contained in the ore of platinum, associated with osmium and iridium, two metals discovered about the same time by Mr. Tennant. In 1809 he showed that the supposed new metal, tantalum, was identical with columbium, previously discovered by Mr. Hatchett; and shortly before his death, he transmitted to the Royal Society a communication, constituting the Bakerian lecture of 1828, in which he fully describes his ingenius method of rendering platinum malleable. From this invention he is stated to have acquired more than 30,000*l.*

Dr. Wollaston's knowledge was more varied, and his tastes less exclusive, than any other philosopher of his time, except Cavendish; but optics and chemistry are the two sciences in which he made the greatest discoveries. To him we owe the first demonstration of the identity of galvanism and common electricity, and the first explanation of the cause of the different phenomena exhibited by them. Dr. Wollaston was accustomed to carry on his experiments in the greatest seclusion, and with very few instruments; he was also endowed with an extreme neatness of hand, and invented the most ingenious methods of determining the properties and constituents of very minute quantities of matter. It is related by Dr. Paris (in his Life of Davy), that a foreign philosopher once calling on Wollaston with letters of introduction, expressed a great desire to see his laboratory. "Certainly," replied Wollaston, and immediately produced a small tray, containing some glass tubes, a blowpipe, two or three watch-glasses, a slip of platinum, and a few test-tubes.

Another anecdote is told of him, that, having been engaged one day in inspecting a monster galvanic battery constructed by Mr. Children, he accidentally met, on his way home, a brother chemist, who knew of Mr. Children's grand machine, and uttered something about the inconvenience of it being of such an enormous size; on this Wollaston seized his friend by the button, led him into a bye corner, where, taking from his waistcoat pocket a tailor's thimble which contained a galvanic arrangement, and pouring into it the contents of a small phial, he astonished his friend by immediately heating a platinum wire to a white heat. He also produced platinum wire so extremely fine as to be nearly imperceptible to the naked eye.

Towards the close of the year 1828, Wollaston became dangerously ill with disease of the brain. Feeling his end approaching, and being unable to write himself, he employed an amanuensis to write accounts of such of his discoveries and inventions as he was unwilling should perish with him; and in this manner some of his most important papers were communicated to the Royal Society. It is a curious fact, that, in spite of the extensive cerebral disease under which he laboured, his faculties continued unclouded to the very last. When almost at the point of death, one of his friends

having observed, loud enough for him to hear, that he was unconscious of what was passing around him, Wollaston made a sign for
pencil and paper, and then wrote down some figures, and after
casting up the sum, returned the paper: the amount was found to
be correct.

Dr. Wollaston died on the 22nd of December, 1828, at the age of
sixty-two—only a few months before his great scientific contemporaries, Sir Humphry Davy and Dr. Thomas Young. He was buried
in Chiselhurst churchyard, Kent. Dr. William Henry* gives the
following summary of his character:—

" Dr. Wollaston was endowed with bodily senses of extraordinary
acuteness and accuracy, and with great general vigour of understanding. Trained in the discipline of the exact sciences, he had
acquired a powerful command over his attention, and had habitu-
ated himself to the most rigid correctness both of thought and
language. He was sufficiently provided with the resources of the
mathematics, to be enabled to pursue with success profound enquiries in mechanical and optical philosophy, the results of which
enabled him to unfold the causes of phenomena not before under-
stood, and to enrich the arts connected with those sciences by the
invention of ingenious and valuable instruments. In chemistry
he was distinguished by the extreme nicety and delicacy of his
observations, by the quickness and precision with which he marked
resemblances and discriminated differences, the sagacity with which
he devised experiments and anticipated their results, and the skill
with which he executed the analysis of fragments of new substances,
often so minute as to be scarcely perceptible by ordinary eyes.
He was remarkable, too, for the caution with which he advanced
from facts to general conclusions; a caution which, if it sometimes
prevented him from reaching at once the most sublime truths, yet
rendered every step of his ascent a secure station, from which it
was easy to rise to higher and more enlarged inductions."—*Weld's
History of the Royal Society, with Memoirs of the Presidents.* London,
1848.—*Sketches of the Royal Society, &c., by Sir John Barrow, Bart.,
F.R.S.* London, 1849.

* Preface to *Elements of Experimental Chemistry*, Eleventh Edition.

THOMAS YOUNG, M.D., F.R.S., &c.

MEMBER OF THE INSTITUTE OF FRANCE.

Born June 13, 1773. Died May 10, 1829.

Dr. Thomas Young, celebrated for his universal attainments, was born at Milverton, in Somersetshire. He was the eldest of ten children of Thomas and Sarah Young; his mother was a niece of Dr. Richard Brocklesby, a physician of considerable eminence in London. Both of his parents were members of the Society of Friends, and to the tenets of that sect, which recognizes the immediate influence of a Supreme Intelligence as a guide in the ordinary conduct of life, Dr. Young was accustomed in after years to attribute, in no slight degree, the formation of those determined habits of perseverance which gave him the power of effecting any object upon which he was engaged, and by which he was enabled to work out his own education almost from infancy, and with little comparative assistance from others. At the age of two years Young could read with considerable fluency, and before he was four years old had read the Bible through twice, and also Watts' hymns. He was likewise from his earliest years in the habit of committing to memory pieces of poetry, in proof of which there exists a memorandum, written by Young's grandfather, on the margin of a copy of Goldsmith's 'Deserted Village,' to the effect that his grandson Thomas had repeated to him the whole poem, with the exception of a word or two, before he was five years old. In 1780 he was placed at a boarding-school at Stapleton, near Bristol, and here the deficiency of the instructor appears to have advanced the studies of the pupil, as Young now became his own teacher, and used to study by himself the last pages of the book taught almost before he had reached the middle under the eye of the master.

In the year 1782 he became an inmate of the school kept by Mr. Thompson, at Crompton, in Dorsetshire, remaining there nearly four years, during which period he rapidly acquired knowledge upon various subjects. Having commenced the study of botany, he was led to attempt the construction of a microscope, with the assistance of an usher in the school of the name of Benjamin Martin, in order to examine the plants he was in the habit of gathering. In his endeavours to make the microscope Young found it necessary to procure a lathe, and for a time everything gave way to a passion for turning. This was, however, at length succeeded by a desire to become acquainted with the nature of fluxions, and after reading through and mastering a treatise upon this subject, he turned his attention to the study of Hebrew and other Oriental languages. Ultimately at the age of fourteen Thomas Young was more or less

H

versed in Greek, Latin, French, Italian, Hebrew, Persic, and Arabic, and in forming the characters of these languages had already acquired a considerable portion of that beauty and accuracy of penmanship which was afterwards so remarkable in his copies of Greek compositions, as well as those subjects connected with the literature of ancient Egypt. A story is related of him, that when requested a few years later, by a friend of Dr. Brocklesby, who presumed somewhat upon Young's youthful appearance, to exhibit a specimen of his penmanship, he replied by writing a sentence in his best style in fourteen different languages.

In 1787 Young was engaged, in conjunction with Mr. Hodgkin, as private tutor to Hudson Gurney, grandson of Mr. David Barclay, of Youngsbury, near Ware, in Hertfordshire, and he remained thus occupied during the space of five years, extending his knowledge as far as possible. The number of books he read through at that time was comparatively small, but whatever book he began to read, he read completely and deliberately through, and it was perhaps this determination always to master what he might happen to be engaged on before attempting anything else, which enabled Dr. Young to attain so great knowledge on such various subjects. He himself had little faith in any peculiar aptitude being implanted by nature for any given pursuits. His favourite maxim was, that whatever one man had done another might do, and that the original difference between human intellects was much less than it was supposed to be; in this respect he resembled his great predecessor Newton, and his cotemporary Dalton, both of whom had unbounded confidence in the powers of patient thought.

In the autumn of 1792 Thomas Young removed to London, in order to study medicine, which profession he had determined to adopt, being greatly influenced in his choice by the wishes of his uncle Dr. Brocklesby. This gentleman had kindly undertaken the charge of his education, and Young was by him introduced to the members of the most distinguished literary circles in the metropolis, including Burke, Drs. Lawrence and Vincent, Sir Joshua Reynolds, Sir George Baker, and others. In the autumn of 1793 he became a pupil at St. Bartholomew's Hospital, and in October 1794 proceeded to Edinburgh, still further to prosecute his medical studies. While residing at Edinburgh Dr. Young mixed largely in society, began the study of music, took lessons on the flute, and also private lessons in dancing, and frequently attended performances at the theatre. From this period he gave up the external characteristics of the Quakers, and ultimately ceased to belong to their body, although he practised to the end of his life the general simplicity of their moral conduct.

During the year 1795 he commenced a tour on the Continent, staying at the University of Gottingen during nine months, in order to prosecute his studies and take a doctor's degree. In February,

1797, he came back to England, and was almost immediately after his return admitted a Fellow-Commoner of Emmanuel College, Cambridge; the Master of the College, Dr. Farmer, saying as he introduced Young to the fellows, " I have brought you a pupil qualified to read lectures to his tutors."

In December 1797 Young's uncle, Dr. Brocklesby, died, bequeathing to his nephew the sum of 10,000*l*., besides his house, furniture, and a choice collection of pictures. Dr. Young was now entirely at liberty to form his own scheme of life, and he determined to commence practice as a physician, for which purpose, after having completed his terms of residence at Cambridge, he took a house in Welbeck Street (No. 48), which he continued to occupy for five-and-twenty years. His practice as a physician, although respectable, was never large. He wanted that confidence or assurance which is so necessary to the successful exercise of the profession. He was perhaps too deeply informed, and therefore too sensible of the difficulty of arriving at true knowledge in the science of medicine ever to form a hasty judgment; while his great love of, and adherence to truth, made him often hesitate where others would have felt no difficulty in expressing an opinion. It was perhaps a happy circumstance for the fame of Dr. Young that this should be the case, as he was thereby enabled to devote a considerable portion of his time to those literary and scientific studies in which so few could compete with him. In 1799 he published his memoir entitled ' Outlines and Experiments respecting Sound and Light,' which was read before the Royal Society and printed in their ' Transactions.' Other papers, ' On the Theory of Light and Colours,' followed, which the council of the Royal Society selected for the Bakerian lectures. In the year 1801 Dr. Young accepted the office of Professor of Natural Philosophy at the Royal Institution, which had been established the year previously. The conducting of the journal of the Institution was also entrusted to his care, in conjunction with his colleague Sir Humphry Davy, at that time Professor of Chemistry. Dr. Young remained at the Royal Institution two years, during which period he gave a course of lectures on ' Natural and Experimental Philosophy,'. a syllabus of which he published in 1802, announcing for the first time his great discovery of the general law of the interference of the undulations of light. His lectures were not, however, popular; they embodied too much knowledge to be intelligible to any considerable portion of his hearers; and the matter was so abundant and the style so condensed, that students tolerably versed in science might have found it extremely difficult to follow him in his masterly discussions.

Dr. Young had been elected a Fellow of the Royal Society as early as the year 1794, when he had just completed his twenty-first year; he was now appointed (1802) Foreign Secretary to the same Society, an office which he held during the remainder of his life, and for which he was well qualified by his knowledge of the principal languages of Europe.

In 1804 he married Eliza, the daughter of James Primrose Maxwell, of Cavendish Square, and this union is said to have been attended with uninterrupted happiness; his wife who survived him left no children.

In 1807 appeared his most elaborate and valuable work, 'A Course of Lectures on Natural Philosophy and the Mechanical Arts,' being the embodiment of the sixty lectures delivered while at the Royal Institution, together with the labour of three more years occupied in further arranging and improving them. This work comprises a complete system of natural and mechanical philosophy, drawn from original sources, and is distinguished not only by the extent of its learning and the accuracy of its statements, but by the beauty and originality of the theoretical principles. It also contains a disquisition upon the doctrine of interference in the undulatory theory of light mentioned before, the general law of which he thus enunciates: "When two undulations from different origins coincide, either perfectly or very nearly in direction, their joint effect is a combination of the motions belonging to each."* Sir John Herschel, speaking of this discovery, says that it alone "would have sufficed to have placed its author in the highest rank of scientific immortality, even were his other almost innumerable claims to such a distinction disregarded." Amongst other laborious and difficult matters of investigation, Dr. Young made the first and most important steps in reading the Egyptian Hieroglyphics, in which he preceded Champollion; and he afterwards, in 1823, published a work on this subject, under the title of 'An Account of some recent Discoveries in Hieroglyphical Literature and Egyptian Antiquities; including the author's original Alphabet as extended by Mr. Champollion; with a Translation of five unpublished Greek and Egyptian Manuscripts.' In the year 1808 Dr. Young was admitted a fellow of the College of Physicians, and in 1810 was elected physician to St. George's Hospital, a situation which he retained for the remainder of his life. In 1813 he published 'An Introduction to Medical Literature, including a system of practical Nosology intended as a guide to Students and as an Assistant to Practitioners.' In 1816 Dr. Young was appointed Secretary to the Commission empowered to ascertain the length of the second's pendulum, and thereby establish an uniform system of weights and measures. Two years subsequent to this he became secretary to the Board of Longitude, and on the dissolution of that body, became sole conductor of the 'Nautical Almanac.' Dr. Young at various times contributed eighteen articles to the 'Quarterly Review,' of which nine were on scientific subjects—the rest on medicine, languages, and criticism.

* *Life of Thomas Young, M.D., &c., by George Peacock,* page 143.

Between 1816 and 1823 he wrote sixty-three articles for the 'Supplement to the Encyclopædia Britannica,' Sixth Edition, of which forty-six were biographical. In the year 1821 he made a short tour in Italy with his wife, and, in August 1827, was elected one of the eight Foreign associates of the Academy of Sciences at Paris, in the place of Volta, who died in 1826; the other competitors for this honour being the astronomers Bessel and Olbers, Brown the botanist, Blumenback, Leopold, Von Buch, Dalton, and Plana the mathematician.

Dr. Young's course of life, considered apart from the variety of his occupations, was remarkably uniform. He resided in London from November to June, and at Worthing from July to the end of October, continuing this regular change of residence for fourteen successive years. In the year 1826 he removed from his house in Welbeck Street, where he had resided for a quarter of a century, to another in Park Square, which had been built under his own directions, and fitted up with great elegance and taste. He continued to live here for the remainder of his life. During the month of February, 1829, he began to suffer from what he considered repeated attacks of asthma. His health gradually got worse, but though thus under the pressure of severe illness, nothing could be more striking than the entire calmness and composure of his mind, or could surpass the kindness of his affections to all around him. In the very last stage of his complaint, in an interview with Mr. Gurney, his perfect self-possession was displayed in the most remarkable manner. After some information concerning his affairs, and some instructions concerning the hieroglyphical papers in his hands, he said, that perfectly aware of his situation, he had taken the sacrament of the Church on the day preceding; that whether he should ever partially recover, or whether he were rapidly taken off, he could patiently and contentedly await the issue. His illness continued, with some slight variations, until the morning of the 10th of May, when he expired without a struggle, having hardly completed his fifty-sixth year. The disease proved to be an ossification of the aörta, the large arterial trunk proceeding from the left ventricle of the heart. It must have been in progress for many years, and every appearance indicated an advance of age, not brought on probably by the natural course of time, nor even by constitutional formation, but by unwearied and incessant labour of mind from the earliest days of infancy. His remains were deposited in the vault of his wife's family, in the church of Farnborough, in Kent.—*Life of Thomas Young, M.D., &c., by Dr. George Peacock, Dean of Ely.* London, 1855.—*Memoir by Dr. D. Irving, Encyclopædia Britannica,* Eighth Edition.—*English Cyclopædia.* London, 1858.

APPENDIX.

JOSEPH BLACK, M.D.

PROFESSOR OF THE UNIVERSITIES OF EDINBURGH AND GLASGOW.

Born 1728.*   Died November 26, 1799.

Dr. Joseph Black was born at Bourdeaux, where his father, a native of Belfast but of Scotch descent, was settled as a wine merchant; and being a man of engaging disposition and extensive information was much esteemed by his friends, among whom he reckoned Montesquieu, at that time one of the presidents of the court of justice in the province where Mr. Black resided. At the age of twelve Joseph Black was sent to a school at Belfast, where he remained for some years. In 1746 he was removed to the College at Glasgow and ever afterwards lived in Scotland, which was, properly speaking, his native country. While at the College of Glasgow he studied under the celebrated Dr. Cullen, then professor of anatomy and lecturer on chemistry, and in the year 1751 removed to Edinburgh to complete the course of his medical studies. In the following year Black made his first great discovery of the cause of the causticity of lime, a property till then supposed to be due to the absorption by the lime of some igneous agency. He placed this question on a scientific basis by ascertaining the chemical difference between quick-lime and other forms of the carbonate, and first announced his discovery in a Latin Thesis upon the occasion of his taking his degree of Doctor of Medicine in 1754. It was not, however, given in its fullest details until the year afterwards, when he published his celebrated work entitled, ' Experiments on Magnesia, Quick-lime, and other alkaline substances;' a work which Lord Brougham describes as being incontestably the most beautiful example of strict inductive investigation since the 'Optics' of Sir Isaac Newton. In 1754, as has been mentioned, Black took his medical degree at Edinburgh ; in 1756 he was appointed to succeed Dr. Cullen as professor of anatomy and lecturer on chemistry in the University of Glasgow. Soon after, however, he exchanged this for the professorship of medicine at the same university, as being more congenial to his tastes. Dr. Black continued at the University of

* Lord Brougham gives the date of Dr. Black's birth as 1721.—*Lives of Philosophers.* Third Edition, 1855.

Glasgow for the next ten years, and it was during this period, between the years 1759 and 1763, that he brought to maturity his speculations concerning *heat*, which had occupied his attention from the very first commencement of his philosophical investigations. His two great discoveries were the doctrines of ' Latent Heat,' and ' Specific Heat.' The theory of ' Latent' Heat, which mainly urged Watt to the adoption of improved arrangements in the steam-engine, may be briefly described as the absorption of heat by bodies passing from the solid to the fluid state, and from the fluid to the aëriform, the heat having no effect on surrounding bodies (being, therefore, insensible to the hand or thermometer), and only by its absorption maintaining the body in the state which it has assumed, and which it retains until the absorbed heat is given out and has become again sensible, when the state of the body is changed back again from fluid to solid, from aëriform to fluid.

The doctrine of ' Specific Heat,' or as it was called by Dr. Black the *capacity* of bodies for heat, is summed up in the facts, that different bodies contain different quantities of heat in the same bulk or weight; and different quantities of heat are required to raise different bodies to the same sensible temperature. Thus it was found that a pound of gold being heated to 150° and added to a pound of water at 50° the temperature of both became not 100°, the mean between the two but 55°, the gold losing 95° and the water gaining 5°, because the capacity of water for heat is 19 times that of gold. So twice as much heat is required to raise water to any given point of sensible heat as to raise mercury, the volumes of the two fluids compared being equal. The true doctrine of combustion, calcination of metals, and respiration of animals, which Lavoisier deduced from the experiments of Priestly and Scheele upon oxygen gas, and of Cavendish on hydrogen gas, was founded mainly upon the doctrines of latent and specific heat; and it was thus the sin-gular felicity of Black to have furnished both the pillars upon which modern chemistry reposes.

In 1766 Black succeeded Dr. Cullen in the professorship of che-mistry at the University of Edinburgh, and in the new scene on which he entered his talents became more conspicuously and more extensively useful. Dr. Robison thus characterises him as a lecturer —" He became one of the principal ornaments of the university, his lectures were attended by an audience which continued increasing from year to year; his personal appearance and manners were those of a gentleman, and peculiarly pleasing. His voice in lecturing was low but fine, and his articulation so distinct that he was perfectly well heard by an audience consisting of several hundreds. His discourse was so plain and perspicuous, his illustration by experi-ment so apposite, that his sentiments on any subject never could be mistaken even by the most illiterate." Dr. Black continued to lecture at the University of Edinburgh for thirty years; he then

retired and died three years afterwards, in 1799. His health, never
robust, was precarious at all times from a weakness in the bronchia
and chest, but he prolonged life by a system of strictest abstinence,
frequently subsisting for days together on watergruel and diluted
milk. He was never married. He lived in a select circle of friends,
the most illustrious men of the times in science and in letters;
Watt, Hutton, Hume, Robertson, Smith; and afterwards with the
succeeding generation of Scottish worthies, Robison, Playfair, and
Stewart. He was extremely averse to publication, contemning the
impatience with which so many men of science hurry to the press,
often while their speculations are crude and their inquiries not
finished. He never published any work himself with the exception
of his 'Experiments on Magnesia, &c.,' and two papers, one in the
'London Philosophical Transactions' for 1775 on the Freezing of
boiled Water; the other in the second vol. of the 'Edinburgh Transactions,' on the Iceland Hot Springs.

Dr. Black expired in the seventy-first year of his age, without any
convulsion, shock, or stupor to announce or retard the approach of
death. Being at table with his usual fare, some bread, a few prunes,
and a measured quantity of milk diluted with water, and having the
cup in his hand when the last stroke of the pulse was given, he set
it down on his knees, which were joined together, and kept it steady
with his hand in the manner of a person perfectly at his ease; and
in this attitude he expired without a drop being spilt or a feature in
his countenance changed. His servant coming in saw him in this
posture and left the room, supposing him asleep. On returning soon
after, he saw him sitting as before and found that he had expired.—
Brougham's Lives of Philosophers. London and Glasgow, 1855.—
Encyclopædia Britannica, Eighth Edition.

RICHARD CORT.

Born 1740. Died 1800.

The sad history of this great inventor, who has been well sur-
named "The Father of the iron trade," is comparatively soon told.
Although his discoveries in the manufacture of iron were so important as to have been one of the chief causes in the establishment of
our modern engineering, little is known of the life of the unfortunate
inventor. He was born in 1740 at Lancaster, where his father
carried on the trade of a builder and brickmaker. In 1765, at the
age of twenty-five, he was engaged in the carrying on of the business of a navy agent in Surrey Street, Strand, in which he is said to

have realized considerable profits. 'While conducting this business Cort became aware of the inferiority of British iron in comparison with that of foreign countries, and entered on a series of experiments with the object of improving its manufacture. In 1775 he relinquished his business as a navy agent and took a lease of some premises at Fonltey, near Fareham, where he erected a forge and an iron-mill. He afterwards took into partnership Samuel Jellicoe, son of Adam Jellicoe, then deputy-paymaster of seamen's wages, a connection which ultimately proved the cause of all Cort's subsequent misfortunes. Ford in 1747, Dr. Roebuck in 1762, the brothers Cranege in 1766, and Peter Onions, of Merthyr Tydvil, in 1783, had all introduced valuable additions to the then known processes of iron manufacture. In 1783-4 Cort took out his two patents which, while combining the inventions of his predecessors, specified so many valuable improvements of an original character, that they established a new era in the history of iron manufacture, and raised it to the highest state of prosperity. Mr. Truran,* in speaking of Cort, remarks " The mode of piling iron to form large pieces, as described in his inventions, is the one at use in the present day."—" The method of puddling iron now in use is the same as that patented by Henry Cort. There has been no essential departure from his process. Iron bottoms have been substituted for sand and by building the furnace somewhat larger, a second charge of cast-iron is introduced and partially heated during the finishing operations in the first, as conducted at the present day. All that has been done in the last seventy-three years has been in the way of adding to and perfecting Cort's furnaces, as experience has from time to time suggested." Cort's method of passing the piled wedged-shaped bars of iron through grooved rollers has been spoken of by another competent authority as of " high philosophical interest, being scarcely less than the discovery of a new mechanical power in reversing the action of the wedge, by the application of force to four surfaces so as to elongate the mass instead of applying force to a mass to divide the four surfaces." The principal iron masters soon heard of the success of Cort's new inventions, and visited his foundry for the purpose of examining his process, and of employing it at their own works if satisfied with the result. Among the first to try it were Richard Crawshaw of Cyfartha, Samuel Homfray of Penydarran (both in South Wales), and William Reynolds of Coalbrookdale. The two first-named at once entered into a contract to work under Cort's patents at 10s. a ton royalty; and the quality of the iron manufactured by the new process was found to be so superior to other kinds, that the Admiralty directed it, in 1787, to be used for the anchors and other iron-work in the ships of the Royal Navy. The merits of the invention were now generally conceded,

* *Mechanics' Magazine*, vol. v. (new series), page 276.

and numerous contracts for licenses were entered into with Cort
and his partner, by the manufacturers of bar-iron throughout the
country, and licenses were taken at royalties estimated to yield
27,500l. to the owners of the patent. Cort himself made arrangements for carrying on the manufacture on a large scale, and with
that object entered upon the possession of a wharf at Gosport
belonging to Adam Jellicoe, his partner's father, where he succeeded
in obtaining considerable government orders for iron made under
his patents. This period, apparently the crowning point of Cort's
fortunes, was but the commencement of his ruin. In August, 1789,
Adam Jellicoe died, and defalcations were found in his public
accounts to the extent of 39,676l. His papers and books were at
once seized by Government, and on examination it was found that
a sum of 54,853l. was owing to Jellicoe by the Cort partnership for
moneys advanced by him at different times to enable Cort to pursue
his experiments, which were necessarily of a very expensive character. Among the sums advanced by Jellicoe to Cort was found
one of 27,500l. entrusted to Jellicoe for the payment of seamen
and officers' wages. As Jellicoe had the reputation of being a rich
man, Cort had not the slightest suspicion of the source from which
the advances made to the firm were derived, nor has any conni-
vance whatever on the part of Cort been suggested. The Government, however, bound to act with promptitude in such a case, at
once adopted extraordinary measures to recover their money. The
assignments of Cort's patents, which had been made to Jellicoe in
consideration of his advances, were taken possession of, but, strange
to say, Samuel Jellicoe, the son of the defaulter, was put in possession of the properties at Fonltey and Gosport and continued to
enjoy them, to Cort's exclusion for a period of fourteen years. Notwithstanding this, the patent rights seem never to have been levied
by the assignees, and the result was that the whole benefit of Cort's
inventions was made over to the ironmasters and to the public,
although there seems little reason to doubt, that had they been duly
levied, the whole of the debt due to the government would have
been paid in the course of a few years. As for Cort himself, on the
death of Jellicoe he left his iron works a ruined man. He subsequently made many appeals to Government for the restoration of
his patents, and offered to find security for payment of the debt due
by his firm to the Crown, but in vain. In 1794 an appeal was made
to Mr. Pitt by a number of influential members of parliament, on
behalf of the inventor and his destitute family of twelve children,
when a pension of 200l. was granted to him, which he enjoyed until
the year 1800, when, broken in health and spirit, he died at the age
of sixty. He was buried in Hampstead Church, where a stone
marks the date of his death and is still to be seen; a few years ago
it was illegible, but it has been restored by his surviving son
Richard Cort.

Mr. Smiles thus concludes a long and interesting account of Cort in his 'Industrial Biography:'—"Though Cort died in comparative poverty, he laid the foundations of many gigantic fortunes. He may be said to have been, in a great measure, the author of our modern iron aristocracy, who still manufacture after the processes which he invented or perfected, but for which they never paid him one shilling of royalty. These men of gigantic fortunes have owed much, we might almost say everything, to the ruined projector of 'the little mill at Fonltey.' Their wealth has enriched many families of the older aristocracy, and has been the foundation of several modern peerages. Yet Henry Cort, the rock from which they were hewn, is already all but forgotten; and his surviving children, now aged and infirm, are dependent for their support upon the slender pittance,* wrung by repeated entreaty and expostulation, from the state."—*Smiles's Industrial Biography.* London, 1863.—*Mechanics' Magazine,* 1859–60–61.

JAMES IVORY, F.R.S., &c.

Born 1765.   Died September 21, 1842.

This distinguished mathematician was born at Dundee and received the elements of his education in the public schools of that town. His father was a watchmaker and intended that his son should become a clergyman of the church of Scotland, for which purpose he sent him, when fourteen years old, to the University of St. Andrews. Here Ivory remained for six years, and had for his fellow student, Mr. (afterwards Sir John) Leslie, with whom, at the end of the above period he removed to the University of Edinburgh, where he remained one year to complete the course of study required as a qualification for admission into the church of Scotland. Circumstances, however, seem to have prevented Ivory from carrying out the intentions of his father, for, on leaving the university in 1786, he became an assistant teacher in an academy at that time recently established in Dundee. After remaining at this academy for three years, Ivory, in company with several others, established a factory for spinning flax at Douglastown, in Forfarshire. In this apparently uncongenial occupation he remained for fifteen years (from 1789 to 1804), but the undertaking proved unsuccessful and in 1804 the company ceased to exist. Mr. Ivory then obtained the

---

* After many appeals, a pension of 50*l.* a-year was granted by the Crown to Richard Cort, the sole surviving son of Henry Cort.

appointment to a professorship of mathematics in the Royal Military College at Marlow, in Buckinghamshire (afterwards removed to Sandhurst), with which establishment he remained until his retirement from public service.   This was the most active period of his life, for while fulfilling assiduously the duties of his professorship he continued unremittingly his scientific studies.   His earliest writings were three memoirs, which he communicated in the years 1796, 1799, and 1802, to the Royal Society of Edinburgh.   The first of these was entitled, 'A New Series for the Rectification of the Ellipse;' the second, 'A New Method of Resolving Cubic Equations;' and the third, 'A New-and Universal Solution of Kepler's Problem;' all of them evincing great analytical skill, as well as originality of thought. Mr. Ivory contributed fifteen papers to 'The Transactions of the Royal Society of London,' nearly all of them relating to physical astronomy, and every one containing mathematical investigations of the most refined nature.   The first, published in the 'Transactions of 1809,' and entitled, 'On the Attractions of Homogeneous Ellipsoids,' is his most celebrated paper, in which he completely and definitely resolved the problem of attraction for every class of ellipsoidal bodies.   Many of Ivory's remaining contributions, ranging through a period of nearly thirty years, related to the subject of the attraction of spheroids and the theory of the figure of the Earth, and some of them are considered masterpieces of anylitical skill. One of the last subjects which occupied his attention was the possible equilibrium of a spheroid with three unequal axes when revolving about one of the axes, a fact which Jacobi had discovered. This Ivory demonstrates in the volume for 1838 of the 'Philosophical Transactions.'   The volumes in 1823 and 1838, contain Ivory's two papers on the 'Theory of Atmospheric Refraction,' a subject which, next to the Theory of Attractions, engaged most seriously his attention on account of its great importance in astronomy and the curious mathematical difficulties which its investigation presents.   For each of these papers he was awarded the Royal medal by the Society.   Of all his contributions to the 'Transactions,' only one is purely mathematical; this is contained in the volume for 1831, and is entitled, 'On the Theory of Elliptic Transcendants.' Besides these contributions to the Royal Society, Ivory wrote several papers in the Philosophical Magazine of 1821–27; in Maseres's 'Scriptores Logarithmici;' in Leybourne's 'Mathematical Repository;' and in the Supplement to the sixth edition of the Encyclopædia Britannica.   In the beginning of 1819 Ivory, finding that his health began to decline under the great exertions which he made in carrying on his scientific researches, and performing his duties as professor, resigned his professorship at Sandhurst and retired into private life.   In consideration, however, of his great merit, the pension due for the full period of service required by the regulations was granted to him, although that period had not been completed.

After his retirement, Ivory devoted himself entirely to his scientific researches, living in or near London until his death. In 1814 he had received the Copley medal for his communications to the Royal Society; in 1815 he became a Fellow of the same society. He was also an honorary fellow of the Royal Society of Edinburgh; an honorary member of the Royal Irish Academy and of the Cambridge Philosophical Society; a corresponding member of the Institute of France, of the Royal Academy of Sciences at Berlin, and of the Royal Society of Göttingen.

In the year 1831, in consideration of the great talent displayed in his investigations, Ivory was recommended by Lord Brougham, whom he had known in early life, to the notice of the King (Wm. IV.), who, with the Hanoverian Guelphic Order of Knighthood, gave him an annual pension of 300*l*., which he enjoyed during the rest of his life; and in 1839 he received the degree of Doctor in Laws from the University of St. Andrews.

Mr. Ivory attained the age of seventy-seven before his death; he was essentially a self-taught mathematician, and spent most of his leisure in retirement. He fathomed in private the profoundest writings of the most learned continental mathematicians, and at a period when few Englishmen were able to understand those difficult works; he even added to their value by many original contributions, and must always be remembered with special interest when the singular destitution of higher mathematical talent, which had reigned in this country for so long a period before his time, is considered.— *English Cyclopædia.* London, 1856. — *Encyclopædia Britannica.* Eighth Edition.

JOSEPH PRIESTLY, LL.D.

Born March 24, 1773. Died February 26, 1804.

Joseph Priestly was the son of a cloth-dresser at Burstal-Fieldhead, near Leeds. His family appear to have been in humble circumstances, and he was taken off their hands after the death of his mother by his paternal aunt, who sent him to a free school at Batley. There he learnt something of Greek, Latin, and a little Hebrew. To this he added some knowledge of other Eastern languages connected with Biblical literature; he made a considerable progress in Syriac and Chaldean, and began to learn Arabic; he also had a little instruction in mathematics, but in this science he did not make much proficiency. Indeed his whole education was exceedingly imperfect, and, excepting in Hebrew and Greek, he never afterwards improved it by any systematic course of study. Even in chemistry, the science which he best knew, and in which he made so important a figure, he was only half-taught, so that he presents one of the memorable examples of knowledge pursued, science cultivated, and even its bounds extended, by those whose circumstances made their exertions a continued struggle against difficulties which only genius like theirs could have overcome. After studying for some years at the Dissenting Academy founded by Mr. Coward at Daventry (afterwards transferred to London), Priestly quitted Daventry and became minister of a congregation at Needham Market, in Suffolk, where his salary never exceeded thirty pounds. He had been brought up in the strictest Calvinistic principles, but he very soon abandoned these, and his tenets continued in after life to be those of the moderate Unitarians, whose leading doctrine is the proper humanity of Christ, and who confine all adoration to one Supreme Being. Priestly's religious opinions proving distasteful to his congregation at Needham Market, caused him to remove in 1758 to Nantwich, in Cheshire, where he obtained a considerable number of pupils, which greatly increased his income and enabled him by strict frugality to purchase a scanty scientific apparatus, and commence a study of natural philosophy. In 1761, Priestly removed to Warrington, where he was chosen to succeed Dr. Aitken as tutor in the *belles lettres* at that academy. On settling at Warrington he married the daughter of Mr. Wilkinson, an ironmaster in Wales, by whom he had several children. His literary career may be said to have commenced here, and having once begun to publish, his appeals to the press were incessant and on almost every subject. The universality and originality of his pursuits may be judged from his delivering at Warrington a course of lectures on anatomy, while his published works during the next seven or eight years comprise:—' The Theory of Language and Universal Grammar,' 1762; ' On Oratory and Criticism,' 1777; ' On History and General Policy,' 1788; ' On the Laws and Constitution of England,' 1772; ' On Education,' 1765; ' Chart of Biography,' 1765; ' Chart of History,' 1769. During the same period appeared, in 1767, his work entitled, ' A History of Electricity,' &c., which was so well received that it went through five editions. This was followed in 1772 by a ' History of Vision.' In 1767, on account of a dispute with the Warrington trustees, Priestly removed to Leeds, where he became minister of the Mill-Hill Chapel, and wrote many controversial books and pamphlets. In after times he wrote—' Letters to a Philosophical Institution;' ' An Answer to Gibbon;' ' Disquisitions on Matter and Spirit;' ' Corruptions of Christianity;' ' Early Opinions on Christ;' ' Familiar Letters to the Inhabitants of Birmingham;' ' Two different Histories of the Christian Church;' ' On Education;' ' Comparison of Heathen and Christian Philosophy;' ' Doctrine of Necessity;' ' On the Roman Catholic Claims;' ' On the French Revolution;' 'On the American War;' besides twenty volumes of tracts in favour of Dissenters and their Rights. His general works fill twenty-five volumes, of which only five or six are on scientific subjects; his publications being in all 141, of which only seventeen are scientific. When residing at Leeds Priestly's house immediately adjoined a brewery, which led him to make experiments upon the fixed air copiously produced during the process of fermentation. These experiments resulted in his discovering the important fact that atmospheric air, after having been corrupted by the respiration of animals, and by the burning of inflammable bodies, is restored to salubrity by the vegetation of plants; and that, if the air is exposed to a mixture of sulphur and iron-filings, its bulk is diminished between a fourth and a fifth, and the residue is both lighter than common air and unfit to support life; this residue he termed ' phlogistic air,' afterwards called azotic or nitrogen gas.* For these experiments the Copley medal was awarded to him in 1773 by the Royal Society. The following year to this, from experiments with nimium or red lead, Priestly made his great and important discovery of oxygen gas. This was followed by his discovering the gases of muriatic, sulphuric, and fluoric acids, ammonial gas and nitrous oxide gas. He also discovered the combination which nitrous gas forms suddenly with oxygen; diminishing the volume of both in proportion to that combination; and he thus invented the method of eudiometry or the ascertainment of the relative purity of different kinds of atmospheric air.

In considering the great merits of Priestly as an experimentalist, it must not be forgotten that he had almost to create the apparatus by which his processes were to be performed. He for the most part had to construct his instruments with his own hands, or to make unskilful workmen form them under his own immediate direction. His apparatus, however, and his contrivances for collecting, keeping, transferring gaseous bodies, and for exposing substances to their action, were simple and effectual, and they continue to be still used by chemical philosophers without any material improvement. Although Priestly was the first to discover oxygen, and thus give the basis of the true theory of combustion, he clung all his life with a wonderful pertinacity to the Phlogistic Theory,† and nothing in after life would make him give it up. In 1773 Priestly accepted an invitation from Lord Shelbourne (afterwards first Marquis of Lansdowne), to fill the place of librarian and philosophic companion, with a salary of 250*l*., reducible to 150*l*. for life should he quit the employment; 40*l*. a-year was also allowed him for the expense of

* Discovered at the same time by Dr. Rutherford of Edinburgh.

† The Phlogistic Theory explained the phenomena of combustion by supposing the existence of a hypothetical substance termed Phlogiston, the union of which with bodies made them combustible, and the disengagement of which was the occasion of combustion.

apparatus and experiments, and homes were provided for his family in the neighbourhood both of Lord Shelbourne's town and country residence. Priestly remained with the Earl of Shelbourne for six or seven years, at the end of which period, in 1780, he settled at Birmingham and became minister of a dissenting body there. While residing at Birmingham he engaged fiercely in polemical writings and discussions, particularly with Gibbon and Bishop Horseley. He also displayed a warm interest in the cause of America at the time of the quarrel with the mother-country, and likewise took an active and not very temperate part in the controversy to which the French Revolution gave rise; and, having published a 'Reply' to Burke's famous pamphlet, he was in 1791 made a citizen of the French Republic. This gave considerable offence to the inhabitants of Birmingham, an ironical and somewhat bitter pamphlet against the high church party still further excited their feelings against him; and a dinner which was given on the 14th of July, to celebrate the anniversary of the attack upon the Bastile, became the signal for a general riot. The tavern where the party were assembled was attacked, and, although Dr. Priestly was not present, his house and chapel were immediately afterwards assailed, he and his family escaped, but his house, library, and manuscripts were burnt. Although his losses were made up to him partially by an action at law and partially by a subscription among his friends, Priestly felt that he could no longer live at Birmingham, he therefore removed to London and succeeded his friend Dr. Price as principal of the Hackney Academy. He, however, still found himself highly unpopular and shunned even by his former associates in silence. This determined Priestly to leave England, and in the spring of 1794 he withdrew with his family to America and settled at Northumberland, in Pensylvania, where he purchased 300 acres of land. Here he remained the rest of his life, occupied in cultivating his land, in occasional preaching, and in scientific studies. He continued writing and publishing until his death, in February 1804, in the 72nd year of his age. He expired very quietly, and so easily that having put his hand to his face those who were sitting close to him did not immediately perceive his death.—*Brougham's Lives of Philosophers.* London and Glasgow, 1855.—*Encyclopædia Britannica.* Eighth Edition.

MEMOIRS OF

THE DISTINGUISHED MEN OF SCIENCE OF GREAT BRITAIN, LIVING A.D., 1807-8.

OPINIONS OF THE PRESS ON THE FIRST EDITION.

ONCE A WEEK.

Accompanying the picture, &c., there is a volume by Mr. W. Walker, junior, giving a brief memoir of the salient points of each individual history. This is well executed, and forms a useful book of reference for those who would know more than the picture can tell.

ENGINEER.

Messrs. Walker's great historical engraving of the "Distinguished Men of Science," noticed some weeks ago in these columns, is accompanied by a well written and handsomely printed octavo volume of 228 pages, containing condensed biographical sketches of the fifty-one subjects of the picture itself. The book appears to have been first undertaken with the view of furnishing a mere outline of the life and achievements of these eminent men, but the inevitable delay attending the production of a large engraving, and the gradual accumulation of personal and historical details, at last led Mr. Walker, Jun., to revise and considerably extend the scope of his work, which now forms a very complete and desirable compendium of long-neglected, and, popularly speaking, almost inaccessible biography, of interest and value as well to those who cannot possess themselves of the picture as to the subscribers to that work. The whole is preceded by an introduction, not wanting in suggestive matter, from the pen of Mr. Robert Hunt, F.R.S. . . . . . There is probably no work, certainly none so well within the reach of the general public, which gives anything like as full and yet concise an account of the great men of science who lived and flourished half a century ago. The arrangement of the book is such as to facilitate the readiest reference to any part, and, while the matter is abundant, the style is clear and pleasing. We believe the book will be in large request.

In our notice last week of Mr. Walker's engraving of the distinguished men of science, we were only able to make a passing mention of the book of memoirs which accompanies it. As, however, this book is to be obtained separately, and has evidently been written with care, we will now speak further as to its deserts. In the preface the writer claims the merit only of a compiler, with one or two exceptions, and he expresses a hope that he may have performed his task with clearness and brevity, not neglecting, at the same time, to present his facts in a readable form. The combination of these three qualities is not often to be met with in a series of short biographies, and we are, therefore, glad to be able to say that Mr. W. Walker has, in a great measure, succeeded in accomplishing this. We would particularly call attention to the notices of Cavendish, Samuel Crompton, Dr. Jenner, Count Rumford, and Dr. Thomas Young, as instances of the successful manner in which good sketches of character have been interwoven with plain records of the facts occurring in the lives of these eminent men. The memoir of James Watt is also well put together, and it must have cost the writer considerable labour to compress into the space of six pages so clear an account of the numerous works of this great philosopher and engineer.

The biographies which claim particular notice, from containing original information, are those of Tennant, Maudslay, and Trevithick. The life of Charles Tennant, the founder of the celebrated chemical works at St. Rollox, Glasgow, gives to the public for the first time a sketch of the career of one whose inborn energy of character and clear intellect (to use the author's words), placed him among the foremost of those men who, by uniting science to manufactures, have entitled their occupations to be classed among the ranks of the liberal professions.

But the memoir the perusal of which will afford the greatest interest to engineers is that of Trevithick. Without pretending to anything like a life worthy of the genius of this extraordinary man, it is, notwithstanding, the most complete biographical notice which has yet been published of him. We trust the book may be extensively read, as it affords interesting information, in an easily accessible shape, of men, the memory of whose deeds is too liable to pass away.

ENGRAVING OF

THE DISTINGUISHED MEN OF SCIENCE OF GREAT BRITAIN, LIVING A.D., 1807-8.

THIS Great Historical Engraving represents, assembled at the Royal Institution, authentic Portraits of the following illustrious men:—WATT, RENNIE, TELFORD, MYLNE, JESSOP, CHAPMAN, MURDOCK, the first to introduce gas into practical use; RUMFORD, HUDDART, BOULTON, BRUNEL, WATSON, BENTHAM, MAUDSLAY, DALTON, CAVENDISH, SIR HUMPHRY DAVY, WOLLASTON, HATCHET, HENRY, ALLEN, HOWARD, SMITH, the father of English Geology; CROMPTON, inventor of the Spinning Mule: CARTWRIGHT, TENNANT, RONALDS, the first to successfully pass an electric telegraph message through a long distance; CHARLES EARL STANHOPE, TREVITHICK, NASMYTH, MILLER of Dalswinton, and SYMINGTON, the inventors and constructors of the first practical Steam Boat; PROFESSOR THOMSON, of Glasgow; TROUGHTON, DONKIN, CONGREVE, HERSCHEL, MASKELYNE, BAILY, FRODSHAM, LESLIE, PLAYFAIR, RUTHERFORD, DOLLOND, BROWN, the botanist; GILBERT and BANKS, the Presidents of the Royal Society at that epoch of time; CAPTAIN KATER, celebrated for his pendulum experiments; DR. THOMAS YOUNG, and JENNER the benefactor of mankind.

Engraved in the best style of Stipple and Mezzotinto by WM. WALKER and GEORGE ZOBEL. From an original drawing in Chiaroscuro. Designed by GILBERT; drawn by J. F. SKILL and W. WALKER.

~~~~~~~~~~

PUBLISHED BY W. WALKER & SON, 64, MARGARET STREET, CAVENDISH SQUARE, LONDON, W.

Size of the Engraving, without Margin, Forty-one by Twenty and a half Inches.

Plain Impressions, £5 : 5.

Proofs, with Title and Autographs, £8 : 8.

Artist Proof, with or without Autographs, £10 : 10.

———

OPINIONS OF THE PRESS.

———

TIMES.

An Engraving before us comprises the portraits of 50 distinguished Men of Science of Great Britain who were living in 1807-8, and who are here represented as assembled in the Upper Library of the Royal Institution . . . . we can easily conceive, as the preface to an accompanying volume of biographies informs us, that the collection and combination of these portraits occupied five years,—for some of them, at this distance of time, must have been discoverable with very great difficulty. Thus we have among them portraits of some of the inventors of whom we know very little in proportion to their acknowledged capacities, such for example as Trevithick the friend of Robert Stephenson, and Murdock the Achates of James Watt and introducer of gas . . . . there can be little doubt that the 50 physiognomies are derived from authentic originals in every case, great diligence having been employed in searching for such in the hands of their representatives . . . . as we said, this engraving must not be regarded only as a work of art, but as a collection of portraits of special interest, some of which are not attainable in any other form; while, as a whole, they are an appropriate monument of *our greatest scientific epoch.*

DAILY TELEGRAPH.

We may fairly commence the following remarks with unqualified praise of a work of art, which is intended to honour the distinguished men of science who were living in Great Britain early in the present century, and who, with one surviving exception, having passed into a deathless fame, are yet remembered by philosophers equally great, who were their contemporaries. Mr. Wm. Walker, with the assistance of Mr. Zobel, has produced a really great historical engraving from a design by Mr. Gilbert, representing an assemblage of fifty eminent chemists, engineers, astronomers, naturalists, electricians and mechanical inventors, grouped in the library of the Royal Institution. The scene is thoroughly appropriate, for these men were living in the years 1807-8, while the Royal Institution itself dates from 1800, having been founded to promote the application of science to practical uses. The period marked by the pictorial gathering in question, belonged to an era as complete and brilliant as any that British science has yet passed through. A glance round the circle of intensely thoughtful faces composing this great portrait group will revive many a page of instructive and ennobling history. We see in the centre, seated round a table, James Watt, Sir Isambard Brunel, John Dalton, &c. . . . . Such men were our fathers—patient, indomitable, calmly and wisely bold, modestly self-reliant; ever watching, ever toiling, ever adding to the store of knowlege that was to benefit not them alone but the great human race. Such men are their sons who carry on the appointed work of improvement and civilization. To such men do we point as examples for our children. Their sterling qualities may be best summed up in the words of Lord Jeffrey, written of that same John Playfair to whom we have already referred. Their's was the understanding "at once penetrating and vigilant, but more distinguished, perhaps, for the caution and sureness of its march than for the brilliancy or rapidity of its movements: and guided and adorned through all its progress by the most genuine enthusiasm for all that is grand, and the justest taste for all that is beautiful."

ATHENÆUM.

Messrs. Walker and Son have published a large engraving of fifty-one distinguished men of science, alive in 1807-8, grouped together in the library of the Royal Institution. This engraving, which is a beautiful production, is described as designed by Gilbert, &c. . . . . . It is accompanied by a book, the frontispiece of which is a reduced copy of the engraving, for reference, &c.

ONCE A WEEK.

An earnest artist named William Walker, not being wholly absorbed in the pursuit of gain, but working with enthusiasm on his own perceptions of what is great in humanity and fitting in a nation, has for many years devoted himself to the task of gathering and grouping together the great men who were living in the early part of the present century. . . . . This is of a verity a picture of great men—men whose instinct it was to work for the world and fight against misery: some of them wealthy and some of them poor; with visions perchance of wealth to come, but still working for the world's welfare as the only path through which to ensure their own,—the race of path-finders who are ever setting copies for the English nation to work by, and thus gain more results by the development of national energy. Accompanying the picture, which contains upwards of fifty portraits, some full figures, and some more or less hidden, but all admirably grouped, there is a volume, by Mr. Walker's son, giving a brief memoir of the salient points of each individual history; this also is well executed, and it forms a useful book of reference for those who would know more than the picture can tell. . . . . . Grateful are we to men like Mr. Walker, who has thus gathered together in groups the world's workers, with their images and superscriptions, that men may know their benefactors, and render to their memory that justice which was too rarely accorded to their lives. So, all honour to the work of both the father and the son, the picture and the book, in teaching the men of the present what they owe to men of the past.

Perhaps no class of men have deserved more of their country and of mankind than the great inventors and discoverers in astronomy, chemistry, engineering and other departments of science; yet very little is known of many of them in proportion to the acknowledged good which has resulted from their labours. We possess works of art commemorating the achievements of heroes in the field, and of statesmen in parliament, but until now no work of any magnitude has ever been executed in honour of men whose doings have laid the foundation of our commercial prosperity. We are, however, able to state that this can no longer be said, as Mr. Walker, of 64, Margaret-street, Cavendish-square, has, after an extended period of labour, produced an engraving which must remain an enduring record of our greatest era in science—the early part of the present century. At that epoch of time, steam, under the hands of Watt, Symington, and Trevithick, was commencing its marvellous career; astronomy and chemistry began to reveal their long-hidden secrets; while the discovery of vaccination, by Jenner, had already rescued thousands from death to enjoy the blessings left as a legacy by many a silent worker in science. . . . . . We may fairly state that we have never seen so large a body of men arranged in a group, where it is necessary that all should, in a measure, present their faces turned towards the spectator, so free from that stiffness which is the general fault of works of this class. For this, great praise is due to John Gilbert, by whom the original picture (drawn by J. F. Skill and W. Walker) was designed. The engraving has been executed by W. Walker and George Zobel; while in order to render the work complete, a series of memoirs have been drawn up by Mr. W. Walker, Jun., and furnished with a short introduction by Mr. Robert Hunt, F.R.S., keeper of the Mining Records. We can only now say of the book, that while many of the memoirs are necessarily brief, one, that of Trevithick, contains the most information yet published regarding that eminent engineer.

BUILDING NEWS.

We are glad to be able to inform our readers, that a large engraving has just been completed by Mr. Walker, of 64, Margaret-street, Cavendish-square, in honour of the men of science who have done so much towards the establishment of our present commercial prosperity. This work, which may well be called historical, represents fifty-one illustrious men, living in the early part of the present century, assembled in the Upper Library of the Royal Institution. The picture is divided into three groups, and comprises authentic portraits of our greatest inventors and discoverers in astronomy, chemistry, engineering machinery, and other departments of science. . . . . . The grouping of so large a number of figures must have been a difficult task; this has, however, been successfully accomplished by John Gilbert, the designer of the original picture, who, by a skilful combination of various attitudes, has given both grace and ease to the figures represented. The engraving has been executed by William Walker and George Zobel, and the greatest care seems to have been taken to secure faithful and authentic likenesses. The work is rendered complete by a series of well-written memoirs, compiled to accompany the engraving. This book is also published separately, and we should think there would be many who would buy the memoirs although unable to purchase the engraving.

W. DAVY & SON, PRINTERS, 8 GILBERT STREET, W.

LIST OF BOOKS

PUBLISHED BY

E. & F. N. SPON,

16, BUCKLERSBURY, LONDON.

———◦◇◦———

ARCHITECTURAL SURVEYORS HAND BOOK.—

A Hand-book for Architectural Surveyors, and others engaged in Building, by J. T. Hurst, C.E., royal 32mo, roan, 4s. 6d.

BIRT (W. R.)—

The Manifestation and Operation of Volcanic Forces in modifying the Moon's surface, by W. R. Birt, F.R.A.S., 12mo, sewed 6d.

BREWING.—

Instructions for making Ale or Beer in all temperatures, especially adapted for Tropical Climates, by John Beadel, on a sheet, 6d.

CHALMERS TARGET (The).—

England's Danger, The Admiralty Policy of Naval Construction, by James Chalmers, 8vo, sewed, 2s.

CHANNEL RAILWAY (The).—

Connecting England and France, by James Chalmers, plates, royal 8vo, cloth, 3s. 6d.

COTTAGES.—

Designs for Schools, Cottages, and Parsonage Houses for Rural Districts, by H. Weaver, fol., half-bound, 7s. 6d.

CHOCOLATE AND COCOA.—

Cocoa; its growth and Culture, Manufacture, and Modes of Preparation for the Table, Illustrated with engravings, accompanied by easy methods of analysis, whereby its purity may be ascertained, by Charles Hewett, post 8vo, price 1s.

COFFEE AND CHICORY.—

Coffee and Chicory: their culture, chemical composition, preparation for market, and consumption, with simple tests for detecting adulteration and practical hints for the producer and consumer, by P. L. Simmons, F.S.S., Author of "The Commercial Products of the Vegetable Kingdom," "Dictionary of Trade Products, &c. &c. &c , post 8vo, sewed, 1s.

COTTON CULTIVATION.—

Cotton Cultivation in its various details, the Barrage of Great Rivers, and Instructions for Irrigating, Embanking, Draining, and Tilling Land in Tropical and other Countries posessing high thermometric temperatures, especially adapted to the improvements of the cultural soils of India, by Joseph Gibbs, Member Institute Civil Engineers, with 5 plates, crown 8vo, cloth, 7s. 6d.

COTTON SUPPLY.—

Considerations relative to Cotton Supply, as it was, as it is, and as it might be, by Joseph Gibbs, Member Institute Civil Engineers, 8vo, sewed, 1s.

EARTHWORK TABLES.—

A general sheet Table for facilitating the Calculation of Earthworks for Railways, Canals, &c., by F. Bashworth, M.A., on a large sheet, 6d.

EARTHWORK TABLES.—

A general Table for facilitating the Calculation of Earthworks for Railways, Canals, &c., with a Table of Proportional Parts, by Francis Bashforth, M.A., Fellow of St. John's College, Cambridge, in 8vo, cloth, with mahogany slide, 4s.

"This little volume should become the hand-book of every person whose duties require even occasional calculations of this nature ; were it only that it is more extensively applicable than any other in existence, we could cordially recommend it to our readers, but when they learn that the use of it involves only half the labour of all other Tables constituted for the same purpose, we offer the strongest of all recommendations, that founded on the value of time."—*Mechanics' Magazine.*

ELECTRICITY.—

A Treatise on the Principles of Electrical Accumulation and Conduction, by F. C. Webb, Associate Institute Civil Engineers, part I, crown 8vo, cloth, 3s. 6d.

ELECTRICITY.—

Scientific Researches, experimental and theorectical in Electricity, Magnetism, Galvanism, Electro-Magnetism, and Electro-Chemistry, illustrated with engravings, by William Sturgeon, royal 4to, cloth, 21s.

ELECTRO-METALLURGY.—

Contributions towards a History of Electro-Metallurgy, establishing the Origin of the Art, by Henry Dircks, crown 8vo, cloth, 4s.

ENGINEERS' POCKET BOOK.—

A Pocket Book of useful Formulæ and Memoranda for Civil and Mechanical Engineers, by Guildford L. Molesworth, Member Institute Civil Engineers, Chief Resident Engineer Ceylon Railway, sixth edition, with a supplement, royal 32mo, roan, 4s. 6d.; the supplement can be had separate, price 3d.

"Mr. Molesworth has done the profession a considerable and lasting benefit by publishing his very excellent Pocket-Book of Engineering Formulæ. What strikes us first, is, the very convenient size and form of the book adopted by the author, and next in glancing over its contents we are pleased to find many really useful things not found elsewhere in any Engineering Pocket-Book. Mr. Molesworth's treatment of Hydraulics and Hydro-Dynamics, and Motive Power, generally, is excellent. To the latter branch of his subject, Mr. Molesworth has evidently devoted considerable attention, and his collection of formulæ will be found most useful. But to stop to detail everything that is good and useful in this book would be nearly equal to re-printing a list of its contents."—*Artizan*, April, 1863.

ENGINEERS' PRICE BOOK.—

Appleby's Illustrated Hand-book and Prices current of Machinery and Iron Work, with various useful Tables of Reference, compiled for the use of Engineers, Contractors, Builders, British and Foreign Merchants, &c., 8vo, cloth, 2s. 6d.

FRENCH CATHEDRALS.—

French Cathedrals, by B. Winkles, from drawings taken on the spot, by R. Garland, Architect, with an historical and descriptive account, 50 plates, 4to, cloth, 18s.

GLACIERS.—

Expeditions on the Glaziers, including an ascent of Mont Blanc, Monte Rosa, Col du Géant, and Mont Buét, by a Private of the 38th Artists, and Member of the Alpine Club, post 8vo, sewed, 2s.

GOLD-BEARING STRATA.—

On the Gold-bearing Strata of Merionethshire, by T. A. Readwin, F.G.S., 8vo, sewed, 6d.

HEAT.—

An enquiry into the Nature of Heat, and into its Mode of Action in the Phœnomena of Cumbustion, Vaporisation, &c., by Zerah Colburn, 8vo. boards, 2s.

HYDRAULICS.—

Tredgold's Tracts on Hydraulics, containing Smeaton's experimental Papers on the Power of Water and Wind to turn Mills, &c., &c., Venturi's Experiments on the Motion of Fluids, and Dr. Young's Summary of Practical Hydraulics, plates, royal 8vo, boards, reduced to 6s.

IRON BRIDGES.—

Diagrams to facilitate the Calculation of Iron Bridges, by Francis Campin, C.E., folded in 4to, wrapper, 2s. 6d.

IRON BRIDGES.—

A practical Treatise on Cast and Wrought Iron Bridges and Girders as applied to Railway Structures and to Buildings generally, with numerous examples drawn to a large scale, selected from the Public Works of the most eminent Engineers, with 58 full-page plates, by William Humber, Associate Institute Civil Engineers, and Member of the Institution of Mechanical Engineers, imperial 4to, half bound in Morocco, £1 16s.

"Mr. Humber's admirable work on Iron Bridges."—*The Times.*

IRON (APPLICATION OF).—

Two Lectures on Iron, and its application to the manufacture of Steam Engines, Millwork, and Machinery, by William Fairbairn, C.E., F.R.S., demy 8vo, sewed, 1s.

JONATHAN HULLS.—

A description and draught of a new invented Machine for carrying Vessels or Ships out of or into any Harbour, Port, or River, against Wind and Tide, or in a calm, by Jonathan Hulls, 1737, reprint in fac-simile, 12mo, half morocco, reduced to 2s. sewed 1s.

LIFE CONTINGENCIES.—

A brief View of the Works of the earlier eminent writers on the doctrine of Life Contingencies, by Thomas Carr, 8vo, sewed, 1s.

LOCKS AND SAFES.—

A Treatise on Fire and Thief-proof Depositories and Locks and Keys, by George Price, in one large vol. (916 pages), with numerous wood-engravings, 8vo, cloth, gilt, 5s.

LOCKS AND SAFES.—

A Treatise on Gunpowder-proof Locks, Gunpowder-proof Lock Chambers, Drill-proof Safes, Burglars' methods of opening Iron Safes, and the various methods adopted to prevent them; why one maker's safes are better than another's; the Burnley Test, its history and results, by George Price, author of "A Treatise on Fire and Thief-proof Depositories and Locks and Keys," demy 8vo, cloth, with 46 wood engravings, 1s.

MARINE STEAM ENGINE.—

A Catechism of the Marine Steam Engine, for the use of young Naval Officers and others, by Thomas Miller, Captain R.N., F.R.G.S., F.S.A., 12mo, cloth, 2s.

MECHANICAL DRAWING.—

An elementary Treatise on Orthographic Projection, being a new method of teaching the Science of Mechanical and Engineering Drawing, intended for the instruction of Engineers, Architects, Builders, Smiths, Masons, and Bricklayers, and for the use of Schools, with numerous illustrations on wood and steel, by William Binns, Associate Institute Civil Engineers, late Master of the Mechanical Drawing Class at the Department of Science and Art, and at the School of Mines, formerly Professor of Applied Mechanics at the College for Civil Engineers, &c., third edition, 8vo, cloth, 9s. Mr. Binns' system of Mechanical Drawing is in successful operation in all the Art Schools of the United Kingdom.

"Mr. Binns has treated his subject in a practical and masterly manner, avoiding theoretical disquisitions on the art, and giving direct and applicable examples, advancing progressively from the correct orthographic projection of the most simple to the most complex forms, thus clearing away the mist from the mind of the student, and leading him gradually to a correct and thorough appreciation of what he has undertaken, and to that which it is his desire to attain."—*The Artizan.*

MEMOIRS OF SCIENTIFIC MEN.—

Memoirs of the Distinguished Men of Science of Great Britain, living A.D. 1807-8, by H. Walker jun., with an Introduction by Robert Hunt, F.R.S., second edition, revised and enlarged, post 8vo, cloth, 4s. 6d.

MINING.—

A Practical Treatise on Mine Engineering, by G. C. Greenwell, 61 plates, royal 4to, half bound, £2 15s.

MINING.—

Records of Mining and Metallurgy, or Facts and Memoranda for the use of the Mine Agent and Smelter, by J. Arthur Phillips and John Darlington, in crown 8vo, cloth, illustrated by wood engravings by F. Delamotte, reduced to 4s., in boards, 3s.

MINING.—

A Treatise on the Ventilation of Coal Mines, together with a Narrative of Scenes and Incidents in the Life of a Working Miner, by Robert Scott, 8vo, sewed, 1s.

OBLIQUE BRIDGES.—

A practical Treatise on the Construction of Oblique Bridges with spiral and with equilibrated courses, with 12 plates, containing 100 figures, by Francis Bashforth, M.A., Fellow of St. John's College, Cambridge, 8vo, cloth, 6s.

OPTICAL ILLUSIONS.—

The Ghost as produced in the Spectre Drama, popularly illustrating the marvellous optical illusions, obtained by the apparatus called the Dirksian Phantasmagoria, by Henry Dircks, C.E., crown 8vo, cloth, 2s.

ORNAMENT.—

The book of Ornaments of every style, applicable to Art and Industry, for the use of Lithographers, Engravers, Silversmiths, Decorators, and other Art Workmen, by Jos. Scheidel, 5 numbers at 1s. 6d. each.

ORNAMENT.—

Gleanings from Ornamental Art of every style, drawn from examples in the British, South Kensington, Indian, Crystal Palace, and other Museums, the Exhibitions of 1851 and 1862, and the best English and Foreign Works, in a series of 100 plates containing many hundred examples, by R. Newberry, 4to, cloth, 30s.

PERPETUAL MOTION.—

Perpetuum Mobile, or Search for Self-motive power during the 17th, 18th, and 19th centuries, illustrated from various authentic sources in papers, essays, letters, paragraphs, and numerous patent specifications, with an introductory essay by Henry Dircks, C.E., with numerous engravings of machines, crown 8vo, cloth, 10s. 6d.

"A curious and interesting work. Mr. Dircks' chief purpose was to collect together all the materials requisite to form a record of what has been done, or attempted, rather in this curious branch of *quasi* science, and most instructive in one sense it is. Mr. Dircks' volume is well worth looking into ; it contains a vast deal of entertaining matter."—*Builder.*

RAILWAYS.—

Railway Practice, a collection of working plans and practical details of construction in the Public Works of the most celebrated Engineers, comprising Roads, Tramroads and Railways, Bridges, Aqueducts, Viaducts, Wharfs, Warehouses, Roofs and Sheds, Canals, Locks, Sluices, and the various

Piers and Jetties, Tunnels, Cuttings, and Embankments, Works connected with the Drainage of Marshes, Marine Sands, and the Irrigation of Land, Water Works, Gas-works, Water-wheels, Mills, Engines, &c., by S. C. Brees, C.E. Text in 4to, with 279 plates in folio, together 2 vols. half-bound morocco, £3 10s.

RAILWAY MASONRY.—
The Guide to Railway Masonry, containing a complete Treatise on the Oblique Arch, by Peter Nicholson, third edition, revised by R. Cowen, C.E., with 42 plates, 8vo, cloth, 9s.

ROPEMAKING.—
A Treatise on Ropemaking as practised in public and private Rope-yards, with a description of the manufacture, rules, tables of weights, &c., adapted to the Trade, Shipping, Mining, Railways, Builders, &c., by R. Chapman, formerly foreman to Messrs. Huddart and Co., Limehouse, and late Master Rope Maker of H.M. Dockyard, Deptford, 18mo, cloth, 2s.

SCREW CUTTING.—
Screw Cutting Tables for the use of Mechanical Engineers, showing the proper arrangement of Wheels for cutting the threads of screws of any required pitch, with a Table for making the Universal Gas Pipe Threads and Taps, by W. A. Martin, Engineer, royal 8vo, oblong, cloth, 1s., sewed, 6d.

SCREW PROPELLER.—
The Screw Propeller, what it is, and what it ought to be, by R. Griffith, 8vo, sewed, 6d.

SEWING MACHINE.—
The Sewing Machine: its History, Construction, and Application, translated from the German of Dr. Herzberg, by Upfield Green, illustrated by 7 large lithographic plates, royal 8vo, ornamental boards, 7s. 6d.

SOCIETY OF ENGINEERS.—
Transactions of the Society of Engineers, 1860 to 1862, plates, 12mo, sewed, 7s. 6d. The volume for 1863, just ready, cloth.

STEAM BOILERS.—

The Modern Practice of Boiler Engineering, containing observation on the Constructions of Steam Boilers, and remarks upon Furnaces, used for Smoke Prevention, with a chapter on Explosions, by Robert Armstrong, C.E., revised with the addition of Notes and an Introduction by John Bourne, Esq., with engravings, fcap. 8vo, cloth, 2s.

"The collected experience of a practical Engineer, who, for thirty years of his life has directed his attention to the construction of Steam-Boilers and Furnaces, is a valuable addition to the stock of Engineering knowledge, and it will be generally more appreciated because it is condensed within so small a volume as the one before us."—*Civil Engineer and Architects' Journal.*

STEAM BOILERS.—

Steam Boiler Explosions, by Zerah Colburn, 8vo, sewed, 1s.

STEAM ENGINE.—

Practical illustrations of Land and Marine Engines, shewing in detail all the modern improvements of High and Low Pressure, Surface Condensation, and Super-heating, together with Land and Marine Boilers, by N. P. Burgh, Engineer, 20 plates in double elephant, folio, cloth, with text. £2 2s.

STEAM ENGINE.—

Rules for Designing, Constructing and Erecting Land and Marine Engines and Boilers, by N. P. Burgh, Engineer, Royal 32mo, roan, 4s. 6d.

STEAM ENGINE.—

The Steam Engine, for Practical Men, containing a theoretical investigation of the various rules given in the work, and several useful Tables, by James, Hann, A.I.C.E., and Placido and Justo Gener, Civil Engineers, 8vo, cloth, 9s.

"To the practical and scientific Engineer, and to the Assistant Engineer, who aspires to pass his examination for chief with credit to himself, and the Service, we can cordially recommend the work."—*The Nautical Standard.*

STEAM NAVIGATION.—

High-speed Steam Navigation and Steamship Perfection—Can perfection be defined in the form of a Steamship, a Propeller, or any other mechanical contrivance? a proposition for the solution of the Scientific World, and for the consideration of the British Admiralty, by Robert Armstrong, of Poplar, 8vo, sewed, 1s.

SUGAR MACHINERY.—

A Treatise on Sugar Machinery, by N. P. Burgh. Engineer, with 16 plates drawn to a large scale, royal 4to, cloth, 30s.

SURVEYING.—

An Introduction to the present practice of Surveying and Levelling, being a plain explanation of the Subject and of the instruments employed, illustrated with suitable plans, sections, and diagrams, also with engravings of the Field Instruments, by S. C. Brees, C.E., 8vo, cloth, 3s. 6d.

SURVEYING.—

A practical Treatise on the science of Land and Engineering Surveying, Levelling, estimating quantities, &c., with a general description of the several Instruments required for Surveying, Levelling, Plotting, &c., and Illustrations and Tables, by H. S. Merrett, royal 8vo, cloth, 16s.

TRADE OF NEWCASTLE-ON-TYNE.—

History of the Trade and Manufactures of the Tyne, Wear, and Tees, comprising the papers prepared under the auspices of a Committee of Local Industry, and other documents of a similar character, read at the second meeting in Newcastle-on-Tyne of the British Association for the advancement of Science, revised and corrected by the writers, second edition, 8vo, boards, 3s. 6d.

TURBINE.—

A practical Treatise on the construction of the Turbine or Horizontal Water-wheel, with seven plates specially designed for the use of operative Mechanics, by William Cullen, Millwright and Engineer, 4to, sewed, 6s.

TURNING.—

Turners' and Fitters' Pocket-book for calculating the change wheels for screws on a Turning Lathe, and for a Wheel-cutting Machine, by J. La Nicca, 18mo, sewed, 6d.

TURNING.—

The practice of Hand-turning in Wood, Ivory, Shell, &c., with Instructions for turning such works in Metal, as may be required in the practice of Turning in Wood, Ivory, &c.; also, an Appendix on Ornamental Turning, by Francis Campin, with wood engravings, crown 8vo, cloth, 6s.

WAGE TABLE.—

Delany and Okes' Wage Table for Engineers, Shipbuilders, Contractors, Builders, &c., from one-quarter of an hour, in regular progression to nine and three-quarter hours, from one day to ten days, at one shilling to eight shillings per day, on one sheet, 1s.

In 2 vols., royal 8vo, half morocco, neat, price £3 3s.

APPLETON'S

DICTIONARY OF MACHINES,

MECHANICS' ENGINE-WORK, AND ENGINEERING,

WITH 4000 ENGRAVINGS ON WOOD, AND MANY STEEL PLATES.

SECOND EDITION.

London: E. & F. N. Spon, 16, Bucklersbury.

Royal 4to, cloth, Illustrated by 84 Plates of Furnaces and Machinery, price £3 10s.,

THE IRON MANUFACTURE OF GREAT BRITAIN,

THEORETICALLY AND PRACTICALLY CONSIDERED;

Including Descriptive Details of the Ores, Fuels, and Fluxes, employed; the Preliminary Operation of Calcination; the Blast, Refining and Puddling Furnaces; Engines and Machinery; and the various Processes in Union, &c.

By WILLIAM TRURAN, C.E.,

Formerly Engineer at the Dowlais Iron Works, under the late Sir John Guest, Bart. subsequently at the Hirwain and Forest Works, under Mr. Crawshay.

SECOND EDITION.

Revised from the Manuscript of the late Mr. W. Truran,

By J. ARTHUR PHILLIPS,

Author of "A Manual of Metallurgy," "Records of Mining," &c.;

AND

W. H. DORMAN, C.E.

OPINIONS OF THE PRESS.

"The book treats of every detail connected with the arrangement, erection, and practical management of Iron Works, in the most minute and careful manner; and the various ores and the materials employed in reducing the ores, and in producing the metal in its various stages up to the finished metal—in the form of Rails, Merchant Bars, Rods, Hoops, and Plates—are most thoroughly and scientifically dealt with, and in the most intelligible manner brought before the reader."—*Artizan*, October, 1862.

"The most complete and practical treatise upon the Metallurgy of iron to be found in the English language."—*Colliery Guardian*, November 29, 1851.

"Mr. Truran's work is really the only one deserving the name of a treatise upon, and text-book of the Iron Manufacture of the Kingdom. It gives a most comprehensive and minute exposition of present practice, if the term may be applied to Iron Manufacture as distinguished from strictly professional subjects. The Author does not go out of his way to theorise how Iron should or may be made, but he describes how it is made in all the Iron Districts of the Kingdom."—*Engineer*, December 26, 1851.

"It has seldom fallen to our lot to introduce to the notice of the scientific public, a more valuable work than this. It is evidently the result of long, careful, and practical observation, and it forms at once a glorious monument to the memory of its author, and an excellent guide to those who are directly and indirectly interested in the great subject of which it treats."—*Mechanics' Magazine*, Sept. 26, 1852.

"To the valuable character of Mr. Truran's work, we fully referred upon the publication of the first edition, and we cannot say more in praise of the very handsome volume before us, than that whatever information was wanted in the former has now been carefully supplied, and that the whole work appears to have been subjected to an amount of careful revision which has rendered it as near as may be perfect, and consequently gives it a just claim to the highest position as a standard work upon the Metallurgy of the Metal of which it treats. Scientific knowledge and practical experience have been brought to bear in its production, and all the valuable elements of each have been most judiciously combined."—*Mining Journal*, September 20, 1862.

London: E. and F. N. SPON, 16, Bucklersbury.